KV-416-957

THE GENTLE WIND'S CARESS

After the deaths of her mother and sister, Isabelle Gibson and her brother are left to fend for themselves in a workhouse. However, when the matron's son attempts to rape her, Isabelle escapes him by marrying Farrell, a moorland farmer. But he's a drunkard and in a constant feud with his landlord, Ethan Harrington. When Farrell bungles a robbery and deserts her, Isabelle and Ethan are thrown together, but both are married and must hide their growing love. Meanwhile, when faces from the past return to haunt her, a tragedy is set to strike that will change their lives forever.

ANNE WHITFIELD

---◆---

THE GENTLE WIND'S CARESS

Complete and Unabridged

ULVERSCROFT
Leicester

First published in Great Britain in 2007 by
Robert Hale Limited
London

FILP
20182491R
CLACKMANNANSHIRE
LIBRARIES
U   1108

First Large Print Edition
published 2008
by arrangement with
Robert Hale Limited
London

The moral right of the author has been asserted

Copyright © 2007 by Anne Whitfield
All rights reserved

British Library CIP Data

Whitfield, Anne
    The gentle wind's caress.—Large print ed.—
Ulverscroft large print series: saga
1. Yorkshire (England)—Social conditions—19th
century—Fiction 2. Great Britain—History—
Victoria, *1837 – 1901* —Fiction 3. Love stories
4. Large type books
I. Title
823.9'2 [F]

ISBN 978–1–84782–103–4

Published by
F. A. Thorpe (Publishing)
Anstey, Leicestershire

Set by Words & Graphics Ltd.
Anstey, Leicestershire
Printed and bound in Great Britain by
T. J. International Ltd., Padstow, Cornwall

This book is printed on acid-free paper

16.99

20182491R

20182491R

his book is to be returned on or be

2018245974

SPECIAL MESSAGE TO READERS

This book is published under the auspices of

THE ULVERSCROFT FOUNDATION

(registered charity No. 264873 UK)

Established in 1972 to provide funds for research, diagnosis and treatment of eye diseases. Examples of contributions made are: —

A Children's Assessment Unit at Moorfield's Hospital, London.

•

Twin operating theatres at the Western Ophthalmic Hospital, London.

•

A Chair of Ophthalmology at the Royal Australian College of Ophthalmologists.

•

The Ulverscroft Children's Eye Unit at the Great Ormond Street Hospital For Sick Children, London.

You can help further the work of the Foundation by making a donation or leaving a legacy. Every contribution, no matter how small, is received with gratitude. Please write for details to:

**THE ULVERSCROFT FOUNDATION,
The Green, Bradgate Road, Anstey,
Leicester LE7 7FU, England.
Telephone: (0116) 236 4325**

**In Australia write to:
THE ULVERSCROFT FOUNDATION,
c/o The Royal Australian and New Zealand
College of Ophthalmologists,
94-98 Chalmers Street, Surry Hills,
N.S.W. 2010, Australia**

Anne Whitfield was born in Australia and currently lives in the beautiful Southern Highlands area of New South Wales. Many of her novels and stories are set in England and take inspiration from the Yorkshire area, where both of her parents grew up.

No man of a woman born,
Coward or brave, can shun his destiny.

Homer, *Iliad*, *VI* (Bryant trans.)

1

Halifax, Yorkshire
September 1876

Isabelle stood dry-eyed at her sister's grave. Morning rain trickled down her collar and sent icy shivers across her skin. A blanket of dirty-grey clouds lay low as though pressing her misery deeper onto her shoulders. The muffled bustle of Halifax came from behind, reminding them that life continued no matter what.

For a fleeting moment, Isabelle panicked. Alone. She and Hughie were all alone. The world suddenly seemed too large, too frightening without Sally's calm presence. Sally was the soothing voice to Isabelle's flights of fancy. Her madcap schemes and grand plans for leaving Halifax always made Sally smile tenderly and nod, but her elder sister knew, in her sweet and quiet way, that their lives were already mapped out for them. Isabelle Gibson couldn't change that. But dreams for a better life kept the workhouse inmates alive, Sally had known that and wouldn't dispel Isabelle's imaginings, for

1

it was all they had.

A cold hand inched into her own and Isabelle looked at her brother Hughie with his cropped dark hair and the sad grey eyes of their mother.

'Poor Sally,' he said with a sniff, using his sleeve to wipe away the moisture from his nose. 'At least she's with mother now and grandfather. They will watch over us together.'

Isabelle couldn't speak. Her emotions at her sister's death only surfaced as anger. Anger at losing yet another member of her family. Sally, like their delicate mother, had been too gentle, too good for this harsh life. After their grandfather's death there had been no one to look after them, no one to save them from entering the private workhouse. For her mother, a proud woman, this situation was humiliating and ultimately killed her.

A stooped old man stepped forward. 'Er, I need ter fill it in, lass. So, yer'd best be heading off now.'

Wrenched from her thoughts, she looked at the gravedigger as though she had never seen one before, then nodded once and turned away. Grabbing Hughie's hand tighter, she dragged him behind her as she twisted this way and that around the numerous grave markers.

They crossed the lane and entered the back gate of the workhouse grounds, which was barren of all colour. No trees or plants softened the sharp lines or grey drabness of the stone buildings. The only greenery was the rows of late summer vegetables. The rest of the yard didn't even have the luxury of cobbles but was simply dirt — dusty in the dry weather and thick mud in the rain.

'What'll we do now, Belle?'

After stepping through the doorway into the side entrance of the main building, Isabelle stopped, took off her flat woollen hat and shook the rain from it. 'We aren't staying here any longer, that I do know.'

'Where'll we go then?'

'I don't know.'

'Maybe our father will come and get us?'

'Don't talk daft.' She frowned. 'He's been gone eight years and I doubt he'll be back now. Why do you always think of him? You hardly remember him!'

Hughie shrugged and looked down at his boots.

She slapped her hat against her leg, annoyed, as always, that Hughie continued to hold the image of their father as some hero who would come and sweep them away to a wonderful life of riches and pleasures. Sighing, she paced the narrow, dim hallway, hardly aware of the multitude of noises penetrating from other rooms above her head.

'We need to be able to look after ourselves and not be split up. Now Sally has gone, Matron might do it. Yesterday, the dragon mentioned sending you down the pit. And me,' she snorted in disgust and fear, 'well, I can only imagine where she'd like to send me.'

'She'll put you into service.' Hughie nodded like a wise old man.

'Oh no, she won't.' Isabelle slowed her pace. 'I'll not swap one form of servitude for another unless it's to my benefit. I promised Mother.' She pressed her temples and squeezed her eyes shut to concentrate. The sound of movement further along made her glance up. Neville Peacock was leering at her from a doorway. Revulsion made Isabelle shiver far more than the cold did.

Peacock sauntered towards them, hands in his trouser pockets. 'So, your dear Sally is six foot under now?'

Isabelle clenched her fists, fighting the urge to scratch his eyes out. 'One good thing is that she's out of your clutches! As soon will I be!' she retorted.

His evil laughter echoed around the shadowed hallway. 'And here I was thinking you enjoyed my advances.'

Isabelle straightened and fixed him with a look of contempt. A tuft of beard grew from his chin and that, with his long sallow face, reminded her of a lean, dangerous wolf, always on the prowl. 'I would rather swim in the midden than let you touch me.'

His face tightened. 'You enjoy my attention.'

'I put up with it before to keep you away from my sister!'

His nostrils flared and a flush crept up his neck. He stared at her breasts before dragging his gaze up to her face. 'I will have you, Miss Gibson, and you will take pleasure in it.'

'Leave my sister alone!' Hughie stepped up beside her.

Peacock raised his fist, but Isabelle thrust herself between them. 'Don't you dare touch him.'

He moved back and lowered his hand, chuckling. 'I'll not waste my time. He's but a minnow in a very large river.'

Isabelle tossed her head and narrowed her eyes. 'And you are nothing but a slimy eel.'

Mrs Toombs, a patron of the workhouse, scurried by at the end of the corridor, but halted on seeing Isabelle. 'Why, dear, I just heard the news. Poor Sally. You must feel wretched? Mrs Peacock already misses Sally's quiet presence, I'm sure.' She ruffled Hughie's damp hair. 'Never mind, at least Sally has gone to a better place now.'

Neville Peacock slunk away into the shadows and disappeared from sight.

Isabelle sighed and pushed his nauseating image from her mind. She smiled at the plump, elderly woman. 'Thank you, Mrs Toombs. Yes, Sally will be greatly missed.'

'Indeed. So, what will you do now?'

'I thought I might marry, Mrs Toombs, should I find someone willing to take both myself and Hughie.'

'Excellent idea, my dear. Everyone should be married and for a young bright girl like you it would be the perfect solution.'

Isabelle nodded. 'That was my thoughts exactly, Mrs Toombs.'

The older woman adjusted the basket hooked over her arm. Her navy blue taffeta skirts rustled with every movement. 'Well, I must be going. My husband will not wait much longer for me, but he is generous in allowing me to bring my small donations to Mrs Peacock's establishment.'

A grim smile lifted Isabelle's lips. 'You are very kind, Mrs Toombs.'

As the patron hurried back along the corridor, Isabelle chewed her bottom lip in thought.

'She's nice,' Hughie said, breaking into her thoughts.

'Yes, and you know why?'

'No.'

'Because she is married. A respectable married woman gains the high opinion from the community. Once you are married you are free, only answerable to your husband, and if you can bend him to suit your needs, well, there is no limit in what you can do.' She nodded. 'Being married is the best thing a woman can do. You just have to make sure you marry the right person and not a drifter like our father!'

Hughie shuffled on the spot, his expression bored.

'I need to speak with Matron.' She squeezed his hand and let go 'Go back to your chores. We'll meet after the noon bell behind the garden shed in the west corner.'

'Can't we go into the glasshouse? It's warmer in there.'

'No. There's always people about.'

Once Hughie had left her, Isabelle straightened her shoulders, placed her hat back on at a slight angle and took a deep breath. Marriage. The word burned in her soul. If she could marry she could keep Hughie with her and they'd be free from the workhouse, away from Matron's demanding rule and away from the slime, Neville Peacock.

Lifting her brown skirt, she ran down the corridor, turned left and marched along a wider hallway with numerous doors on both sides. At the end of the hall, she turned right and paused in front of a black painted door, which bore a brass plaque with the words: MRS PEACOCK, MATRON.

Isabelle automatically tidied her hair, knowing Matron's fastidious nature in all things. Smoothing her skirt, she prayed silently that the woman wouldn't make her angry, which was often the case whenever their paths crossed. Isabelle stiffened her spine and raised her hand to knock. *I am a vicar's granddaughter, not some scum off the street.* With this in mind she rapped sharply on the door.

Within seconds it opened and Mr Beale, the matron's right-hand man, glared at her from behind thick, steel-rimmed lenses. 'How dare you knock on this door!'

'Excuse me, Mr Beale, but I wish to speak to Matron.'

'Why you insolent — '

'I shall not waste her time, I promise you.' Isabelle pushed open the door and stepped inside, making the little man stumble back, gaping at her.

8

Mrs Peacock, a large woman always dressed in black, flung down her pen and glared. 'What is the meaning of this?'

'I ask for your forgiveness, Matron, but I have urgent needs that I must discuss with you.'

'Urgent needs?' Matron snorted, full of loathing. 'Don't talk nonsense, leave me at once.'

'I wish to prepare for my future.'

Matron laughed a shrill noise that grated on Isabelle's ears. 'Your future? You have no future now Sally has gone! She was the one worthy thing you had and it is your fault she died.'

Isabelle frowned. 'Sally died from pneumonia.'

'Yes, and how did she catch it?' Matron stood and placed her hands flat on the desk. 'She chased after you into the rain. You and your impertinent ways led her to her death. If you hadn't run off that day, she would still be here!'

'And why did I run?' Emotion boiled inside Isabelle's chest at the matron's unjust accusation. 'I ran because your filthy son wanted to lift my skirts and you didn't care.' She tossed her head. 'As if I would willingly let him touch me!'

Matron went white around the lips. 'That is

a lie. My son wouldn't sully his hands with you. I would never allow it.'

Isabelle grunted. 'Yes, I suppose you speak the truth there. You didn't want him touching me. You wanted him to beget a child on Sally. Isn't that right!'

'How dare you.'

'Sally had the qualities of my mother. She was refined, delicate and pure.' Isabelle's lips curled in disgust. 'Something the Peacocks and this establishment do not have.'

Matron thumped the table. 'Get out!'

Isabelle closed her eyes. *I've done it again*. Every time she was in front of the matron they ended up in conflict. It had been the one thing she and Sally fought about; her lack of patience and quick temper.

She opened her eyes and let out a long breath. 'I did not come here to argue, Matron. I did wish to discuss with you my future plans.'

'As I said you have no future.' Matron seethed between clenched teeth.

'I believe differently.'

'Believe what you like, Gibson, but I know the truth of it.' Matron walked to the window that overlooked the grass area at the front of the workhouse before the high stone wall blocked the rest of the view. 'You are not your sister. You do not have her qualities. Do you think you can compare with her or take her place in my affections?'

'No.'

'No, you cannot.' She glanced over her shoulder at Isabelle. 'You are past eighteen years of age. It is high time you left here and began working. Most girls your age have been working for many years. Your mother spoilt you all, believing you were to be better than you are. She, like you, had ideas above her station.'

Isabelle clenched her fist in her skirts. 'My mother was a vicar's daughter, educated and trained as a lady's companion.'

Matron dismissed her words with a wave. 'I gave it some thought as Sally lay dying and I found a position for you as a scullery maid in Lodge House on the outskirts of Halifax.'

'I will not go into service.'

Matron's mouth thinned to a mere slit in her face. 'For too long you have benefited from my benevolence towards your sister, who put her talents to good use and helped Mr Beale with the account books. However, all that has changed now.'

'I won't be a scullery maid and you have no say in what I do.'

Matron took three large strides and stood just inches from her. She reeked of onion. 'I can put you out on the street, my girl, you and your brother, so think on that!'

'I will *not* be a servant, spending my days on my knees scrubbing floors.'

A stinging slap on the face stunned Isabelle. Pain bit deep. Matron's thin lips drew back in a snarl. 'That is all you are good for!'

Isabelle refused to cradle her flame-hot cheek in front of them. She raised her chin. 'I am a vicar's granddaughter. I can read and write. I want to be married and be respectable.'

'Married?' Matron laughed loudly. 'You'd be lucky to wed a hermit.'

Anger raced through Isabelle's veins like fire through dry grass. She ached to tell the old dragon exactly what she thought of her but she knew it would not help her and Hughie. Taking a deep breath, she arranged her expression to be docile and tried to act as her mother would. 'Matron, I am thankful for your offer, but I consider being married as the best alternative for both me and Hughie.'

Mr Beale stepped forward and Matron scowled at him. 'Excuse me, Matron, but I do think I have an answer to your problem,' he said and turned to Isabelle. 'Could you please wait outside while I talk with Matron?'

Isabelle left the room and paced the corridor. She buried her anger and took a deep breath. There was no point in losing her temper, it never got her anywhere except into more trouble. Marriage was all she hoped for and she mustn't lose sight of her dreams. If she became a servant living in a big house she would lose Hughie. Servitude wouldn't give her the freedom or the respectability of a married woman. She stamped her foot in frustration. 'Why wasn't I born pretty like Sally and mother?' Her mutterings echoed loudly in the empty corridor. She went to a small window overlooking the lawns and peered at her reflection: boring, curly brown hair and boring light blue eyes. She was too tall for a girl and her boyish figure irritated her. Why couldn't she have soft round curves and golden hair? Then men would be falling over themselves to offer proposals.

The door opened behind her and she turned to face Matron and Mr Beale. A glint of something she couldn't name shone in Matron's small, beady eyes. 'Mr Beale knows of a bachelor, a second cousin of his, who tenants a farm near Heptonstall.'

Isabelle frowned. 'Heptonstall?'

'West of here — '

'Yes, I've heard of it.'

'So you should have. Sally told me your family are distant relations of the Gibson's of Greenwood Lee.'

'My father's people claim some connection, I believe.' Isabelle dismissed all thought of her father instantly. A knack she learnt soon after he left.

'To be a farmer's wife is nothing to scorn, you know.'

Isabelle swallowed. 'But, I was thinking more of a man with a small business. I could help in his shop maybe. Surely there must be someone who needs a wife and lives here in Halifax? I've never lived anywhere else.'

Matron's eyes narrowed. 'Do you want to be married or not?'

Isabelle nodded. 'Of course, but a farmer? I know nothing of farming.'

'Work is work. You'll soon learn.'

'Very well, I shall write to him. Or maybe visit?'

Mr Beale stepped forward. 'Er, no, that's not necessary. I will write to him and have him come to Halifax.'

'He is a good man? And he will take on Hughie too?'

Matron looked at Mr Beale and, at his nod, smiled. 'Yes, Hughie shouldn't be a problem. He can work on the farm too.'

'A farm.' Isabelle mulled the words around in her mind. Gradually her imagination came alive and sparked her interest. A farm with fields of baby animals, wild flowers; living in the country away from the fumes of the city, away from the traffic and noise.

'He is a moorland farmer,' explained Mr Beale.

Her mind whirled. To move away or to stay in town? To marry a farmer or a man with a business? She had seen advertisements for wives in the paper, especially men venturing to a new country. Maybe she could take an enormous gamble and marry someone emigrating to Canada, America or Australia? But would they take the expense of Hughie? She put her hand to her head, her mind spinning. Here she was contemplating the other side of the world when she couldn't even comprehend living just miles away further up the valley!

Matron tapped her foot. 'Well?'

Isabelle bit her bottom lip. 'Is there any other person you know who might want a wife? Maybe I should place an advertisement in the newspaper?'

Matron held up her hand. 'Let us speak with Mr Beale's cousin and see what we make of that first, yes? A farmer's wife is a desirable position.'

Isabelle remembered Sally's words. *Take little steps, Belle, little steps.* Suddenly, she nodded. 'Thank you, Matron and you, Mr Beale.'

She left them and walked back along the corridor deep in thought. A farm. The air would be fresh and clean, not full of smoke like Halifax. It might be just what they needed. Hughie was good with plants; he often worked in the workhouse gardens. He would grow into a fine man living in the clean air and eating fresh food. Reaching the hallway leading to the kitchens, Isabelle paused and nibbled at her fingertips. Her thoughts ran wild, warming to the idea. She could be a farmer's wife, she was certain of that. She *could* keep chickens and bake bread like her grandfather's old cook taught her. She straightened her shoulders at the thought. Yes, that would do nicely.

Abruptly, a hand clamped over her mouth. Isabelle jerked in terror. Grabbed around the waist, she was wrenched off her feet and carried into the nearest room — the linen room. She fought against the restraint, kicking widely, but her skirts muted any impact she made. In a swift movement, her attacker banged her up against the wall of shelves holding sheets, towels and pillow-cases. Faded light filtered in through a high dirty window and it was enough for her to see the excited eyes of Neville Peacock. She thrashed her head but he pushed it hard against the wooden shelf.

'Keep still, my lass.'

His grip over her mouth made it impossible to shout out and she dragged in quick shallow breaths through her nose.

'You'll like it, I promise.' His knee edged her legs apart, but he soon realized that to lift her skirts he would have to free one hand. He took his hand away from her mouth and next his tongue bombarded her lips, edging its way past her teeth.

Bile rose in Isabelle's throat. She wrenched her face away, but his lips followed, leaving wet kisses across her cheek. She gagged. Cold air touched her thighs as he raised her skirts high over her stockings. Furious at the invasion, she growled and bit his tongue so hard blood spurted into her mouth.

He howled in pain and backhanded her in the face. 'You bitch!'

Stars burst before her eyes like fireworks on Guy Fawkes night. The confined room spun round her. Dazed, she gripped a shelf to steady herself. Tears blurred her vision as she spat and coughed. Neville leant against the opposite wall, one hand over his mouth, his eyes closed. Blood trickled between his fingers and ran down his chin to drip on his white shirt. Isabelle heaved and dashed for the door. Whipping it open, she glanced back at him before hurrying out.

Matron was in the corridor and stopped mid-stride, startled by Isabelle's flight. Her gaze narrowed as she swept it from Isabelle to the linen room door.

Wordlessly, Isabelle shook her head and darted away. Her heart pounded, threatening to explode in her chest. The echoes of her running footsteps bouncing off the walls sounded loud in her ears. She had to leave this place!

2

The cold wind outside tried to wheedle its way into the corridors of the workhouse as Isabelle rushed to the matron's office to meet with her intended husband. For a split second she baulked at the prospect, but knowing her desire to leave rested on this meeting, she quelled her nerves and hurried on. The draughts whistled around her ankles and a quick glance out of the small windows she passed showed another grey gloomy day heralding winter. Summer had only just finished yet she missed it already. The thought of spending another winter inside these frigid walls spiralled her into a mood of gloom.

She knew she should be thankful she lived in a private workhouse and not a parish one, but still the conditions were primitive and the future bleak unless she took some chances. Living this way had taken her mother and sister. Their gentleness left them as they became unable to cope once outside the safety of the vicarage. Still, her mother always said that she, Isabelle, was the strongest in the family. The idealist. The one to weather the harsh demands of a world devoid of compassion. She would show them all that her mother was right. Her family might have fallen lower than the low but that didn't mean she wouldn't do all in her power to claw them back to their rightful place.

Within a week of speaking of her desire to be married, to have a home of her own, Mr Beale had arranged it for his cousin to visit. It had been a week of hiding from Neville. After the incident in the linen room, he had given her a few days reprieve before hounding her unmercifully. He hid in corners and loomed out of shadows. He watched from windows and sent her peculiar notes. She became distressed when he struck up an interest in Hughie, which included giving him little presents.

Two nights ago, she had gone to bed and found a dead kitten under the blankets. Frightened and not sure what to do, she had stayed up all night with only her umbrella as protection. From then on, Isabelle lived in fear of Neville. She caught scraps of sleep during the day when she could, knowing that each night would see her maintaining her vigil over her bedroom door and window.

And this morning, a note was pushed under the door. Neville had written exactly what he was going to do with her when he caught her and that she would never marry anyone but him. Thankfully, after breakfast, Matron had sent him off to visit family in Leeds and for this Isabelle had sent a prayer of thanks heaven-ward.

★   ★   ★

The office door opened before she could lift her hand to knock and Mr Beale ushered her in. 'You're late.'

'I'm sorry.' She puffed. 'I was helping in the kitchens.'

Matron, all congeniality, beckoned with a tight smile. 'Come in, girl, and present yourself to Mr Farrell.'

Isabelle stepped further into the room and looked at the man who might become her husband. Her heart hammered against her ribs as she took in his ruddy complexion, sharp blue eyes and black hair. She knew him to be thirty-eight, but he looked ten years older. Once, he would have been a good looking man, powerfully built. Only now, his muscle had run to heaviness, but she felt he would still be strong — the width of his arms strained his coat sleeves and his neck was as thick as a bull's.

'Miss Gibson.' He held out his wide hand, looking uncomfortable in his suit too small

21

for him, but his shy smile calmed her a little.

'Good day, Mr Farrell.' She barely touched his fingers before she withdrew her hand to hide it behind her back. 'Thank you for coming to see me.'

'I heard yer were in the need for a husband.' His unblinking stare wasn't unsympathetic.

'Yes. I am. I need a home for my brother and me.' She smiled, trying desperately to still her anxiety. 'You . . . you require a wife to help you run your farm?'

'Aye.' He glanced at Mr Beale and then at Matron.

As if taking her cue, Matron bustled forward. 'Miss Gibson is a hard worker indeed, Mr Farrell. You'll not go wrong in having her for a wife.'

Isabelle frowned in surprise at Matron's sunny nature. She'd never had a good word to say about her before. Turning her attention back to Mr Farrell she focused on his answer.

'Being a farmer's wife is no easy life.' He peered at her as though sizing up her worth. 'Yer sure yer up to it?'

'Of course!' She straightened, alarmed that he'd think her weak. She'd have no one say she couldn't pull her weight. She wasn't frightened of hard work. 'I'm healthy and strong.'

He nodded. 'Yer'll need to be.'

She raised her chin. 'Hard work doesn't deter me, Mr Farrell.'

'Yer'd be no use to me if it did,' He snorted. 'There'll be many chores that are yours alone. The farm's been without a woman since me mam died some years back. I haven't time to do everything now.'

'Of course. You can depend on me. I promise you.'

'Right. Good.'

'Mr Beale tells me your farm is on the moors beyond Heptonstall.'

'Aye.'

'When I was small I remember my father taking me onto the moors near Sowerby. We walked forever that day. It was like being on top of the world and — ' Isabelle stopped, embarrassed at the other's silence.

Farrell shifted uneasily, a flush staining his cheeks. 'Well, I don't know about that, but it's not bad in't summer. Winter can be a bloody nuisance.'

'Indeed, Mr Farrell!' Matron eyed him severely for his language. 'I'm certain Isabelle will enjoy all the delights a moorland farm can offer.'

'Right, yes.' Farrell fiddled with the hat in his hands.

'Well, what do you think, Isabelle?' Matron

beamed. 'Doesn't it all sound romantic?'

Romantic? Isabelle stared at her. Who was this new woman? She much preferred the old matron, at least then she knew what to expect. Matron's extraordinary behaviour confused her already jumbled thoughts, but before she could speak, Farrell strode to the chair near the door and picked up a small posy of wildflowers. He thrust them at Isabelle without meeting her eyes.

'There aren't many flowers left now. These were all I could find about the place.'

She took the squashed bunch of flowers. The unexpected gesture astonished her. If he could bring her flowers then he couldn't be that bad, surely? 'Thank you. Do they grow near your home?'

'Aye. Near the stream.' His tone became distant and, scowling, he looked away as if disappointed by something.

Isabelle sniffed their faded fragrance and was filled with the sense of outdoors. She longed to be up on the moors, to experience the vastness of them where there were no walls to keep her in or to hide the world from her view. She felt she couldn't breathe here any more.

★ ★ ★

Later that afternoon, Isabelle and Hughie, sat huddling in their thin coats in a secluded corner of the yard playing cards. They put up with the cold because it was better than the other option — staying inside and being at Matron's beck and call.

'So, this Mr Farrell seems nice?' Hughie asked, shuffling the cards.

'Yes, he seemed to be.' Isabelle shrugged, not really knowing one way or the other. 'He didn't stay long otherwise I would have sent for you to meet him, too.'

'Will he like me, do you think?'

'Of course he will.' She winked. 'Why would he not?'

'It might be good to live on a farm and care for animals.'

She snorted. 'Anywhere is better than here.'

'I know. Matron slapped me around the ear this morning for eating too fast, but I'm always hungry.'

'Just think of what they must eat at the farm. Fresh eggs, milk, hams and cheese.'

Hughie groaned and rubbed his stomach. 'Remember how at grandfather's we used to have two eggs every morning after prayers? We're lucky to get one egg a week!'

Warm memories flowed as Isabelle remembered the pleasant times of living with their grandfather; his gentle voice reading to them at night in front of the fire, the long walks on Saturday afternoons, and the Christmas festivities he enjoyed so much. He had taken them in when Aaron Gibson, her father, abandoned them. Life had been good at the vicarage until a sudden seizure took their darling grandfather from them. With no home or income of their own they had no option but to take the charity of Peacock's Private Workhouse.

In good faith, her mother gave Matron all her jewellery to help towards their keep. But once their mother died, the Matron's true nature emerged and her false benevolence turned to coldness. Since then, only Sally's sweet nature kept up the pretence of civility.

'Does Mr Farrell have family?' asked Hughie.

Isabelle frowned. 'Not sure. He mentioned his mother died a few years ago. That's all I know. I imagine he has workers. A farm needs men to run it.' She paused and gazed at the elderly men toiling in the vegetable gardens. By the far wall two women, old before their time, sat on stools knitting or sewing surrounded by numerous children. Everything and everyone was colourless, dreary, desperate and sad. This wasn't her fate, to be left existing behind a high, stone wall, shut away from the world. Of that she was certain. She hated each moment she spent here.

'Will you marry him then?'

She looked at Hughie and reached for his hand. 'I think I might. I haven't decided. I wanted to speak to you about it first.'

'Have there been any other men you'd might want to marry instead?'

'No. None. I guess I could ask Mr Thwaite, the grocer in Nelson Street. He always smiled at me whenever Sally and I used to pass by. He's widowed.'

'And old, too.' Hughie laughed. 'His daughter was as old as Mother.'

Isabelle sighed, too anxious to share in the jest. Something had to be done. A chance must be taken. She wouldn't be trapped here with the years stretching out before her in a never-ending drudge of work and Neville's attention. Her youth would be gone, stolen by Matron's harsh demands and Neville's malicious attacks.

Hughie peeked up from under his lashes. 'Matron said I'm to go down the pit.'

'You aren't! I promised Mother.' Isabelle pressed her fingers to her throbbing temples. The pressure built within and she couldn't control it, couldn't escape it. Too many decisions. Too many uncertainties. But what choices did she have? What should she do?

'Can't we just run away? Now Sally has gone, we can do it. Just you and me. I'm old enough, nearly thirteen!'

Isabelle shook her head slowly, sadly. 'I can't risk it. If something was to happen to you, I'd never forgive myself. And if something happened to me, you'd be alone.'

'Anything is better than rotting in here.'

'Dying by the side of the road isn't.'

He nodded, but Mildred, another workhouse inmate, caught their attention as she ran towards them: 'Isabelle! This just arrived for you.' She held out a brown box.

'For me?' Surprised, Isabelle stood and took the box from her.

'Let me know what's in it later. I must get back. Matron is doing her inspections.' Mildred ran off towards the kitchens before Isabelle could thank her.

Intrigued, Hughie jumped up to stand beside her. 'What is it, Belle?'

'It must be from Mr Farrell. How lovely.' Opening the box, Isabelle pulled back the brown paper inside and gasped. Several withered pink roses dipped in black ink lay at the bottom of the box.

Hughie stepped back in disgust. 'Eww, that's awful! If that Farrell sent you this as a gift I'd not marry him, Belle.'

Isabelle swallowed and found it difficult to

speak. How could anyone send such a thing to her? A card lay underneath one rose but she didn't pick it up. Forcing a smile, she turned to Hughie. 'It must be someone's joke. They aren't from Mr Farrell. It's nothing to worry about. Why don't you go in and see if you can charm a cup of tea from Cook, while I throw this away.'

Once Hughie had left, she carefully tugged the card from beneath the disfigured flowers and read it. 'You will never marry anyone but me. N.'

She dropped the box in horror. Spilt like a bottle of ink, the flowers tumbled out at her feet.

3

Isabelle's stomach lurched as wildly as the cart did every time its wheels rolled into a rut. She hid her shaking hands by folding them tightly in her lap. Her new husband, Len Farrell, slapped the reins hard on the poor, skinny beast pulling them. Isabelle took a trembling breath. Spirit fumes emanated from Len as though he had bathed in gin. His coat, although not new, looked decent that morning when she first saw him in church, but now dark telltale signs of spilt food and drink mottled it. She had vague memories of the ceremony and the small tea party afterwards. Their conversation, albeit some-what stilted and under the watchful gaze of Matron and Mr Beale, remained on safe ground with him telling her about the moors and wildlife near his farm.

She allowed her gaze to shift up to his face and she bit her lip in alarm. This man was her husband. How had it happened so quickly? Four weeks after burying Sally she had married a stranger. Despite her apprehension and fear of what she had just committed to, she couldn't but help to feel relieved at escaping the Peacock's Workhouse. The last four weeks had been nothing but torture. Neville continued to torment and harass her at every opportunity until she felt too ill to care anymore. All that kept her going was the thought that soon she would be married and away from him. Neville hated the thought of her marrying anyone but him. However, it was his violence that drove her into the hasty marriage with Farrell. If he'd left her alone, she could have taken her time, been more selective. She sighed and thought: *Oh well, what's done is done.*

The cartwheel fell into a hole, jerking Isabelle back to the present. She forced herself to relax. Yes, she had married a stranger, but what had been the alternative? Living on the streets would have been much worse and she had to think of Hughie's future too. She raised her chin and concentrated on her surroundings. They'd left Halifax immediately after the wedding tea and driven straight to Hebden Bridge, where Len stopped to purchase goods, which, for some reason, he grumbled about. Now, they drove up the steep, winding Heptonstall road and her new husband had barely spoken to them. She couldn't blame him really. Obviously, the situation wasn't easy for him either. She expected that men were equally nervous as

31

women when they married.

Craning to look past Hughie, Isabelle marvelled at the magnificent scenery of the valley below. The grey stone terrace houses of Hebden Bridge hugged the slopes as though they had been hewn from the valley sides. The silver ribbon of the River Calder coiled through the town like a lazy snake. Beside it, caught in glimpses between trees and buildings, lay the Rochdale Canal.

Familiar names in a new and unfamiliar life.

The muted noise of the small village of Heptonstall greeted them like a soft caress on the wind. The narrow, quiet streets reflected the lateness of the day; many would be inside enjoying their tea. Isabelle took eager interest in the old church and Weaver's Square, and counted seven public houses, but all too soon they left the stone thoroughfare of Towngate and headed northwest on Smithwell Lane and out of the village. She would have to investigate the village properly at a later date.

Isabelle stifled a yawn; she had been awake since before dawn. The day's toll flagged her strength. She still couldn't believe she was now married. Opening her eyes wide to keep alert, she surveyed the countryside as it opened up on both sides of the road. The higher they rose, the cooler the weather became and the bleaker their environment. This was moor country. The crisp autumn air awoke her senses. Her gaze lingered on the hues of the heather covered moor. *How beautiful it is*, she thought. Maybe being married and living in the country would be an enjoyable experience.

Len slapped the reins against the horse's rump and grunted. One-handed he pulled out a small hipflask and unscrewed the top. He made gurgling sounds as the liquid went down his throat, as though he couldn't take it in fast enough. Isabelle shivered. Drink was new to her. His loud belch made her jump, and she looked at him in rebuke. He clearly wasn't used to being in a woman's company, but she could teach him.

Sighing, she lifted her chin and decided to learn more about this husband of hers. 'So, Mr Farrell, have you always lived at your farm? I mean, has your family always been there?'

'Aye.'

'Do you have many relatives living nearby?'

'No.'

This news saddened her. She had been looking forward to the company of female family members. Since losing her darling mother and sister, she had missed the closeness they shared. It would have been nice to share recipes and gossip.

Hughie leant forward to address his new brother-in-law. 'How many animals do you have, Mr Farrell?'

'The both of yer can stop calling me Mr Farrell. Me name's Len or just Farrell.' He took another swig from his flask.

Hughie grinned at Isabelle, excited to be on an adventure. 'Well, Len, how many have you got?'

'Enough to keep yer busy.'

'What kind?'

'Sheep.'

The one-word answers soon quelled Hughie's interest, and he leant back in his seat in a huff.

Isabelle tried to ignore the uneasiness that plagued her. She had asked to be married. This was what she wanted, so she'd better make the best of it. There was much she had to learn, Hughie too. There'd be adjustments on both sides. Farrell had never been married before, so sharing his house with strangers was bound to make him tetchy. All would be well though, she believed. They'd have a home, food and each other to care for. She was to be mistress of a house and farm. She'd have respect. Suddenly a thought entered her head. Did she have servants? Turning to Len she tried to keep the eagerness out of her voice. 'Are there servants at your farm?'

He stared at her for a half a minute, then laughed so hard it made him cough. After he finished spluttering he gave her a quick look. 'What do yer think I am? Gentry?'

'Well no, not gentry.' She frowned, not liking his ridicule. 'So there is no one?'

'Of course there ain't. I ain't medd of money.'

'Is your farm not very big then?'

'It's big enough for yer needs, madam. Now stop with the questions, me head's fair thumping.'

She looked at Hughie and managed a tight smile. Such an important day, not to mention a very long one, made them all tired.

The journey passed by in silence until Len cleared his throat and shifted in his seat. He turned the horse into Draper's Lane and they headed north. The landscape sloped downhill gently. He pointed to a depression in the land on his right that broke the pattern of undulating moors. 'See that over there? That's me farm. Meadow Farm it's called. Further on this lane goes down to Hebden Water.'

Isabelle gazed at the cluster of farm buildings hidden amongst a clump of trees a mile or so away. Meadow Farm was situated on a flat plateau inside the depression. Though they were high up, hills in the west rose again even higher. Down to their left, the land fell away at a gentle angle towards another valley some miles off. Sheep dotted the landscape.

'Meadow Farm. What a lovely name.' Isabelle nudged Hughie, where he rested against her side, dozing. 'Look Hughie, over to the right, that is Meadow Farm, our new home.'

Being high in the cart seat, she could see over the stone walls and hawthorn hedges that grew in number the closer they got to the farm. The moor gave way to patches of farmland as men wrested the land from nature. Excited, Isabelle scanned the surrounding fields. Some lay fallow, others were neatly ploughed. As they drove down the slope, the natural indentation of the landscape offered them some protection from the wind. Nearing the farm, the road widened. A cart full of milk cans rattled towards them.

Isabelle smiled at the passing driver. 'Is there another farm close by, Len?'

'Aye.' He pointed further along the road. 'This lane leads to Lee Wood Road and to Bracken Hall where the bastard landlord lives. He owns all the fields we just passed and plenty more besides.'

She peered over her shoulder at the

well-tended fields. 'I thought they were yours.'

'Nope. The bastard from Bracken Hall took 'em off me when I went to sign up for a new lease.' Len spat over the side of the cart. 'He left me with just ten acres. Not enough to make money with, barely enough for me to live on. I had to sell half my flock. Bastard.' He spat again. 'He'll get what's coming to him one day and I hope to God I play a part in it.'

Isabelle swallowed back her comment on spitting and any further questions as an angry red stain flushed Len's neck and cheeks. A feud. That was the last thing she expected. Her husband hated his landlord.

The large chestnut trees encircling the farm loomed closer. Without their summer leaves they exposed the features of the farm. She spied the brick farmhouse and a few outer buildings, before a tall hawthorn hedge blocked their view. Ducks and geese squawked and honked as Len drove the horse and cart through the rotten timbered gates that lay drunkenly against the hedge. A deep pothole in the drive caused the cart to nearly throw them out. Isabelle and Hughie were shoved against each other. Len swore and reined in the horse, threw the reins onto the seat and climbed down.

Straightening up, Isabelle adjusted her hat, then stopped and stared. Disbelief shattered her excitement. Stench from an unseen source made her cover her nose. The filth of the yard amazed her. Thick mud from previous rain lay inches deep and coated brickwork where it had splashed up. The whole yard seemed to be of one colour, a dirty dark grey. Age discoloured the farm-house and only under the eaves did the true pale grey brick reveal itself. Doors hung off the outer buildings and missing slates left gaps in the roofs like a toothless mouth. Smaller farm buildings had peeling paintwork around glassless windows. Oozing straw, piled high, filled one corner of the yard and, in another corner, lay a broken wagon upon which sat a few scrawny hens. A cat hissed from a fence post before disappearing into the wild scrubland behind the house.

Almost afraid to, Isabelle turned her attention to the house and shuddered. The same decay and neglect of the yard attached itself to the house. Thick grime covered the attic's window matching the dirt and cobwebs on the downstairs mullioned windows. Despite the ravages of disregard awarded to the house, its structure hinted at a long ago dignity. Weed-infested gardens hugged the walls and an overgrown climbing rose was so monstrous in size and so heavy that it had peeled back from the house wall and hung in a cascade of thorny tangles.

'Are yer getting down or what?' Len shouted, taking the bags out of the back of the cart.

Hughie jumped down and landed in a mud puddle. Squelching with each movement, he turned and helped Isabelle down. She refused to meet his eyes.

Len thrust their bags at them and then collected the boxes of provisions. He placed the boxes on the ground in the mud. 'Go away inside, I've got things to do in Hepstonstall. I'll be back tomorrow.'

'Tomorrow?' Isabelle gaped at him.

'That's what I said.' He pulled himself up into the cart and then looked at Hughie. 'See to the animals. Yer've got to earn yer keep or yer out!'

'Wait!' Isabelle struggled to gather the skirts of her best and only dress with one hand and hugged her bag to her with the other. 'Can your business not wait until later? We've only just arrived . . . '

Len leant down as far as he could and sneered in her face. 'Don't be thinking yer can tell me what to do just because I gave yer me name. I'm me own man and I'll do as I please. Got it?' He straightened up and whipped the horse forward.

Isabelle and Hughie watched him turn the horse and cart around in the confines of the yard and then trundle back out through the gates.

'Oh, Belle,' Hughie whispered, looking at her with wide frightened eyes.

She had to be strong. She mustn't let him see her weaken with fear. Taking a deep breath, she straightened her shoulders and tossed her head. 'Come, Hughie. Let us look inside our new home.'

He baulked. 'You mean we are staying?'

'Of course we are staying.'

He didn't move when she stepped towards the house. 'But Belle, look at this place.'

Concentrating on treading around lumps of manure and the worst of the mud, she didn't look back at him. 'Yes, it is not what we expected, but we'll just have to make do for now. My husband obviously needs more help.'

Hughie muttered under his breath and trudged after her. They found the front door locked and she experienced a moment of panic, envisaging being locked out all night. She then decided to check the back of the house.

Their first glimpse of this part of the yard did not raise their hopes — it was in the same

40

terrible state as the front and side yards, with the only difference being the open fields beyond softening the view somewhat. A stone path partially covered by weeds led to one of the two back doors through which there must have been a kitchen garden once. A clump of nettles guarded the other door, so she assumed the black painted door in front of her was the main one used by Len.

She gripped the handle and turned it. Surprisingly, it opened easily and she sagged with relief. However, her heart plummeted as she stood on the step facing a dim and grubby kitchen. It reeked of dampness. A large table littered with all sorts of tins, jars, stale food, ale bottles and utensils occupied the middle of the room.

Isabelle dumped her bag on the dusty stone-flagged floor and stepped to the range along the far wall. Cold seeped into her bones. She grimaced at the mound of ashes in the grate. Sighing, she turned and viewed the large dresser. It held little of any interest. Walking around the table, she went to the window and, using her elbow, scrubbed away a circle of grime to let in more light. It did nothing to improve the room.

'Let us look in here.' She indicated the room behind Hughie and he turned and followed her into the scullery. In here was the copper pot for washing, the larder and a door leading down into the black cellar. The other back door led into this room from outside.

In the kitchen once more, Isabelle hesitated. She looked through the doorway into the dark, narrow hall. Quietness shrouded the house like a dense fog. She felt like an intruder. Biting her lip, she inched down the hallway and opened the door to the front room. After peering into its bleak coldness, Isabelle quickly closed the door. She would have a proper look later.

'We aren't going up there, are we?' Hughie pointed upstairs.

Isabelle took his hand, fighting off her own trepidation. 'It's where we are to sleep. So, I suppose we should.' She led him up the narrow, uncarpeted staircase to the small landing above. Two doors led off the landing. Each door opened into a bedroom. One bedroom was empty, the other held a double bed, a washstand and a chest of drawers. Nothing in the room indicated that it was Len's room. There were no personal touches, but Isabelle guessed he slept there because it held the only bed.

In the corner of the landing, a rickety ladder went up into a hole in the ceiling. Hughie climbed it first and poked his head through. 'It's just got some boxes and crates in it. There's a chest in the corner and a baby's cradle.'

'Come back down. We'll go and light a fire. I'm fair frozen.'

In the kitchen, Isabelle took off her coat and then used the iron poker to clear the ashes to one side of the grate. 'Find me some paper and kindling, Hughie.'

He went into the scullery and soon returned with what she needed. At first, the fire refused to blaze and smoked so badly it made her cough.

Hughie watched with a pained expression. 'What do you want me to do, Belle?'

'Go outside and bring those boxes in. I'll make us a cup of tea if I can ever get this fire going.'

Once Hughie had placed the two boxes on the table, Isabelle unpacked them. The pound weight bags of sugar, tea and salt, plus small sacks of flour and oats she took and placed in the empty larder while Hughie stacked the bottles of ale. Isabelle took the empty bucket from the scullery and went outside. The pump was near the large clump of nettles and she wondered how often Len drew water, for the path was not well used.

'I think the chimney isn't drawing.' Hughie told her as she entered the kitchen with the full bucket. 'It needs to be swept, but that's hardly surprising is it? I doubt Mr Farrell does little around here.'

'Shhh, Hughie, we don't know his circumstances. Best not to judge just yet.' She filled the kettle with water and then swung it over the flames.

'Why did you marry him, Belle? Couldn't you have waited for someone better?'

She turned from searching in the cupboards for teacups and looked at him. On no account did she want to worry him about the lengths Neville went to in frightening her. 'Who do you think would have married me? Gentry?'

'I'm sure it could have been someone better than Farrell. A tradesman maybe.'

'I could have turned old and grey waiting, Hughie. I didn't want to take the risk. I couldn't have stayed at Matron's much longer. She wanted me out.'

'Mrs Peacock's establishment wasn't so bad was it?'

'For me, yes it was. Neville made things difficult. Besides, you know how much the Matron and I argued.'

'That was because you were always telling her what she needed to do to make the place run better.'

'Well, someone had to!'

'Mother always said you were too . . . ' he

searched for the right word, 'opinionated.'

'I tried not to be.' Isabelle shrugged. 'Sally was the buffer between me and Matron, but once she left us . . . Well, never mind that now. I made my choice and I must live with it.' Isabelle stomped into the scullery and in the large stone sink found dirty plates, cups and an iron pot. She took two chipped cups and dunked them into the water bucket and rubbed them clean. It wasn't ideal, but quenching her thirst was more important. They'd had nothing to eat or drink since their short wedding breakfast that morning and here it was nearly sundown. They drank their tea without milk and in silence until a cow's bellow made them jump.

Hughie's eyes widened. 'What about the animals he said I had to see to?'

Isabelle frowned. 'Oh dear.' She looked through the dirty window. The light outside was fading fast. Sighing, she shrugged on her coat again. 'Very well. Let us see what has to be done.'

Outside, Isabelle paused. The three out-buildings on the other side of the yard did not look inviting. She gazed out over the fields. A small flock of sheep grazed farther away, but closer by a few cows wandered about in the house field, and one actually came up to the gate and bellowed to them. The ancient trees surrounding the house and yard were strung out in a line along a shallow stream towards the small woodland in the distance. White flecks against the stream's banks showed that the ducks and geese had left the yard.

Taking a deep breath, Isabelle strode towards the first outbuilding and pulled back the dilapidated old door. The dank smell of rotten straw clogged her throat. She waited for her eyes to adjust to the dimness and then peered around. A haphazard pile of old straw bales dominated one corner while in another, numerous farm implements lay scattered and forgotten.

'There is so much in here.' Hughie said walking over to three barrels placed against the far wall. He took the lid off one and grimaced. 'Whatever it was in this barrel is all mouldy now.'

Isabelle opened a sack by the door and found it full of potatoes. She dragged the sack out into the yard so she could see better. Most of them had gone to seed, but some were edible. She took out four large potatoes. The cow by the gate bellowed again. 'I think we need to milk that cow. What do you think?'

Hughie glanced from her to the cow and back again. 'We don't know how.'

'Looks like we'll have to learn a lot of

things.' The noise from the cow grew louder and more frequent. Isabelle gave the potatoes to Hughie. 'Take them inside and bring me back the bucket.'

She walked slowly towards the demanding beast and paused. Its udder seemed huge. Isabelle bit her lip and stepped closer. She unlocked the gate and the cow bellowed into her face, frightening her so much she screamed. Her heart raced as though she had run a mile. She grasped the cow's head rope. 'What am I to do?' she whispered, close to tears.

'Here, Belle.' Hughie thrust the bucket at her. 'Put it under the cow and pull those things there.' He pointed in the direction of the udder.

'Well, you hold this rope.' She placed the bucket under the udder and squatted down. Taking a teat in each hand, she pulled and jumped in surprise when milk squirted over her boots.

'You did it!' Hughie's yell made the cow step sideways.

'Hold it still and be quiet.' Isabelle steadied herself again and alternatively pulled at the teats. Some milk made it into the bucket, but within minutes, her arms and back ached from the unusual position.

'How much is enough?' Hughie asked.

'I don't know.' She turned to look at him and at the same time the cow's hind leg jutted forward and knocked the bucket over, spilling its precious contents.

'Damn! Blast!' Isabelle slapped the cow's rump and it trotted away. Collecting the overturned bucket, she scowled at the offending creature. 'It can bellow all it wants for I'm not doing that again.' Sighing, she walked through the gate and closed it. 'Mr Farrell will have to deal with it in the morning when he returns.'

'We'll not be having milk in our tea then.'

'I'm sure we'll survive.'

Hughie strolled over to the last outbuilding in the row. 'What's in here do you think?'

'No doubt more of the same that's in the first one.'

The door was split in half, with the top section open and tied against the crumbling stonework, the lower half shut. Hughie looked over and then turned to grin at her. 'Come look, Belle.'

Peeking over the door, she spotted a fat pig asleep in the corner, but hearing them, the pig rocked onto its feet and snuffled over to the door making hideous noises.

'It might be hungry.' Hughie reached down to scratch its tough hairy head.

'Careful, it might bite.' Isabelle pulled him

away. 'Go look in the middle shed and see if there is some food in there or any other animals. I'll search in the bushes over there for eggs.'

The hens scattered when she approached and headed into the first barn. Tall grass, weeds and stinging nettles surrounded the broken wagon like a fortress. Swishing them aside with a stick, Isabelle hunted for eggs. She found three on top of the wagon and gently placed them in her pockets. Ducking under the wagon, she spied a hen sitting near the wheel. It moved for a moment revealing a dozen or so eggs and Isabelle grinned and reached in for them. A stinging pain on her hand made her fall backwards. The hen had pecked her. 'You rotten thing! Keep your eggs then!' Straightening up, Isabelle rubbed her sore hand as Hughie joined her.

'I've fed the pig some grain I found.' He shrugged. 'It might not be what it eats but there's nothing else.'

'Don't worry about it now.'

They walked into the house as the light faded completely. The fire was low, but gave out enough light for Isabelle to see by as she rummaged around the kitchen for candles. Beneath all the rubbish covering the table, she found a small candle stub in a holder with matches. Its light was pitiful, but better than nothing.

'Look in the scullery for a lamp, Hughie, and we need more water. Can you get it while I start — ' Isabelle screamed as a mouse ran over her boot and under the table.

'It's all right, Belle.' He grinned. 'It's only a mouse.'

She closed her eyes momentarily. Tiredness sapped her spirit. The whole situation she was in was a nightmare she hoped to wake up from. Treacherous tears formed behind her lids, but she knuckled them away. She wouldn't cry. She couldn't give in.

4

Isabelle woke with a start, wincing at the pain and stiffness in her neck, and lamented the folly of sleeping upright in a kitchen chair. Across the table, Hughie slept on with his head cradled on his arms.

She yawned and stood up, stretching her legs to get the blood flowing again. A weak light filtered in through the grubby window and she sagged against the table at the enormity of her situation. She had married a stranger and now lived in a filthy neglected farm. Her bottom lip trembled as tears welled, but she swallowed them back. This weakness of wanting to cry annoyed her. Crying never did any good. It hadn't brought her mother or Sally back or even her father when he had walked away from them when she was only ten years old. No, crying was for old women regretting their lost youth. She, Isabelle Gibson, now Farrell, had her whole life ahead of her and she intended to make a go of it.

With this in mind, she went into the scullery and changed out of her good dress and into her old black skirt and cream blouse, the only other clothes she possessed. That done, she went outside and filled the bucket with water.

Hughie was adding wood to the fire when she entered the kitchen. She grinned at him. 'Today is a new day, Hughie. A fresh start for both of us.'

His face lit up. 'We are leaving?'

She shook her head. 'No. I am married. I have to stay and so we are going to make the best of it. Len Farrell might be accustomed to living in squalor but we are not. We are going to clean and tidy this place.'

Hughie groaned and buried his head in his hands. 'I want to leave, Belle. I don't like it here.'

'You've hardly given it a chance. Yes, we've had a bad beginning, but it will get better. I'm sure of it.' She put the kettle on to boil as the cow's bellow rang in the clear morning air. 'Now, go and milk that cow while I make a start on getting this kitchen to rights.'

Hughie threw up his hands. 'I can't milk the dreaded thing.'

'Yes, you can.' She poured the water into the kettle and then pushed the bucket at him and waved him away. 'Now go. And watch that its back leg doesn't clout you one.'

After a quick cup of weak black tea, Isabelle filled the iron pot with hot water and added caustic soda that she had found under the stone sink in the scullery. Placing an empty box on a chair, she threw anything resembling rubbish into it and then scrubbed the table with a rag dipped in the soda water. She left the table to dry and washed the window inside and out. Then, she wiped over the dresser and all the shelves. Next, she found a broom in the cellar and brushed away the numerous cobwebs coating the ceiling beams.

The sudden light shining through the clean window showed how dirty the kitchen floor was and so, bunching up her skirts, Isabelle got down on her knees and scrubbed that too.

As she threw the mucky water over the nettles, Hughie ran to her grinning. 'Look!' He thrust the bucket at her. 'It must be at least an inch deep.'

'Wonderful.' She tussled his hair. 'We can have tea with milk this morning, and since we ate the eggs and potatoes last night, I have oats simmering for porridge.'

'Good, I'm starved!'

Chuckling, they went in for their breakfast. Things were brightening up. They could do this, she knew it.

Hughie whistled in surprise at the cleaner kitchen. 'You've done grand, Belle.'

'Yes, well, there is so much more to do.'

She tipped the milk into a clean jar and put it on the table. 'I have plenty more cleaning to do, so you'll have to keep me supplied with buckets of water.'

'Do you think the pig needs feeding in the mornings too?'

Isabelle stirred the oats and turned to him, but her words died in her throat as Len Farrell stood in the doorway. She hadn't even heard him arrive.

Her husband, filthy and bloodied, staggered into the kitchen and fell into a chair. Isabelle's heart missed a beat as his bloodshot eyes peered at her. He reeked of stale beer.

'Well, wife . . . ' He slipped sideways in his chair and only kept upright by holding onto the table edge. 'Made yersen at home I see.'

Isabelle swallowed. 'I . . . we ..'

'Silence!' he roared.

Hughie jumped and ran to stand beside her and she held him tight.

Farrell winkled his nose as though he smelt something unpleasant. 'Eating me food! Sleeping in me house!' He thumped the table. 'Get out!'

Isabelle trembled. 'What do you mean?'

'I said get out!' Farrell sprung to his feet, but the motion was too quick for him in his befuddled state. He toppled over and landed with a sickening thud on the stone floor.

'Dear God in Heaven,' she whispered. Pushing Hughie away, she stepped around the table and stared at her prostrate husband.

'Is he moving, Belle?' Hughie murmured, his fear evident in his white face.

Isabelle touched Farrell with the toe of her boot. He groaned and she let out a pent up breath. 'He's alive.'

'What are we to do?'

'Nothing for the moment. He's drunk. We'll let him sleep it off. Maybe then he will be more sensible.' She ushered Hughie outside. 'Go look for some more eggs and fill the bucket with water. Then come in for your breakfast.'

Once Hughie was gone from sight, Isabelle looked down on her unfortunate choice of husband. He frightened and repulsed her, but she had made her decision to stay. Besides, she had no money, no family and nowhere to go. Sighing, she went to the range. Maybe her husband was a good man when he wasn't drunk?

While he slept Isabelle continued with her scrubbing. Farrell didn't stir for two hours, then, as she was sorting out the best of the old potatoes from the sack, he moaned. Isabelle's dirt-covered hands stilled and she peeped over at him.

He groaned on sitting up. His eyes

narrowed, trying to focus. 'What's going on?'

Disgusted she sneered, 'Nothing. You fell down drunk!'

Farrell grunted. Gripping the table edge, he hauled himself to his feet, sniffing and coughing. 'Get me a drink.'

'There's tea in the pot.' She rose and poured out a cup of tea for him and then inched it over in his direction.

He took a sip before flopping down onto the chair at the end of the table. Red eyes narrowed as he surveyed the kitchen before scowling back at her. 'Yer make too free with me things.'

Isabelle swung the kettle onto the heat to boil and to give her shaking hands something to do. 'Pardon?'

'Who said yer could touch me things?'

'I am your wife. It is my duty to clean our home.'

'It is my home.'

She stared at him as though he was a simpleton. 'And, since our marriage, it is mine also.' She put two cups on the table. Hughie would be in for his tea soon. 'Do you want to continue living in filth? I cannot imagine what — '

'Shut yer mouth!' His fist caught the side of her head. She spun like a top and banged into the range. The fire's heat threatened and she darted away, dizzy, swaying with stars sparkling in front of her eyes.

'You . . . You hit me.' She held her head and stared at him through her tears.

He turned away and sat back down. 'It's yer own fault.'

Her fault? Why? *Because you opened your mouth!* Isabelle swallowed. When would she learn not to judge and give her opinions so freely? She badly needed to sit down but her limbs wouldn't move.

'I'm hungry,' Farrell growled, his head hung low.

Stiff and hesitant, Isabelle moved to the range. Her mind went blank. What to feed him? She couldn't think. 'We . . . we don't have much. No meat.'

His face reddened in anger. 'I bought bread yesterday. Don't yer tell me yer've both eaten it all!'

'No, no. We haven't.' Isabelle held onto the back of the chair to keep upright.

'Christ, woman, are yer dumb or what? Peacock said yer could cook!'

'I . . . I can bake pies. Our old cook showed me . . . '

'I don't care what it is, just feed me.'

She closed her eyes momentarily and left the safety of her end of the kitchen. As she passed his chair, he jerked out a hand and

57

caught her wrist. 'If yer want to stay here, yer'd best smarten up.' His fingers felt like they were crushing her bones. 'If I've got to have a wife, I'll not have a stupid one.' Isabelle nodded.

Hughie clambered in carrying a bucket full of water, but stopped on seeing Farrell clasping her wrist. His gaze flew to her. 'I . . . I . . . got water.'

'Thanks, pet. Put . . . put it over there. I've got some tea in the pot for you.'

'Thanks, pet!' Farrell mimicked in a woman's high voice, then he stood so fast he knocked his chair over. 'Get me something to eat!' he roared. 'I'll not be placed second behind this runt.' With a swipe of his ham fist, Farrell knocked Hughie in the chest, sending him skittling backwards. The bucket fell from his hands and splashed over Farrell's boots.

Farrell leapt to the side, shouting he'd kill the little swine. Hughie ducked Farrell's swinging fist and raced outside. Isabelle went to follow him when she was abruptly yanked back by Farrell's grip on her hair. He glared down at her a mere inch from her face. 'Yer get me something to eat or yer'll be out on the road with nowt but the clothes on yer back!'

She nodded, wincing as the movement made the pull on her hair tighter.

'And clean this mess up.' He flung her away.

With her scalp burning, she stumbled into the scullery and through to the larder. She allowed herself a moment to sag against the cold shelves before straightening up and raising her chin. She'd feed him and keep her mouth shut until his mood left him. Nodding, she gathered the bread and a jar of lard. *All it will take is a little adjusting — on everyone's part*, she said to herself.

★   ★   ★

Isabelle arched her back and winced with pain as the cramped muscles stretched. Sweat dripped off her nose and hot steam buffeted her with every plunge of the washing stick. Sheets filled the large copper tub and her arms ached as she lifted and wrung the water from them. She carried the full wicker basket outside and walked towards the rope she and Hughie had strung between two trees.

'Hey you!'

He's awake. She turned as Farrell called her. 'Yes?'

'I want a cup of tea.'

'I'll be there in a minute. I must hang this washing out to dry or there'll be no sheets for the bed.'

'Bugger that. Get me some tea.'

'I will after I have finished.' She strode to the rope and dropped the basket. She heard him curse violently. Her legs trembled a little at her own defiance and she hurriedly hung the sheets out, hoping he wouldn't beat her once she was inside. A weary sigh escaped her as she turned back towards the house. The man was unreasonable. His bad mood from after his fall yesterday morning had stayed with him all day, and the copious amounts of ale he'd drunk during the rest of the afternoon didn't help lift it. He had sat for hours drinking at the kitchen table. At first whenever she or Hughie were in range of his arm, he'd swing out and strike them.

Stunned by his temper, Isabelle found it impossible to think or do anything worthwhile. She went around in a daze of disbelief. It seemed impossible that she'd been clouted and yelled at. Never in her life had she been hit or treated this way.

Soon they learnt to stay clear of his end of the table, but since he sat closest to the back door they needed to pass him to go outside. He'd ordered them about until he fell into another stupor. She and Hughie had crept around him during the evening until, thankfully, they had gone upstairs to the bedroom that held the bed. Curled up together, they had inspected their bruises on arms and faces. She cleaned up a cut on Hughie's lip and eventually they fell into an exhausted sleep, but they had paid for that sleep this morning. For on waking, they found themselves covered with red fleabites that itched in the most ferocious way. Hence Isabelle's impromptu washing day. She was determined to scrub the whole farm, brick by brick if need be.

Entering the kitchen, she edged around him and went to the range. 'Do you want some boiled eggs?'

'Aye.'

She set about boiling the water and putting plates on the table.

'What happened to yer face?'

Isabelle paused and stared. 'You don't know?'

He had the grace to look away. 'Tell me I didn't do it,' he whispered.

'Well, I doubt that Hughie did, do you?' She tilted her head and raised one eyebrow. 'Or perhaps you think I did it to myself?'

Farrell cleared his throat. 'I wasn't aware I . . .'

'Could be so cruel?'

He glared and opened his mouth to speak further, but instead simply grunted and turned away. 'Where's the boy?'

'My brother, *Hughie*, who was also on the receiving end of your drunken temper, found an orchard behind the barns. He's collecting windfall apples, if there are any, to feed the pig, but I'll use the best ones to fill a pie.' She added more tea leaves to the tin teapot and glanced at him from under her lashes. 'This farm is in a deplorable state.'

He thumped the table and made her jump, spilling the tea. 'Don't dare to tell me about me farm. Yer uppity wench!'

She hid her trembling hands behind her back. *I've done it again.* 'I simply mean that it looks to me like you need some help. A labourer or two.'

His harsh laugh frightened her even more than his violence. 'Where do yer think I can get the money to hire labour?'

'Surely . . . I mean can't you sell some stock?'

'Does it look like there is stock to sell? I've hardly enough here to keep this place going as it is.' He sat heavily in the chair and hung his head, his hair, over long, fell forward. 'I don't need yer to tell me about the state of this farm. I see it each day.' His slumped form filled her with pity, which surprised her. He had no idea how to behave with people but she knew she could assist him, teach him. She simply didn't believe that he was all bad.

'I will help you run the farm. Together we can accomplish much, I am certain.'

He lifted his gaze to meet hers and for once there was no hostility in him. 'Yer nothing but a girl.'

She gave him a cheeky smile that hurt the bruising around her eye. 'I am strong and determined.'

He stared at her as though he was seeing her for the first time. A soft chuckle escaped him. 'Yer've no notion of what it takes to run a farm.'

'I can learn, besides the situation cannot be worse than it already is.'

'What's yer name again?'

'Isabelle.'

He nodded and looked around the kitchen. 'This place wasn't always so dire.' He sighed deeply. 'Me mother wouldn't be impressed to see her kitchen so bare. And I hate to think what me father would say about outside.'

Isabelle poured the tea and passed it to him. 'How did it get so bad?'

He took the cup from her and cradled it in his hands. 'I'll not discuss it.'

Commotion from outside had them both leaping for the back door. Farrell looked out the window and then pushed Isabelle back inside. 'Stay in here and do *not* come out.'

Isabelle stepped back as he promptly shut

the door in her face. She sighed, annoyed that their first proper conversation had been cut short. She went to the window, but Farrell glared at her as he went past so she hid in the shadows and peeked the best she could. The richness of the riders' clothes and magnificent horses interested her at once. She inched towards the window again for a better view. Farrell's aggressive stance swung her attention to him. Voices rose and the first rider thrust his crop in Farrell's chest. Isabelle nibbled her fingernail appalled at the scene being played out. The second rider hung back, she picked him out as a steward or something similar. He didn't have the aura of authority that the first rider did.

Farrell gestured widely, his face crimson in anger. She hunkered below the window and prayed he wouldn't become violent. Shaking his fist, her husband shouted like a madman. The forefront rider sat back in his saddle as though weary of the argument. Isabelle studied him. What struck her first was that he wore no hat. He had thick chestnut brown hair, much darker than her own. From this distance she couldn't see the colour of his eyes, but his strong jaw line and arrogant manner revealed that he was a man of consequence. He oozed influence and power. An unidentifiable tingle ran along her skin.

Suddenly, the man looked straight at the window. Isabelle ducked, her heart pounding in her chest. She admonished herself for being so silly. Why did it matter if he saw her or not? Standing, she glanced out the window, but the men whipped their horses about and trotted out of view.

Farrell flung open the door. 'That bastard!'

Isabelle bit her lip as he threw himself into a chair. 'Who is he?'

'The bloody landlord, blast him to hell.'

'What did he want?'

'Blood!' He spat on her clean floor and she shuddered. 'He wants his rent, which I haven't got. He can go swim in the midden for it as far as I'm concerned.'

'He won't throw us onto the streets will he?'

Farrell banged the table with both hands. 'Let him try!' He slammed his chair back and strode outside.

Isabelle gripped the table. Lord, what had she done marrying this fellow? She forced herself to smile as Hughie sidled into the kitchen.

'You all right, Belle?'

'Of course. The visitors upset Farrell, that's all.' She straightened her shoulders. 'Did you find many windfalls?'

'Some, yes. I fed the pig, but I was thinking

65

that it should be let out into the orchard. Its pen stinks awful bad.'

'Do the best you can, pet.'

Later, they ate their meal in silence silhouetted by one candle stub. Farrell had killed a chicken for her and, after the tedious chore of plucking it, she'd boiled it. She wasn't good at cooking interesting meals, especially with the limited ingredients they had. So, boiling a chicken was about the best she could do, but at least she knew how to bake bread and pastry pies. That, if nothing else would fill them, just as long as Hughie could catch rabbits or the odd pheasant until the summer when the fruit ripened.

Outside darkness enclosed them like a tomb. Isabelle shivered. She glanced at Farrell and wondered whether he wanted her in his bed tonight. Their marriage hadn't been consummated, not that she was eager for his touch, quite the opposite in fact. She wasn't entirely sure what the act involved, but did remember her parents laughing and giggling in the night, so she didn't think it could be all that bad if you liked the person.

Again, Farrell was in a foul temper. Snarling at her attempts of conversation and totally ignoring Hughie's stumbling questions about the farm. She hoped the landlord never came again if this was the result.

She and Hughie jumped when Farrell hastily stood and said. 'I'm off out.'

'Out?'

Farrell slapped on his battered hat and turned at the door. 'That's what I said.'

'But where are you going at this hour?'

His gaze pinned her into silence. 'I need to find the rent for the bastard landlord, don't I?'

She stared at him, puzzled. 'How though?'

'You'd best not know.' The click of the door closing seemed terribly loud in the quiet of the kitchen.

5

Isabelle dug the spade into the soil and turned the sod over. Recent rain made the ground soft and she was thankful for it. She wiped her hair out of her eyes with her forearm and then ploughed the spade in again, moving her way down the vegetable plot. Neglected over time, brambles and nettles crowded over it. However, in some cases the wind had carried the seed of blown vegetables around the plot where they had resown. Isabelle had picked those vegetables until there were none left, which was why she now planted new seeds. She knew a little about growing vegetables having spent time in the garden with her grandfather, who had enjoyed the practice.

'It's Sunday, Belle, you shouldn't be working,' Hughie said, coming up beside her. Grime stained his face while his clothes hung on his lanky frame. In the month living at the farm, he had grown, but not filled out. Hard work and not enough food gave him a haggard beggar's look.

'Well, on the way home from church this morning I thought that if we dug this plot, I could perhaps grow something over winter or failing that, we could have the soil ready for spring,' she replied.

'Where's *he* gone this time?'

'Halifax.'

Hughie took the spade from her and resumed the task. 'Will he be back today?'

'No, he said not.' She picked up the bag of broad beans and dropped a seed into the row behind Hughie.

'I hope he never comes back.'

'Don't Hughie. Farrell is trying . . . ' Isabelle sighed. In truth her husband had tried to be civil, but his social graces lacked considerably. He swung between drunken rages and fits of brooding depression. 'I know it isn't easy living like this but there are worse places.'

'Huh, I'd like to see them.'

Isabelle bit back further comment, too tired to argue with him. A sullen youth had replaced her once cheery brother. She was to blame for this transformation and it hurt. Arching her throbbing back, she stared at the low clouds that hinted at more rain. She dreaded the fast approaching winter. The farmhouse, although cleaner, was still in no better condition and since Farrell had no money to make improvements, it meant them having to face a dismal freezing winter.

'There, that's the end of it.' Hughie knocked the last of the dirt off the spade and gave it back to her. 'I'll go check the traps. We might have a rabbit for tonight's meal. I'm sick of boiled eggs.'

Isabelle watched him walk away; the droop of his shoulders a permanent thing now. Her heart pained at their situation. Getting married was meant to be the answer to their problems. Never had she imagined her decision ruining them. Still, all was not lost. She managed to feed them on the eggs the hens laid so regularly, plus they had milk. The odd pheasant and trout made it into her cooking pot and, each time Farrell brought such a thing home, she shied away from asking him where he got it. Soon they would have bacon and ham. Farrell had managed to hire a boar to mate with the sow and now she carried a belly full of piglets.

The cool November breeze raised goosebumps on her skin. The weather hadn't been pleasant since they arrived, with showers, storms and grey gloomy days. It was as though Mother Nature was in a rush to bring on winter's dreariness. The light wind sprang up sharper, swifter and slammed the kitchen door shut. Above her, the curtains blew in and out through the open bedroom window. To the east ominous dark clouds raced. The cow bellowed and walked faster to the gate wanting the confines of its stall, which, now Hughie had cleaned it out, was the easiest place to milk her.

'It's all right, Mayflower, I'm coming.' Isabelle crossed the yard to the first outbuilding and put away her seeds and spade. Hughie had spent many long hours tidying and cleaning the barns. He had a natural love for the animals and cared for them avidly. Farrell, unconcerned for his beasts' welfare, gladly left the boy to see to them and if he was surprised by the boy's enthusiasm he didn't show it.

Strong wind replaced the breeze, buffeting Isabelle as she left the building. It whipped her hair from its bun and flattened her skirts against her legs making it difficult to walk. Staggering, she unclasped the gate and grabbed Mayflower's halter, pulling the cow down the yard and into the barn. A clap of thunder roared over her head, echoing in the cavernous, empty barn. Isabelle ushered Mayflower into her stall and closed the door. Next, she snatched up the feed dish and filled it with grain. Outside once more, she called to the hens, who quickly followed her into the next barn, and she fed them before shutting them up for the night.

The wind howled through the bare trees,

tossing them this way and that. Isabelle ran around the buildings into the orchard behind and looked for Hughie, but there was no sign of him. The sow, Flossy, as Hughie named her, pushed her snout against Isabelle's skirts. 'Yes, come on then, I'll put you to bed too.' Isabelle unlatched the back door of the last outbuilding and Flossy went in without complaint. 'Hughie will feed you when he gets back,' she told the grunting pig, closing the door.

Fallen leaves carpeted the orchard and crunched under Isabelle's boots. With a last look for Hughie, she left the orchard and went across the yard to the washing line. Large fat raindrops landed, hurrying her to work faster. She threw the clothes into the basket, and head down, ran for the house. Inside, she paused to catch her breath. From the kitchen window, she watched hailstones bounce on the ground and worried for Hughie. Why wasn't he home? She tossed about the idea of going to look for him, and decided against it for she wasn't sure which direction he'd taken once entering the wood.

Isabelle stoked the fire and added more logs. She put the kettle on to boil and stirred the watery cabbage soup she'd made earlier. Unwrapping the bread from a clean towel, she grimaced at its hard flatness. Baking bread was a talent she had not mastered and she was sorry for it. Nevertheless, she cut a few thin slices before going to the larder and collecting a jar each of blackberry jam and the pickles she had begged Farrell to buy on his last trip to town.

For a moment, she wondered what kept him away from the farm for days at a time. Whatever it was, it brought in a little money. Most times, he returned with supplies to keep them going for a few more days. The rent she knew had been paid, but how he'd raised the sum she didn't know. No animals were sold and since the far fields hadn't been in crop for years, he had no harvest money either. It crossed her mind that his business might be illegal, but she was afraid to ask him. When he was home, he was usually drunk and fit for nothing. Sometimes, he arrived bruised and bloodied and she cleaned him up as he slept off his ale. She always made sure he could find no fault with her. Living in dread of him wanting her to leave kept her in a constant state of anxiety. She did her best to improve the house and farm. He must find no reason to be rid of her and Hughie. So far, she believed it to be working. Even though Farrell said nothing about the changing appearance of the yard and house, she hoped he approved anyway.

She tried not to dwell on her marriage. Her hand stilled on the bread knife. *Am I really married?* They still had not consummated the marriage and although the prospect of committing the act to seal the contract still revolted her, she would rather suffer that than live with the fear of him throwing them out on the streets and annulling the marriage.

Movement at the window sent her rushing to open the back door. The wind nearly tore it out of her hands as Hughie staggered in and collapsed against her.

'Oh, Belle.'

'What took you so long? Are you all right?'

'I found it.'

'What?'

'Farrell's hoard.'

Isabelle blinked. 'Hoard?' She sat him down and then walked to the stove to swing the kettle off the heat. 'What do you mean?'

Hughie, eyes wide, panted, trying to get his breath. 'In the wood there's a dugout, it's not big, mind, just wide enough for someone to crawl in sideways. It's tucked into the bank of the stream. I found it by accident. When the storm started I ran and slipped down the bank, I grabbed a tree root and knocked away some of the bush covering the hole. At first I thought it a fox den, but taking a closer look I saw a tin box had

74

fallen nearer to the opening.'

'Hughie — '

'Look, Belle.' From his pockets Hughie drew out snuffboxes, a pearl necklace and three fob watches. 'These are only some of the things.'

'Oh, dear heaven!' Isabelle's stomach clenched in fear. She blinked rapidly, trying to comprehend what this meant. 'Hughie, you shouldn't have touched them.'

The door banged open startling them both. Farrell, his eyes blazing in rage, stared at the glittering treasures on the table. 'How did yer get those?' He yelled, lunging for Hughie. Despite his big build, Farrell could move quickly when the need arose and within seconds he had Hughie hanging by his shirt collar inches clear off the floor.

'Farrell!' Isabelle rushed to him, but he swept her aside.

'Yer dirty, snivelling little toe rag!' Farrell shook Hughie like a limp doll. 'How dare yer help yerself to me things.'

Isabelle beseeched him from the end of the table. 'He's sorry, Farrell. Please, put him down. We'll talk about it.'

Farrell sneered into Hughie's face. 'Want to steal from me do yer? Well I'll teach yer a lesson yer'll not forget in a hurry!' He flung Hughie against the wall with a thump. Cups rattled where they hung from hooks on the dresser.

'No! Stop!' Isabelle ran to Hughie. Farrell flung her away with enough force to smash her against the dresser. Plates rocked on the shelf. Farrell picked Hughie up and smashed his fist into his stomach. Breath exploded from Hughie in a cruel gasp. The boy went down on his knees, an easy target for Farrell's boots.

'No!' Isabelle charged at Farrell and knocked him sideways away from Hughie.

Farrell grabbed the table and spun to face her. 'Get out of me way! I'll not have him stealing from me under me very nose!'

She stood between the two of them, conscious of Hughie crying behind her. 'He didn't mean to. He was going to put them back, I promise you. Hughie just wanted to show me, that's all.'

'Likely story!' He scorned, red in the face, but his temper was lessening.

Isabelle swallowed. 'Sit down and we'll talk. I've got your dinner ready. Please sit down.' When Farrell lowered himself into the nearest chair, Isabelle went to Hughie and helped him upright. 'Come, dearest, I'll pour you a cup of tea.'

Farrell snorted at her fussing but said nothing as she quickly gave them their dinner, shaking so much she spilled some of the soup. She sat in her place at the end of the table closest to the range. Hughie's snivelling had eased but he ignored the simple meal before him.

Isabelle, her stomach in knots, couldn't eat either. 'Try to eat something, Hughie.'

'Leave me alone.'

Farrell's eyes narrowed. 'Eat! I'll not have food wasted.' Abruptly, he too thrust his soup bowl away and bowed his head. 'It's the only way I can bring in some money.'

Isabelle looked at him. 'Pardon?'

He raised his gaze to her. 'Where do yer think the money comes from? This farm earns nothing. With the flock size reduced, they don't bring in enough.'

A cold shiver tingled down her spine. 'If you are caught what will happen then? How will we survive then?' Farrell hunched his shoulders and looked away. She rose from her chair and went to the fire, tormented by her situation. How could she have married this stranger, this man who could beat her brother so easily?

'Things must change. I will not be married to a criminal. If you spent more time working this farm than you did stealing, happen we'd be doing a whole lot better!'

'Yer so stupid.' His laugh made her clench

her fists. White-hot fury blinded her for a second.

'Never call me stupid, do you hear!' She banged her hands down flat on the table and leaned towards him. 'I'll not have you put us in danger. There will be no more stealing. Instead, you'll work the land. Make this farm pay its way.'

Farrell stood, glaring at her. 'Farm this land? Are yer mad as well as stupid? There isn't enough land to make a livin', the bastard landlord saw to that.'

'Why? Why did he take the land away? Was it because he saw the neglect? The misuse? No doubt he thought he might as well use it than let it go idle.'

Farrell stepped forward, fist raised. 'Yer dare to defend him. He, who ruined me father and who humiliates me at every turn?'

She grabbed the fire poker and held it high. 'Hit me or Hughie ever again and you'll live to regret it.'

He stared at her in amazement.

'Don't think for a second I'll not use this.' Isabelle out-glared him.

'Don't yer threaten me! I put a roof over yer head and food in yer mouth.'

'No you don't, I do!' She jabbed the poker in the air. 'You do nothing but steal and get drunk.'

'I married yer didn't I? I never even wanted a bloody wife.'

'And why you did that I'll never know,' Isabelle sneered.

'Because Peacock paid me to. The old witch wanted rid of yer.'

Her eyes widened. The strength went out of her as the news surged past her anger. 'She . . . she paid you?'

After a moment, he slowly lowered his fist and moved back. 'Put that down.'

'You sit first.'

'Bloody woman,' Farrell muttered, but did as she demanded.

Isabelle leant the poker against the table and thankfully resumed her seat for her legs felt like they wouldn't hold her up a moment longer.

'The matron wanted you out of her son's way. She knew he was after you. I don't know all the details, and I don't care to know,' Farrell explained. He was studying his hands and not looking at her. 'I needed the money for the rent.'

Isabelle nodded. It all made sense. It was a business deal between him and Matron just like it was a contract between Farrell and her. Yet, she couldn't shake away the hollowness she felt. She had the ridiculous feeling of being used.

Hughie, who had a little colour back in his cheeks, took her hand in his. He was all she had in the world, the only one she could trust. Farrell meant nothing to her now, for she knew that no matter how hard she tried he didn't want the same as she. So, she'd do it on her own. With this in mind, she straightened her shoulders and poured them all fresh tea. Yes, Farrell ranted and raved but he no longer scared her and she owed him no loyalty. He would be a means to an end and that's all.

'Right, how much money do you have?'

Farrell jerked in his seat. 'I'll not be telling yer, woman. It's me own business.'

Isabelle seethed at his foolishness. 'We need to buy more livestock and make repairs. The roofs leak, timber has rotted in the barns and we need to buy grain and tools. Can that horse of yours pull a plough?'

'Now, wait just a minute.' He jumped to his feet again.

'For heaven's sake sit down!' She had a strong urge to throw her teacup at his ruddy face. 'Can you not have a simple conversation without huffing and puffing like an enraged old bull?'

'Yer fancy plans won't work here. Me father and mother went to an early grave trying to make this farm something out of nothing.'

'And do you wish to see all their hard work fail? Would you rather walk away and let their deaths be for naught?'

Farrell slumped back into his chair. 'I did try after they went, but it was no good.'

'You were one man alone. Of course it would have been hard.'

'There was no money. Father wasn't interested in making changes and we had some bad harvests. What little money we had dwindled away.'

'Things will be better now, I am certain of it.' She smoothed out her skirts and became businesslike. Farrell didn't have the gumption to take control, so she would. If she had to live the rest of her life here then she was going to damn well make sure the farm was successful. 'You have Hughie and me to help you. Together we will make the changes necessary. Surely the landlord will think differently now he knows you are . . . married.'

'Hardly. That man thinks of nothing but himself.'

Isabelle rose and tidied the table. 'The flock of geese is large. I counted seventeen birds. I think we should send them to market or at least ten or so. Do you agree?' She looked at her husband.

He shrugged. 'If we can catch them. It's

better to grab them at night when they're not so flighty.'

'We'll do it now then.' Isabelle went to the back door, wrapped her black shawl around her shoulders and turned to Hughie. 'Do you feel up to it, dearest?'

He nodded and slipped from his seat to her side. Following Farrell, they left the kitchen and walked out into the darkness.

★   ★   ★

Isabelle carried an armload of firewood into the barn and stacked it neatly along the far wall. Their fuel supply now looked healthier after she had badgered Farrell into cutting up some old trees in the wood. She finished unloading the cart while he and Hughie sharpened the saws and had something to eat. The late December weather, although cold, remained dry, which pleased her after all the rain they endured in November. Once the cart was empty, Farrell and Hughie rumbled out of the yard for another load.

Watching them go, she sighed. Little had changed in her married life. She remained a virgin, and Farrell continued to remain distant and vague about his business. True, he didn't venture out at night as much, but he still disappeared without warning some days and returned with money jingling in his pockets. Christmas and Hughie's birthday had been celebrated only by a visit to church and a special dinner of roast chicken at midday. For a gift, she'd knitted Hughie socks and a scarf, using the last of her supply of wool, but Farrell refused to think of the day as different to any other day and so she complied and made him nothing.

She often wondered what he thought of her, his wife whom he treated like a stranger. Their conversations were strained, mainly consisting of safe topics like the weather or work around the farm. He slept in the kitchen on a straw filled mattress, content to let her and Hughie sleep in the bed upstairs. The situation wasn't ideal, and soon they'd have to buy or build a bed for Hughie in the spare room. He deserved his own room.

As she turned towards the house, needing to check on the rabbit stew simmering on the stove, a horse and rider trotted into the yard. At once, she knew him to be the hated landlord. He reined in a few feet from her. His golden brown eyes narrowed as his gaze swept over her from head to foot. 'Good day, madam.'

She inclined her head and found she couldn't stop staring at him. He held his head at an angle, looking superior. Something hit her between the ribs, robbing her of breath. Her skin tingled, blood pounded in her ears. 'H . . . How do you do.'

'My name is Ethan Harrington. Is Farrell about?' Harrington glanced around the yard before pinning her with another bold stare.

She sounded his name in her mind, liking it. He was no John or Jim or Tom. His eyes were the colour of brandy, a warm brown highlighted with gold flecks. The fine hair on her nape prickled. He wore fawn corduroy trousers with a darker brown riding jacket. His black boots shone even in the dull light from the overcast day. Isabelle was suddenly aware of her own worn dusty skirt and blouse. Shame tinged her cheeks. The beating drum of her heart alarmed her. 'No, he isn't here. He's out . . . gathering wood.'

He frowned and flicked the reins as if undecided what to do next. 'Will he be gone long?'

'Not certain . . . a half hour maybe.' She cursed inwardly at her abrupt inability to talk coherently. What was it about him that made her so aware of him? She absorbed the regal way he sat on his horse and how the fine lines at the corners of his eyes crinkled when he squinted into the distance.

'Who are you?'

His question made her falter. Unexpectedly, she didn't want to reveal to this fine gentleman that she was married to a man like Farrell. Her cheeks grew hotter. Guilt and embarrassment rendered her mute.

He peered down at her, arrogant and proud. 'Have you no answer?'

She raised her chin, remembering from long ago her father's words. *Never be ashamed of who you are, for the time might come when the only person you can rely on is yourself.* 'My name is Isabelle Farrell, formerly Gibson.'

'You are a relative visiting Farrell for a time then.' He made it a statement not a question.

'I live here permanently.' She straightened her shoulders. He wasn't the only one who could be proud. Adele Gibson had instilled in her daughters the same degree of dignity she had conducted herself with until the day she died. How glad Isabelle was now of her mother's teachings.

'I apologize for my lack of manners, Mr Harrington. Would you care to come inside and wait? Or, if you prefer, I can inform my husband that you visited and have him call on you tomorrow?'

Harrington's eyes widened. 'You are his wife?'

Isabelle tried to ignore the note of

incredulity in his voice and quickly dampened down the spark of irritation it caused. What was the matter with him? Did she not look like a wife? At the workhouse she had gained a reputation for having a wild temper and outspoken tongue — such a contrast to her mother and sister. As a married woman she must now rise above such temptations to shout like a fishwife at anything that failed to please her. 'Indeed, sir, as of ten weeks ago.'

'I was not informed.'

'Is it a requirement, Mr Harrington?' She raised her eyebrows, his manner squashing the attraction she originally felt towards him.

He clenched his jaw. His chiselled face seemed as hard as the granite outcrops that littered the moor. 'Obviously, you did not set your standards very high when you chose Farrell.'

'I doubt very much that concerns you, Mr Harrington.' She flicked her skirts aside as though she wore the finest silk and his company sullied them. 'If you will excuse me, I shall be about my business.'

'Your husband, madam, is not a man to be trusted. Unless you want to be walking the streets carrying all you possess, I suggest you make him change his ways. So far he has managed to escape the net, but sooner or later he will pay for his actions.'

A sickly tingle of fear slid down Isabelle's back. She urged some witty retort to spring from her lips but his cold stare silenced her. He gave her the slightest of nods and wheeled his horse about and out of the yard. Standing still for so long had made her cold, yet she knew the iciness she felt was from more than just the weather.

★   ★   ★

Ethan marched into the drawing room, paused to kiss his mother's smooth soft cheek before nodding to Baldwin, the butler, to pour him a nip of the whisky he imported from a distillery from the Scottish Highlands. He rested his forearm along the mantelpiece and stared into the glowing fire. To his left on an emerald velvet sofa, reclined his wife, Clarice, sucking boiled sugar sweets. His stomach churned.

'How was your ride, dear?' Elizabeth Harrington smiled at him, breaking her concentration from her embroidery.

'Cold.' He replied without turning around. The scene of domestic serenity was such a lie that he had the urge to laugh like a madman.

Elizabeth put aside her work. 'Shall I ring for tea?'

Ethan closed his eyes momentarily and

then spun around, doing his best to not look at his wife. He concentrated on his mother, who was the only woman worth his time and love. 'Did you know that Farrell had married?'

'Your tenant, Farrell?' Elizabeth chuckled. 'Why would I be interested in him? That man is such a thorn in your side. I do not understand why you cannot break his lease. I am sure there is some law about it?'

'Father gave the family another ten year lease just before he died. It expires in three years.' Ethan took his drink from Baldwin.

'Your father was always too lenient on those less fortunate.' She gave a sidelong glance at her daughter-in-law and pursed her lips.

Ethan took a gulp of his drink. He needed no reminding of his father's weaknesses. He lived with the consequences every day. He had married Clarice because his dying father had begged him to. Oh, he had done all right out of the deal, he freely acknowledged that, but time had cruelly shown him that money was not everything.

He gazed about the richly decorated room. His mother had sublime taste and the drawing room plus other rooms of Bracken Hall looked elegant; all thanks to Clarice's money. Her father, a wealthy York merchant and his own father's good friend, had left his entire fortune to his only child. That fortune now safeguarded Bracken Hall for the next generation. Yet, the next generation was slow in coming. Ethan shuddered. There would never be an heir for the estate he loved if he couldn't force himself to touch his wife.

'What does it matter whether he has married or not?' Clarice asked, forcing him to look at her. He flinched as she licked her sticky fat fingers and then immediately searched for another sweet at the bottom of the cone paper cup. Beside her, on a small occasional table, was a selection of ornamental jars holding various sugared fruits and chocolates.

'It matters, Clarice, because the man is a wastrel and a thief. He cannot afford to pay his rent on time, so how can he afford to support a wife?'

Clarice shrugged, pulled the nearest jar closer and poured out two brandy-balls, which she promptly popped into her mouth.

Elizabeth clicked her tongue. 'It's four o'clock, Clarice. Time to stop, my dear.'

Ethan cringed. He felt filled with shame that his mother had to chastise his wife like a child. He moved his gaze away from his wife's down-turned mouth. *This is a nightmare.* He had been married for six years to this greedy, unintelligent half woman, half child. For the first year he had tried really hard to find some common ground with her, but they shared none of the same interests. As the years went by, they turned to their own concerns and did their best to ignore each other as much as possible. Clarice was content to sew, read her penny journals and eat. She insisted that his mother continue running the household, and for that he was glad.

'Darling?'

He turned and looked at his mother. Her eyes reflected his own sadness. She understood his pain. He thumped down his empty glass. 'I'll be in the study if you need me.'

She nodded, and as he passed her she reached out and held his hand for an instant. He smiled and left the room. Down the hall was the one room that was entirely his. Ethan paused in the study doorway and surveyed the dark richness of the book-lined walls. The large walnut desk sat beneath the window that overlooked the park. In summer, deer grazed under the sycamores and beech trees. Sighing, Ethan walked to the window and stared out. The bleak greyness of winter echoed his soul. His ridiculous marriage galled him, and until now he had maintained a brave face about it, but today, this moment, he felt as if he couldn't breathe. The image of

90

Farrell's wife swam before his eyes. How had *he*, a useless idler, married someone so striking, someone so full of spirit and pride? Ethan frowned, recalling the meeting. Isabelle, that was her name. He sat at his desk and drummed his fingers on the polished top. Isabelle. He remembered how she had raised her chin and stared at him boldly. A spark had lit her unusually pale blue eyes. Defiance. Character. In only those few minutes together, he saw in her something special. Yes, she wore filthy, shabby clothes and her red hands showed how hard she worked, but despite it all her supple strength of spirit had reached inside him.

He would find out more about her, this woman called Isabelle Gibson. Resting back against the padded leather of his chair, he nodded. Isabelle Gibson — never Farrell.

★   ★   ★

Choking smoke billowed into Isabelle's face. She coughed and flapped the dishcloth. 'Dratted chimney!'

An assortment of cakes and tarts cooled on the table. With practice, she had become more skilled at cooking. Her new plan to sell cakes at the Hebden Bridge markets caused her no end of heartbreak as she perfected her rudimentary skills of pastry making.

Hughie entered through the back door, bringing with him a blast of cold air that circulated the smoke. 'They look good!' He nodded at the display on the table. 'Can I have one?'

'Yes, you can, after you've washed your hands.' She glanced out of the window. Long shadows stretched across the yard. 'Are the ewes in the house field?'

'Yes, all in. Farrell says they'll have to be put in the barns next month before lambing starts. That means I'll have to do more clearing.'

'Is he still out there?'

Hughie sat on the scullery step and pulled off his boots. 'No. He's gone. Hitched up the cart about an hour ago. He didn't say where.' He stood and placed his boots by the back door before going into the scullery to wash.

Isabelle sighed. 'It wouldn't have hurt him to tell his *wife* his whereabouts.' To save her from further unhappiness in soul-searching her bizarre marriage, she dismissed Len Farrell from her mind. He treated her with mediocre respect, but still kept his distance, which suited her admirably.

Last week, Farrell took her for a brief visit to the market, and she bought several items of clothing for herself and new trousers for

Hughie. With the money from the sale of the stolen goods, she had bought a pallet bed for Hughie and placed it in the spare room. The excursion terrified her. Handling 'dirty' money was not something she ever wanted to do again. Her heart nearly gave out every time someone bumped into her, and when she saw the constable at the end of the market, she nearly fainted, certain that he was going to arrest her. Once home, she berated Farrell like a gin-filled fishwife. Never would she endure such an ordeal again. He let her shout until she was exhausted, but didn't retaliate except to ask if she had finished, so he could go for an ale in Heptonstall.

Remembering her fear that day in the market, and knowing that stolen money had bought her goods, Isabelle took a knife and savagely cut a piece of apple pie and placed it on a plate for Hughie as he sat down. Frustrated at her husband's lack of care, for her or anything else, made her voice sharp. 'Did Farrell do any work today?'

Hughie shrugged, taking a large bite. He swallowed and poured himself a cup of tea from the pot on the table. 'When I was chopping wood, he was fiddling around in the end shed. When I looked later, I couldn't see what he'd been doing. He was supposed to be fixing the broken boards on the back wall.'

He took a sip of his tea and then added more milk. 'Oh, he did trim some of the fruit trees in the orchard. There's only about five left to prune now. I'll do them tomorrow.'

Isabelle nodded. 'You're a good boy.'

'So, we're off to market tomorrow?' Hughie asked, wiping his hand across his mouth.

She stood and opened the oven door to check on the golden currant buns cooking. 'Yes, if Farrell brings the cart back in time.'

'I checked his hidey-hole today.'

Isabelle spun to face him, her eyes wide. 'You shouldn't have. You know how he reacts.' She paused, her voice dropping to a whisper: 'Tell me there wasn't anything in there.'

'It was empty.' Hughie stretched and yawned. 'But you can't tell me he's stopped.'

Her heart drummed in her chest. 'He promised he would.'

Hughie snorted, suddenly looking much older than his fourteen years. 'Then where does his ale money come from?'

6

The cries of stallholders carried on the wind and filled the marketplace. Early morning crowds, all eager for a good buy, picked their way past the numerous stalls. Housewives and grandmothers fiddled with sale items, bargaining for the right price, while servants inspected fruit, fish and cheese to make certain their master's money bought only the best.

Isabelle viewed the stream of people from behind her stall. Smiling, she nodded to those who stared at the newcomer. Her tarts, pies and cakes lay on a clean sheet covering the trestle table. Farrell, having driven her to the market, had then disappeared, but promised to pick her up at one o'clock.

Her neighbouring stallholder, a grey-haired elderly man selling garden tools and other ironmonger equipment, stepped nearer. 'I've not seen yer before?'

She smiled in reply. 'No. This is my first time here. I'm Isabelle Gib — Farrell.'

'Farrell?' He took his pipe out of his mouth. 'The only Farrell's I know are from Meadow Farm or out along Sowerby way.'

'I live at Meadow Farm.'

'Yer married Len Farrell?' His incredulous look made her uncomfortable.

'Yes.' She noticed that behind the old man, more stallholders in the row were suddenly very interested in her. Her skin prickled from their scrutiny.

The old man replaced his pipe and shook his head, mumbling. 'More fool you then, lass.'

A customer saved Isabelle from worrying about the old man's comment. Besides, he couldn't tell her anything that she didn't already know or suspect about her husband. She hurriedly assisted the woman whose three children fondled her delicious pies and tarts. Each child received a slap from their mother for their rudeness before she bought an apple pie.

For the next hour, Isabelle remained busy as a slow but constant line of purchasers filed by. Her skirt pocket jingled with coins, and buoyant with her success, Isabelle smiled widely at anyone who looked her way. Yes, she was new and drew interest, but she didn't care. For the first time in her life she had earned money and the success of it made her light-headed. As the midday rush dwindled to a trickle, Isabelle placed the last remaining lemon curd tart in her smallest basket. She stacked two other baskets into the biggest one and then folded the sheet. She glanced up as a large woman with straggly black hair and a hairy chin stopped in front.

'I'm sorry, I only have a tart left, but I'll be back next week . . . '

'No, yer won't!' The woman sneered, bending forward over the table just inches from Isabelle's face. She smelt of stale sweat and ale.

Isabelle stepped back. 'Pardon?'

'Didn't yer 'ear me?' The woman spat to the side. 'Yer ain't coming back to this market!'

Alarmed, Isabelle looked at the gathering crowd, who having heard raised voices thought they might find some free entertainment. The enormous woman placed hands as large as frying pans on her wide hips and stared at Isabelle as though she was filth in the gutter.

'Yer've tekken me trade away. I've sold next ter nowt terday!' She stabbed a fat finger at Isabelle. 'I sell the pies and tarts around 'ere see, and old Mrs Brierly at top end sells her bread. Tis an arrangement we've had fer nigh on ten years.'

'I wasn't aware . . . '

'Well, I'm telling yer now aren't I?' The woman crossed her wobbly arms under her huge pendulous breasts. She was a giant and Isabelle, standing at five foot five, felt like a dwarf.

A few jeers filtered through from the back. Isabelle straightened, trying not to be intimidated. 'I am certain there are more than enough people buying to allow my stall here too.'

As quick as a flash, the woman grabbed a fistful of Isabelle's hair and pulled her across the trestle. Isabelle screamed. The crowd roared. The woman's grip tightened. 'Listen ter me, yer scraggly poacher's woman! I'll not be told what ter do by the likes of you!'

Anger and pain mixed to give Isabelle the rage of a charging bull. She scrambled over the table and grabbed the woman's hand that held her hair as the people at the front spread the word to those at the back that a fight was on.

'Let go of me you filthy cow.' Isabelle tried prising the fat fingers from her hair, but the woman jerked her head. Fit to kill, Isabelle swung her fist and landed one on the woman's chin. In an instant she was free. She sagged back against the table holding her head. Her eyes watered with the throbbing of her scalp.

'What is going on here!' The authoritative voice silenced the commotion. The gathering parted and Ethan Harrington rode straight up to the stall even though his horse was in fear of trampling people and goods together.

Isabelle looked away, embarrassed. He, of all people to see her fighting in public! Her shame grew.

'What's your name?'

Isabelle thought he was asking her and jerked around, but he stared at the large hoyden. She closed her eyes momentarily in relief.

'Marge Wilmot.'

Harrington pointed his riding crop at her. 'Make any more trouble like that again and I'll have you arrested for disturbing the peace.' His hard, unforgiving stare swept the crowd. 'Be gone, all of you!'

Mutters and foot scuffling signalled their departure though Isabelle didn't watch. She turned away and slipped behind the stall to collect her baskets.

'Mrs Farrell?'

At his sympathetic tone, emotion sealed her throat. Never had she been involved in such a spectacle. Her mother and Sally would have been so ashamed. Her grip tightened on the basket's handle. Slowly, she raised her gaze. His toffee-coloured eyes held tenderness before he quickly masked it. Harrington dismounted, lifted his horse's reins over its head and held them. 'Are you hurt?'

'N-no.' Actually her head felt on fire, but she wouldn't have told him that even if she were put to torture. His expression softened and she instinctively knew that he saw through her lie.

'Where is your husband?'

'He is to collect me at one o'clock.' Suddenly she didn't want Farrell to be anywhere near her or Harrington.

Harrington took out his fob watch and opened it. 'He's late.'

'He'll be along any minute.' Her cheeks grew hot under his sharp gaze. Her heart thumped against her ribs. 'Th-Thank you for your help.'

'You are welcome.' He tucked the watch back into his waistcoat pocket and glanced around at the emptying market. 'What was the argument about?'

'She was unhappy about me selling pies. She does the same and today the people shunned her stall and instead wanted to sample my wares.' The moment the words were out of her mouth, Isabelle blushed violently. Lord, she sounded like a whore on a street corner. 'I meant . . . not my wares as in . . . you see . . . what I mean was . . . '

His laughter echoed throughout the empty-ing stalls and the last few people in the market spun to stare at them. 'I do know what you mean.'

She dropped her gaze and bit her lip. *He must think me the oddest fool.*

He grew serious again. 'It might not be wise to come here again. Mrs Wilmot will enlist her cronies to support her next time.'

Swift fury at the injustice of it made Isabelle's voice sharp. 'She cannot keep me from running a stall. I need to earn money. The market is big enough for the both of us. She just doesn't like the competition! My baking is undoubtedly superior.'

Harrington's eyes widened at her speech and the words she used. Unashamed of her mother's teachings, Isabelle raised her chin. She might now live on a farm, but she was educated and above the class of that Wilmot woman.

Harrington's mouth lifted slightly as though he fought a grin. 'I suspect you are correct. Nevertheless, she will make it difficult for you.'

Isabelle tossed her head. 'Let her try.'

Something she couldn't name flared in his brandy eyes, lighting them with gold. The atmosphere surrounding them seemed to suck the air out of her lungs. She stared at him boldly, ignoring the way heat circled her belly. Her gaze dropped to his lips, and she had an unexpected urge to touch them with her fingertips.

Clatter from behind her shattered their fascination with each other. Regretfully, she turned and stared as her husband halted the cart at the end of the stall row. Isabelle swallowed and glanced back to Harrington. 'Thank you for your help.'

Harrington peered at Farrell seated upon the cart and once more became rigid. He bowed to her, stiff and formal. 'Until we meet again, Isabelle Gibson-Farrell.'

Wordlessly, she turned from him and towards her husband. The baskets' wicker handles seemed embedded in her hands so tight did she clutch them. She walked the length of the row on unsteady legs, certain that Ethan Harrington was watching her every step.

'What did *he* want?' Farrell asked the second she was in speaking range.

'Nothing at all.' Isabelle placed the baskets in the back of the cart and then hoisted herself up onto the seat, knowing Farrell wouldn't get down to help.

'I don't want yer talking to him.' He whipped up the horse.

'I can hardly ignore him can I? He is our landlord after all.' She ached to look back to see if he still watched. She didn't understand what had happened between them, but she knew something certainly did. The thought frightened and warmed her.

★   ★   ★

Isabelle sauntered across the snow-covered fields behind the farm. In her pocket she had a handful of grain to throw out for the geese and ducks that dogged her every footstep, even the sheep liked to follow her. The sun was high, though its heat wasn't enough to melt the thick layer of January snow or banish the cold.

She left the animals behind, climbed over the stile and crossed Draper's Lane to enter the frigid winter woodland of Hawden Hole. This area, flowing down the escarpment to Hebden Water had become a favourite place for Isabelle to escape from her endless chores and disgruntled home life. She had thought she could cope living this way, but with each passing day she became aware of how wrong she'd been. The sad thing was, she knew she would be happy living on a farm if only she had the respect of a good man. She wouldn't mind the hard work if she only received a warm smile of gratitude, but living with Farrell meant living with a stranger. It wasn't as if she wanted his love and attention, she didn't, and that's what made the situation even more unbearable, because she was trapped. Trapped in a loveless life. There would be no children for her, and once Hughie married and moved away, she'd have no one to care for or to love her. The years ahead stretched out into an abyss of lonely blackness.

A gentle breeze whistled through the bare trees, lifting the fine hair at her brow that peeped out from under her hood. Strolling, she trailed a stick on the frozen water of a tiny stream. Where rocks poked out ice had broken away and the water trickled through. The sound of the tinkling water soothed her fraught nerves. She had escaped the house after calming both Hughie and Farrell. Their arguments were becoming more frequent as the winter made them spend days cooped up inside. They argued about chores and played her off one against the other until she was ready to scream. Farrell refused to do more than a small amount of work and was determined to treat Hughie like a slave. She understood Hughie's resentment and felt it, but he went out of his way to annoy Farrell and she found that Hughie was quick to shirk work too if he could. Between the pair of them, Isabelle didn't know which was worse, and sometimes being stuck in the middle tested her sanity.

The sound of crunching snow shattered the quiet. Her head jerked up. Ethan Harrington rode out from behind a tree on the opposite side of the stream with his tan dog running beside. He reined in his horse and it snorted steam into the cold air. The dog stopped at once to look at his master for instructions.

Isabelle stared at Harrington. He wore a long, dark grey riding coat lined with sable. His shiny black leather knee-length boots matched his black kid-leather gloves. He wore no hat and the breeze played with his chestnut brown hair. Again she had the urge to touch him. She dropped her stick and tucked her hands inside her cloak's pockets. Silence stretched.

'How are you?' His voice sounded loud within the frozen woodland.

'Well, thank you.'

'I hear you are still causing a stir within the market community.'

She raised her chin. The problems she experienced at the market each week wore down her spirit. She wished she could stop going, but despite the torment from Marge Wilmot, people still bought her pies and she needed the money. 'The trouble is not my doing.'

'I know that.'

Isabelle looked away into the trees. A lone bird flew from a branch. She wondered how this man's presence could unnerve and please her at the same time. Blood pounded in her ears. Every ounce of her body tingled with awareness. Leather creaked as he dismounted. His dog walked beside him as Harrington stepped to the edge of the stream. Across the water they gazed at each other, reaffirming the details of each other they'd memorized before. She knew this and accepted it.

'When do you go to market again?'

Her heart somersaulted at the question. 'Tomorrow.'

'Where does he leave you?'

'At the south end of the market.'

'What time? I'll meet you.'

She swallowed, every bit of her wanted whatever it was he offered, yet some voice inside her head told her to walk away. The image of her grandfather shaking hands with his parishioners on the steps of his church came to mind. He had made her feel so proud. Would he be proud of her wicked thoughts now?

'Isabelle . . . ' His whisper carried to lie gently on her skin.

Her shallow breathing hurt her chest. She

shook her head as though to clear it. 'I have to go.'

'Will you meet me?' His eyes did not plead, did not beg.

She turned away. Her steps quickened. She gathered up her skirts and ran.

* * *

'Where is he!' Isabelle stomped around the kitchen. For the umpteenth time, she went to the window and looked out. Despite the falling snow, she still wanted to go to the market. Her thoughts shied away from the knowledge that Harrington would be there. She needed to go to earn money, that was the most important reason. Her empty purse spurred her on. On the table, her baskets brimmed with pies and tarts. Farrell had left last night without telling her his plans, and it was now past eight o'clock the next morning, and he hadn't returned.

'He'll be here soon.' Hughie sat by the fire darning a sock. 'The snow has likely held him up.'

'What keeps him out night after night?' She stamped her foot in frustration. 'He drinks more than a sailor does on his first day back at port!' Hughie grinned.

The sound of scratching made Isabelle

frown. The snowstorm grew in intensity. She could no longer see the outbuildings. The scratching sounded again. 'What is that?'

Hughie shrugged. 'The trees on the window upstairs?'

Isabelle stepped away from the window, nibbling her fingertips. There would be no market day today. She was going into the scullery when a thump sounded at the back door. She opened it and cried out as Farrell landed at her feet. Hughie dashed to her side and together they stared at her husband's bloody form.

'Heaven's above!' Isabelle bent to touch him. He stirred and moaned. 'Help me bring him inside, Hughie.'

They grabbed him under the arms and dragged him down the step and onto the kitchen floor. His coat was missing and his wet woollen vest cloaked him like another skin.

Farrell opened and closed his eyes. 'Isabelle . . .'

'What happened to you?' She took a dishcloth from the table and knelt to wipe the blood oozing from a cut in his forehead. She gestured to Hughie. 'Get me some blankets off the bed and a pillow too. He's too heavy to lift, so I'll have to make a bed in here for him.'

As Hughie ran to do as she bid, Isabelle quickly made him a cup of sweet tea and held Farrell's head up to pour a little into his mouth. Next, she rubbed his cold hands between her own. Hughie ran into the room with the items she asked for, and Isabelle placed the pillow under Farrell's head. 'Heat a warming pan, Hughie.' Farrell's eyes fluttered, he moaned from blue lips. Isabelle ran into the scullery and found an old pair of gloves. She returned and tugged them onto his icy hands.

'Lord, what have you done to yourself?' He murmured and opened his eyes. She tucked the blanket around him more securely. 'Lie still.'

'No . . . '

She put the cup to his lips again. 'Drink this now. You need to get warm.'

He slowly eased himself up onto one elbow. 'Got to hide.' He wheezed and then coughed. His split lip began to bleed freely again.

'Hide?' She frowned. 'Why?'

'They'll find me here!' He tried to get up, but she pushed him back down.

'Who?'

'Had to run . . . '

Hughie knelt down beside them. 'Has he lost his mind?'

'Heaven knows, silly man. It'd be hardly

surprising if he has, being out in this weather all night.' She made Farrell drink again. 'Take his boots off, Hughie.'

'No!' Farrell reared up. 'I must hide.' He gripped Isabelle's arms until they hurt. His eyes were wide and frightened. 'I can't hide here. They'll find me.'

In a panic, Isabelle glanced up at the door as though the riders from hell would burst through it any moment. She flung away his hands, alarmed. 'What have you done?' Her voice sounded high to her ears.

'They nearly caught me. Had to run.' Farrell panted, throwing off the blanket, struggling to sit up. 'They saw me face. I must go!'

Isabelle stood and hugged herself, fighting rising terror. 'Tell me,' she whispered.

'I've been hiding in the woods all night.' Farrell pulled himself up using the table as a support. Beard growth shadowed his jaw, but colour had returned to his cheeks. He peered out the window at the blizzard raging outside. 'I was at Bracken Hall.'

Isabelle gasped. Her hand flew to her throat. 'No, not there.'

Farrell's face darkened in anger. 'He deserves it!' Shaking, he poured a cup of tea and drank it quickly. Out of his trouser pockets he removed trinkets and jewellery.

They scattered across the table and lay there, glittering in the candlelight beside her baskets.

'Good Lord.' Isabelle thought she would faint. 'You are mad to do this!'

'The bastard stopped me in Heptonstall and told me to look to meself regarding this farm. He said he'd never stop watching me and that I'd better do right by you and the boy and that I wasn't worth having a wife!'

'He said that?'

Farrell sneered. 'Yer calling me a liar?'

'No, of course not.' She gulped. 'What did you say to him?'

'Nowt. How could I? We were in the middle of Towngate with everyone watching!' Farrell reached into one of her baskets and took out all the pies. From another basket he took a small tart and stuffed it in his mouth. He swayed as he pulled off his wet vest and steadied himself by holding the table. Then he unbuttoned his shirt and turned to Hughie. 'Get upstairs and find me some clothes, trousers, shirt and socks. Put extra into a bag. Quickly now.'

'You have to put them back.' Isabelle bit her lip, her hands shook as Farrell began picking up the stolen possessions and thrusting them into his pockets.

'Don't be daft.'

'I won't be a part of this!' Anger surfaced past her fear. 'You are a fool! If you are caught they'll imprison you for years.'

'I'll not be caught.' Farrell drank more tea and ate another tart, regaining some of his strength. He turned cunning eyes to her. 'I'm going away. By the time I come back they'll have forgotten all about it.'

'Go away? Where will we go?'

'Yer ain't going anywhere. Yer staying here. Yer've got to look after the farm, or *he*'ll take it back.'

Hughie ran into the kitchen clutching clothes. Farrell took them and changed. 'Put those pies into that bag and a bottle of tea.'

Stunned, Isabelle did as he directed. She poured the tea from the pot into an earthenware bottle and secured the cork. Her mind whirled, thoughts scattered despite her best attempts to make sense of Farrell's words. She couldn't fathom his intentions, couldn't comprehend what all this would mean to her and Hughie.

On the back of the scullery door, old coats hung on hooks. Farrell sorted through them until he found a large, black shapeless one and shrugged it on, pulling the collar high. He came back into the kitchen and grabbed the bag. 'Right. I'm off. Yer've not seen me today, remember, and yer've no idea where

I've gone. Understand?'

Isabelle blinked, digesting his words. 'But — '

Farrell paused, his hand on the door handle. 'When they come, tell them I've gone away for work, and yer don't know when I'll be back.'

'When will you return?'

He twitched one shoulder. 'A year, more mebbe, whatever it takes. I'll not swing from a rope for him. No chance.'

'If you just give it all back. Please!' Isabelle scrambled for time, for patience, for anything to prevent this disaster from happening. 'Look, it's a blizzard out there. Stay here and we'll think of what to do. They won't come for you in a blizzard.'

'That's right, they won't. It'll give me the perfect chance to scarper and get a head start.'

She rushed to him and gripped his arm in desperation. 'You can't leave us alone here. We've no money. I can't take care of this place. Not by myself!'

'Course yer can. Yer've got the boy to help yer with the lambing. Keep the ewes inside for a few days and then when the thaw starts turn them into the house field for a month.' He opened the door.

'Wait!'

He fished into his pocket and tugged out a pearl necklace. 'I got this from Harrington's wife's bedroom. Sell it. The money will tide you over a good while.'

Horrified, Isabelle recoiled. 'No!'

He shrugged and pushed it back into his pocket. 'Bake more pies to sell then. Now, I've got to go while I can. It'll be hard enough in this weather.'

'But if they saw you . . . ' She tried to swallow past the lump of fear in her throat. 'Harrington won't forget.'

'With a bit of luck, he'll meet with an accident.'

Isabelle swayed, certain she would wake up from this nightmare soon. 'W-where will you go?'

For a moment he looked indecisive. 'South. London's big enough to hide me.'

She closed her eyes. The click of the door closing and the waft of cold air that hit her face told her he had gone.

'What will we do, Belle?' Hughie's eyes were wide in his white face.

She stumbled to her chair by the fireside. Her breakfast threatened to surge back up the way it went down and sweat broke out on her upper lip.

'Belle?'

Sucking in an unsteady breath, she had an

114

overwhelming desire to cry, something she refused to do. Her mind spun like a merry-go-round at a summer fair. 'I don't know what to do.'

'What if Harrington calls the constable? What if they don't believe us? They might arrest us!' Hughie's voice rose high with hysteria. 'They might think we helped him. That we know where to find him!'

She stood and dragged him into her arms. 'It'll be all right, I promise. Harrington will believe me. He will.' Tears filled her eyes as Farrell's revelation came back to haunt her. *Harrington's wife's bedroom.* Her breathing became rapid as an unknown pain sliced her heart. *His wife.*

★ ★ ★

They came two days later. Snowdrifts, five feet high in places, had kept Meadow Farm isolated. In Isabelle's white world she went about her chores without thought or care. The animals were fed. The wood brought in. Paths cleared. Simple meals cooked.

As she fetched water, the distinct sounds of leather creaking and bridle bits jingling alerted her to their presence. Harrington led the way on his magnificent bay horse. Three others, wrapped up well against the cold, filed into the yard behind him. Harrington dismounted and indicated to the others to remain where they were. He trod carefully on the icy path leading from the house to the sheds, but never took his gaze off Isabelle's face. She set the bucket on the ground and waited for him to speak because her throat had closed tighter with every step he took.

He stopped a few feet from her. His eyes gave nothing away. 'How do you fare?'

She didn't expect that question. An ache spread out from her heart to touch each and every nerve in her body. She sighed deeply in acceptance that this man affected her profoundly. Her breath rose between them like a mist. 'I-I am well.'

'He isn't here, is he?'

'No.'

He remained very still. 'When did he leave?'

'Two days ago.' She had thought she'd be embarrassed, but instead she was numb. A cold numbness had settled on her the day Farrell left and she couldn't shake it. Even her monthly stomach cramps hadn't penetrated the deadened weight of hopelessness she felt.

Harrington's eyebrows rose. 'He left you all alone?'

'I have my brother, Hughie. We'll manage

'. . . unless . . . unless you mean to punish *us* for *his* mistakes?' She gripped her freezing hands together.

'Why would I do that? Are you to blame?'

'No.'

A muscle flickered along his jaw. 'Do you think so little of me?'

'I don't know you,' she whispered on a shiver.

Harrington swore softly. 'Let us go inside. You are cold.' He indicated for her to go before him while he turned and told his men to go home.

In the kitchen, Isabelle busied herself by stirring up the fire and putting the kettle on to boil. Harrington's presence filled the shabby room and the fine hairs on her nape prickled in response. Her heart thumped so badly, she was certain he could hear it. Her hands shook as she placed the chipped cups and saucers on the table.

She jumped when in one stride he was beside her, his hands capturing hers. 'Do not be frightened of me.' He gazed earnestly into her eyes and the strength went out of her legs.

'I-I . . . I'm not.'

'No?'

She shook her head, once more robbed of speech.

One side of his mouth lifted in a wry grin.

'Never be frightened of me, Isabelle. You will never have the need.'

The way he said her name, like a soft caress, sent heat pulsing through her veins. A rush of emotion made her want to either run from him or to him. Bewilderment reigned in her mind. Fleetingly, Isabelle wondered if the sensations that coursed through her body would kill her. She couldn't breathe with him so close. Stumbling in her haste, she moved away and broke the contact of their hands.

Harrington stepped back. The tension eased. 'May I have a piece of one of your famous pies?'

Startled at the question, she stared. 'My . . . my pies?'

'If I may?' He took on an innocent expression then smiled. 'You know, all the district talks of your pies since Marge Wilmot made such a spectacle?'

Her gaze flew to the small portion left from her last batch; those made the morning Farrell arrived back with Harrington's wife's jewels. The thought of her pierced her crazed mind. The stab of hurt was quickly ignored and smothered. She located her inner strength that Farrell's leaving had buried. Straightening her shoulders, she tilted her head and raised one eyebrow. 'Maybe your wife would care for some too?'

At once, his manner changed. His eyes darkened. 'Isabelle — '

Hughie clattered into the scullery, kicked off his boots and turned for the kitchen. 'The hens only laid one egg, Belle, do you think — ' He stopped mid-sentence and stared.

'Mr Harrington, this is my brother, Hughie.' Isabelle gestured for Hughie to come further into the kitchen. 'Come and greet Mr Harrington.'

Hughie wiped his hand on his trousers and shook the hand Harrington held out.

'Your sister tells me Farrell has left you both to run the farm?'

Hughie looked from Harrington to Isabelle and back again. 'Yes, sir.'

'It will not be easy come spring when the work starts in earnest. And there is the lambing to come first,' Harrington said.

'We will manage,' Isabelle replied before Hughie was able. She raised her chin. 'Hard work doesn't bother us and we have each other, that is all we need.'

Harrington's eyes narrowed at her subtle meaning.

Isabelle spun to the boiling kettle and lifted it off the heat. 'Please sit down, Mr Harrington and I'll pour the tea.'

'I won't, thank you. I must return to the

estate.' His clipped tones made her wince. She couldn't turn around, couldn't look at him.

'Will you call again, Mr Harrington?' Hughie asked. So like the boy that he was, his fear had been replaced with worship. Isabelle squeezed her eyes tight to stop her sudden tears from falling and waited for his answer.

'I might, lad, should your sister wish it.'

She heard the door open and felt the temperature in the room drop a little. Hughie had walked out with him and their scraps of conversation carried on the still air. Isabelle replaced the kettle over the fire and felt her way to her chair as though she was an old woman. *He is married and so am I.*

7

The church bells chimed the hour of midday. Isabelle rose from her stool and began packing her baskets with unsold pies. She looked around for Hughie. She didn't want to be late in clearing away and leaving the market. Marge Wilmot enjoyed any opportunity to menace her and Isabelle was in no mood for her exploits today.

The clouds sat low, dark and heavy. A freezing wind lifted her hair from beneath the flat felt hat she wore and she sighed in frustration, as there was no sign of Hughie. She hoped he would have the sense to go to the stable behind the public house where the horse and cart were stalled. He'd not been near the market all morning. Today, more than any other market day, uneasiness had cloaked her like a second skin. Repeatedly she felt as though someone was watching her. She peered into the crowds but nothing seemed out of place. Yet, the sensation remained. Her skin prickled.

Juggling the baskets and footstool, Isabelle hurriedly checked she hadn't forgotten anything. For a moment, she wondered if she had enough provisions at home to last a few more days. The pennies that jingled in her pocket wouldn't be enough to buy the flour and sugar she needed to bake the pies for the following weekend trade anyway, and the quicker she got home the better. Something wasn't right here today.

'Didn't do as good terday, did yer?' Marge Wilmot with a few of her followers placed themselves in front of her stall.

Isabelle sighed. 'Go away, Mrs Wilmot. I have nothing to say to you.'

'Nay, but I've got plenty ter say ter yer.' Marge heaved up her enormous breasts with her arm. 'Yer might as well not bother coming anymore. I've put the word around that yer pies are rubbish and they'll mekk whoever eats them sick.'

Fury burnt through Isabelle's veins. 'How dare you!'

'Yer've got a farm ter get yer money, I don't. Me pies are all I have. If yer keep tekking custom away from me, then I'll not be responsible fer me actions.'

'You think people will believe scum like you?' She tossed her head. 'No matter what you say, I still have customers.'

'Not as many as before though, I'll bet.' Marge peered into the baskets she could see. 'Yer've got some left, ain't yer?'

'The market wasn't as busy today. The cold wind kept people home.'

Marge laughed, showing missing teeth. 'I sold all me stuff and I'd have sold a lot more if I'd had it.'

'I'm pleased for you.' Isabelle inclined her head. 'Now, if you'll excuse me, I must find my brother.'

Marge gripped her arm as she passed. Isabelle winced as the fat fingers pinched. 'Let go of me!'

'Listen here, yer silly little bitch.' Marge leaned forward to whisper. 'Yer come here again and I'll have yer. Understand?'

'Your threats do not frighten me.'

'Well, they should.' Marge's piggy eyes narrowed. 'Yer husband's gone and yer've no one ter protect yer.'

Isabelle whipped her arm out of the savage grip and stepped away. The threat didn't frighten her but Marge's words cut deep. She was a married woman without a husband. Trapped in a non-existent role as a wife to no one.

Hughie ran up to her out of breath. 'Sorry. I didn't realize the time.'

Isabelle glanced at Marge before gathering her belongings and walking off with Hughie. 'Where have you been? If you'd arrived on time, I would have avoided her altogether!'

'Sorry, I was down by the canal watching the boats unloading.'

'You should have stayed home and watched the ewes. That would have been more helpful.' She thrust the stool at him and marched on. A scatter of light rain fell and she heaved another sigh at the thought of driving home in such weather.

'Did the old bat give you much trouble?'

Isabelle pierced him with a look. 'What do you think?' Reaching the stable, she placed her baskets in the cart and then gave the stable boy a ha'penny for minding the horse.

Once out on the road, Isabelle concentrated on clearing the people and other transports in Market Street. Hughie sat sullen beside her. It was only when they were climbing up the steep Heptonstall road that she thought to the incident with Marge Wilmot. *What am I to do?* The woman would no doubt resort to violence should she keep attending the market. Besides, her trade had suffered today from Marge's lies, and if it continued there would be no point in keeping her stall. She shivered in her thin coat and pulled up her scarf to better cover her neck and chin.

'We need to plan for the spring.' She glanced at Hughie then back to the road. 'We have little money, certainly not enough for the rent. The stall isn't providing enough.'

Hughie huddled further into his coat. The icy wind slapped them hard at the top of the hill. 'I thought if we could buy more sheep . . . '

'No, we have no money for that.' Isabelle blinked away the sting from her eyes. The flatness of the moor provided easy access for the gale to gather speed. 'We have to put to better use what the farm offers. In April we'll shear the ewes. The fleeces won't bring in much, as the flock is small, but it'll be better than nothing. Then in August we'll sell the lambs. Is it August or September they go to market?' She frowned. 'I'm not sure.'

'I don't know. You'll have to ask someone. We've got the piglets too. We can sell them.'

'Yes, though one or two we'll keep to fatten up for next winter. Maybe we could plough a field of wheat.' Isabelle bit her lip deep in thought. She really didn't know enough about farming. 'I need a husbandry book.'

Hughie's eyes grew wide. 'There is one in the front room.'

Amazed, she twisted to look at him. 'In the sitting-room?'

He nodded and grinned.

'When did you go in there?'

'A few days ago, when it was raining and I was bored.'

Isabelle straightened on the seat and concentrated on the point between the horse's ears. She hardly ever went in the sitting-room herself. The cold mustiness of it reminded her of long dead former occupants. She believed nothing had been touched in there since Farrell's parents had died. 'A book is the last thing I thought the Farrells would own. I didn't expect that they could read.'

'Maybe they couldn't?' Hughie shrugged.

Much later, long after darkness had enveloped the land, Isabelle entered the sitting-room of the house. Holding the lamp high, she paused by the door and surveyed the sparse room. Dust tickled her nose. On the mantelpiece above the large fireplace, portraits of strangers stared at her. She thought the room would frighten her, but suddenly it didn't. Instead, she felt a strange kind of comfort, a sadness. This room once represented the small wealth of a family. A horsehair sofa occupied the area by the fireplace, beside it a small square table held an empty glass vase.

She turned and watched the shadow cast along the wall. The dim light shone on an old painting of a girl with a dog. Moving on, Isabelle went to the bookshelf on the far wall. It held only two books, the husbandry book

Hughie mentioned, and a smaller book of poetry. Next to those were three small tin boxes. Opening them, she found one box held hair, golden curls, the next box a small collection of silk thread. The last box was empty. Again, the sorrow of this room consumed her. It was as though the ghosts of years past lingered, whispering.

'Belle? Belle?'

Hughie's calling brought her out of her reverie. 'In here.'

He stood in the doorway, grinning. 'The first lamb was just born. Come look.'

She smiled and followed him out. Closing the door on the front room, she paused. An inner voice spoke to her and straightened her spine. She wasn't going to repeat the Farrells' failure of the past. She would show them all.

* * *

Ethan ducked his head under a low branch and swore softly when a fluttering of dislodged snow slipped down his collar. He guided Copper away from the fast flowing Hebden Water and edged up the steep wooded incline of Lee Wood. He'd spent the morning discussing the operations of his mill and examining the account books with the mill manager. After touring the four storeys of the building and being cooped up in the fetid heat cast by the weaving machines, he craved the clean crisp air.

Copper knew the track through the woods without any further guidance from him, so Ethan relaxed in the saddle and allowed the cool dampness of the wood to ease his mind away from business. Tomorrow would come soon enough when he would begin another round of visiting his business concerns.

A rabbit darted in the undergrowth and Gyp, his golden retriever raced after it, only to come up short when a convenient hole allowed the rabbit to escape. Gyp nosed around the hole's entrance until Ethan whistled for him. The poor fellow had been kept to lingering in the estate grounds while he was in Liverpool, and as soon as Ethan walked to the stables Gyp had run beside him, as eager as he was to be out.

Although it had been only weeks since his last ride, it felt like months. His trip to Liverpool to check on his business interests there took two weeks. Two weeks of being plagued by the image of Isabelle. What did she have that made him unable to forget her? She belonged to another man. No! The instant he thought it, he swiped it from his mind. She was never Farrell's, but then, she would never be his either. He swore softly.

The more he thought of Isabelle the more he became frustrated by his life. The last two days of rain kept him inside with Clarice and it nearly drove him to madness. His mother's chest cold kept her in bed, the best place for her, he knew, but it also meant he had to suffer his wife's presence alone. His patience to endure her failed him. For too long, he had put the estate above any other needs. Her money had made great changes in the productivity of the estate. It allowed him to build terraced houses in Hebden Bridge and other properties in Todmorden. He had kept his promise to his dying father to better the family's financial situation.

Now, due to his wise investments in cotton mills, glass works and railways, they had more money than ever before, but at the sacrifice of his personal happiness. The family's position had risen to new heights, his name had been mentioned within the community for a parliament position. Yet, none of this gave him the satisfaction it should. His wife's childlike mannerisms and corpulence embarrassed him. She treated him like a stranger, or worse, as someone of no importance. Clarice didn't want a husband and a household, she wanted the inside of a sweets jar. She lived a childlike existence where her greatest decisions of the day were what treats she could eat.

Riding out of the wood, Ethan guided Copper to the right and down Lee Wood Road. He breathed deeply and tilted his head back to the sun. March. Spring blossomed on the horizon. Blood coursed through his veins. He felt alive and edgy and suddenly filled with the need to gallop, to pound over the frozen earth and clear away his frustrations. Copper slipped in the snow, diverting Ethan's concentration back to the present. Ahead a figure walked. Isabelle. His heart thudded and his groin tightened with want. He rode closer and she stopped. Nothing in her manner gave him any hint to her reaction of him. She was thinner. Tired. A surge of affection overwhelmed him. He wanted to crush her to him and kiss her senseless. Above all things, he wanted to protect her, cherish her.

'Good day to you, Mr Harrington.'

Her pale blue eyes seemed to torch his soul. Did she have any idea how alluring they were? He guessed not. In none of their meetings had she shown feminine wiles. Despite that or maybe because of it, he was instantly more aware of her. 'How are you faring?'

She raised her chin. 'Well, for the moment.'

He dismounted and stepped towards her,

thus prompting Gyp to leap over the snow-covered grass to sniff Isabelle's boots.

She smiled and patted his head. 'Aren't you a handsome one?'

Ethan gazed at her, drinking in her loveliness. 'That's Gyp. Be careful, before you know it he'll have you down and be licking the skin off your face.'

She chuckled and bent to tickle behind his ears. 'Good boy.'

Ethan's stomach clenched. He wanted the attention she gave the dog. His mind went blank as he searched for something amusing or intelligent to say. Being lost for words was strange to him, but then, he'd experienced many new things since meeting this lovely creature.

Isabelle straightened and looked out over the moor. 'When is it time to turn the ewes and lambs out?'

Her question stunned him just as much as if she'd asked him to kiss her. 'Pardon?'

She frowned and studied the landscape. 'I don't want to turn them out too soon and lose the lambs to the weather. What do you do?'

He swallowed, trying to gather his scattered thoughts. He ran a hand through his hair. 'Um . . . well, I have shepherds . . . '

'Oh. Yes, of course you would. How silly of

me.' She blushed and turned away.

Instinctively, he moved closer. 'It's too early yet. March is unpredictable. Lambs would die if we had a snowstorm, which is quite likely still. April is much better. The thaw will begin in earnest then.' He paused, knowing he spoke too fast. Only, he didn't want to give her the opportunity to leave.

Isabelle nodded and they fell into step together with Ethan leading Copper by the rein. She darted him a glance. 'Out of twenty-eight ewes we got twenty-four lambs with four sets of twins. Four ewes didn't take with the ram.' Her pale eyes shone with accomplishment and he clenched his hands in an effort not to reach for her. He suppressed a smile, trying to imagine his mother's expression at Isabelle's forthright comments. He found her candour refreshing.

'A successful result indeed. I suggest you cull the four barren ewes. They are likely to be too old now for further use.'

'Right. Yes, good idea.' Her frown appeared again. 'We lost five lambs in one night.'

'It happens.'

'I can't afford to lose any more.'

'Foxes may kill a few once the flock is turned out.'

'Really?' She bit her lip.

He nodded. 'Is Farrell back?'

She made a disparaging sound. 'Not likely. He might never come back.'

He stared at her and she blushed again. His heart sang. Farrell could rot in a gutter somewhere as far as he was concerned. The man didn't deserve Isabelle. He wasn't fit to wipe her boots.

Abruptly, she stopped and turned to him. They were only a foot apart. 'I am sorry he stole from you. Please believe me that neither I nor Hughie had anything to do with what he did.'

'I know that.' He wanted her so badly it hurt. But what did she want?

'It was foolish of him.' She glanced away and her voice lowered. 'His hatred of you makes him do it.'

'Hating someone for your own mistakes and inadequacies shows cowardice and a lack of responsibility. I don't credit him with any intelligence.'

'I'm so ashamed I married him.' She stared down at her boots. 'No one told me what he was like. I see now that it was intentional on their part.'

'Whose part?'

'Those at Peacock's Private Workhouse.'

'He never hurt you?' Anger raced along his veins at the mere thought of Farrell laying one finger on her.

'It no longer matters. I mean nothing to him. He regards me at best as unpaid help, and at worst a stranger who nags him about his whereabouts.' She gave a humourless laugh. 'The only time he showed emotion was when your name was spoken.'

Unable to help himself, Ethan closed the gap between them and with one finger under her chin, turned her face back to him. Her eyes widened and her breath shortened. He was overjoyed that she responded to him. 'What Farrell does or thinks is of no concern to me. Let him hate me if that makes him feel like a man, because the whole district knows he isn't one really. What man would leave his wife to fend alone up here?'

'Why did you take back the land after his father died?' she whispered and he dropped his hand away.

'I only took part of the land back, I let him keep the farm and surroundings acres. Not that he deserved it. I believed after his father died he would keep the farm going, but he is no farmer. Farrell let the moor go to waste. He wouldn't fire it to allow regrowth. His animals died for lack of care because he was too busy supping ale or poaching. There are a lot more reasons, believe me.'

'If you had offered to help him . . . '

'He wouldn't take my help or anyone's.' He

134

looked at her mouth. 'Anyway, enough talk of him. It is you I am concerned about.'

'You have no need to concern yourself over me. I will pay your rent on time.' She swallowed and he watched her slim throat work.

Ethan groaned. 'You mistake my intentions. The rent means nothing to me. I wouldn't take it from you.'

'But I don't understand?' She bit her bottom lip. 'Are you turning us out?'

'No!' He lifted his hands, alarmed that she thought him capable of doing that to her. He had to win her trust and reassure her. 'Please, don't worry about the rent or anything about the farm. I will help you.'

'You will help me until Farrell returns?' Her voice dropped low in shock.

Ethan closed his eyes in frustration. 'Yes, until Farrell returns.'

'You won't report him to the police?'

His gaze roamed over her face, her unique pale eyes. To him, she was beautiful. 'No.'

She reached out and took his hand. 'Thank you.'

He looked down at their joined hands. 'I very badly want to kiss you, Isabelle.' She stiffened, but didn't pull away. 'Would you like that too?'

'I . . . We . . . You . . . ' She sucked in a

breath. 'It is wrong.'

He tilted his head and gave her a wry smile. 'How can it be wrong to feel like this? You do share what I feel, don't you, Isabelle?'

She lifted her chin as though to refuse it, but her expression softened. 'Yes.'

Ever so slowly, he lowered his head. His lips brushed the pulse beating at her temple. Ethan raised his head only inches from her face. He gazed into her eyes, waiting for her to guide him. Amazed, he watched as she peeled off one of her gloves and very slowly raised her hand to touch his face. The simple gesture melted his bones. His loins tightened painfully. Her long fingers, roughened by work, traced the shape of his mouth. Ethan thought he would die of want. Unable to restrain himself any longer, he cupped his hands over her hips and gently pulled her against him. His gaze never left hers. He darted out his tongue and licked her fingers that covered his mouth. Surprised, she faltered. Her chest rose and fell rapidly.

'Do you want me to stop?' Isabelle shook her head a fraction. It was the signal he wanted. Gathering her closer still, he kissed her eyes, her cheeks, her nose and finally found her lips. He liked that she clung to his shoulders, her fingers gripped into the material of his coat. He ran the tip of his tongue over her lips, nudging them open. Gently he probed further until she allowed full access. Their kiss deepened. His spirit soared to the sky above them. She was nectar. She was a Helen of Troy. She was *his*.

They broke apart reluctantly. Ethan dragged air back into his lungs, but didn't let go of her. His mind sang her name, his body sang with her touch. He kissed her nose and smiled. 'Everything changes now.'

She blinked. 'It does?'

'Of course!' He laughed and welcomed the release. It seemed as though he had never laughed in his life before.

She stepped back and frowned. 'I don't see how anything has changed. You are married and so am I.'

His smile slipped. 'But I will take care of you now.'

She took another step back widening the distance between them. 'I'll not be your kept woman.'

'I didn't mean that.'

'What *did* you mean then?'

His mind failed him. Christ what was wrong with him? Whenever he was in her presence, he lost all ability to think.

'Thank you.'

He blinked. 'For what?'

The light died from her eyes and washed

away all colour. 'For answering my question.' She twisted away and rushed to climb the stile over the stone wall bordering the fields. On the other side she gathered her skirts and ran.

Ethan shook his head as though drunk. Confusion now reigned where lust had been. What the hell had just happened?

★ ★ ★

Isabelle tossed the fork load of straw into the wheelbarrow and paused to wipe her hair out of her eyes. The stench of urine-soaked straw made her eyes water and her throat convulse. Lambs bleated non-stop and their mothers gave her baleful stares. Cleaning out the sheds was a hateful task, but necessary to keep disease from claiming her stock. Rain thundered on the roof and she wondered if it would ever stop. For three days, it had tormented them, threatening to ruin her plans of survival.

Once the snow finally thawed, she turned out the sheep into the house field. They feasted on new spring grass for two days and then the rain came, forcing her to bring them all back inside. The weather kept her confined to the house and sheds. She was unable to work in the garden and begin her vegetable bed preparations. But she was able to clean every room in the house. She overhauled the front room ready for her and Hughie to use in the summer. Since this farm was to be her home, then she might as well make it as comfortable as possible. Besides, she wanted her touch in every room. The ghosts of the past had to be replaced with the dreams of the future. She only hoped that she had a future here. She tried not to think of the awkward scene with Ethan. She knew so little of him, if he chose to be vindictive it could make an already difficult situation much worse.

As hard as the work was, at least she and Hughie had a roof over their heads and answered to no one but themselves. She couldn't risk leaving here to find work and another place to live. Thousands of people walked the roads every day looking for work, sleeping in ditches. She couldn't expose Hughie to such a life as that.

Hughie clambered into the shed carrying a straw bale and placed it near the door to join three others. 'That's the last of the dry stuff. Rain coming in through the roof has ruined the rest. That end shed is useless in bad weather. There's more holes in the roof than I can fix. The whole lot of it needs to be replaced.'

'Well I'll put that on the list with everything else, shall I?' she snapped.

He became defensive. 'I'm just saying, that's all.'

She smiled to soften her tone. 'Yes, I know.'

'The stream is high, nearly reaching the top of the banks. I bet Hebden Water is a torrent. I might go look later when I check the traps.'

'Just as long as you don't go close to the edge.' Isabelle sighed. 'Can you finish up in here? I'll go start dinner.'

He took the fork from her. 'What are we having?'

'The chicken I killed this morning.'

'You killed a chicken again?' His eyebrows rose. 'I thought you wanted them kept for laying?'

She paused and wrapped her coat tighter around her, ready to run out into the rain. 'I do, this is the last one for the pot. Then it is back to eating bread and dripping.'

'Bread and dripping.' Hughie shuddered. 'We've had that all week.'

'And we'll continue to have it after the chicken has been eaten too. I have no money to buy food. Until the lambs can be sold, we'll have to rely on the rabbits you trap and the odd egg the hens lay, but their production has slowed in the last month.'

His eyes widened. 'We could starve.'

She touched his arm. 'I'll try not to let that happen. Once the rain stops, I'll go to the market with some pies. I have enough ingredients left to make about half a dozen. With the money from that I will buy vegetable seeds. We'll have vegetables for the summer if nothing else.'

'What about culling those four ewes as Mr Harrington told you to do?'

Isabelle winced at the mention of his name. 'Yes, I must arrange for a butcher to come to the farm. I didn't want to have them slaughtered, as it might not be their fault they didn't take with the ram. Maybe the ram didn't do his job?' She looked out the door. The rain had stopped and the dripping moisture made music of its own. In the distance, blue sky showed between sheets of grey cloud. 'Don't take too long in here.' She called over her shoulder and, head down, ran for the house.

'Isabelle!'

On hearing her name called, she skidded to a halt and splashed dirty puddle water across her boots and up her stockings. 'Damn!'

Ethan Harrington rode further into the yard and dismounted. 'How are you?'

Her heart hammered as though a black-smith lived in her chest. She swallowed and drank in the sight of him. His lack of hat always surprised her, even more so today as the rain had plastered his hair to his scalp. 'This is hardly the weather to be out riding.' *Now why did I say that?* She shook her head.

His gaze pierced her soul. 'It is not enough to keep me from you.'

Isabelle darted a look at the shed, but Hughie wasn't yet aware of their visitor. 'You have no right to say such things.'

'I speak the truth.' He stepped closer.

'We are both married. Had that escaped your notice?'

'Nothing about you escapes me.'

She held up her hand as if to ward him off. 'Please don't.'

'May I be invited in?' He indicated towards the house.

'No.' Isabelle's legs threatened to give way. Memories of his kiss, his touch consumed her until she could barely think. 'Go away, please.'

'I want to be your friend. Let me look after you.'

She was so tempted. For a moment she wanted to lay her head on his shoulder and let him take her worries from her, but at what cost? It would lead to further problems and she didn't have the strength to deal with more. 'What would your wife say about it?'

He took a step closer. 'My wife has nothing

to do with it. We are married in name only. What I do with my time is my business.' His hand cupped her cheek, the leather glove cold against her skin. 'I will promise to simply be a friend and nothing more, if that will convince you to agree.'

'Just a friend?' Her stomach fluttered. 'A landlord type friend?'

He nodded. 'If that is what you wish.'

'It is all it can be.' She gripped his hand and jerked it away from her face. 'Don't you understand? If the gossips find out about your visits here they will taint me as your mistress. I won't have Hughie made miserable or my reputation ruined.'

'I promise you it won't happen.'

She turned from him. 'You can't promise any such thing,' she scoffed.

'Isabelle, look at me.'

Shaking her head, she walked into the house and closed the door.

Ethan swore and spun back to his horse. Hughie stood in the shed's doorway. Startled, Ethan forced a smile to his lips. 'Good day, Hughie.'

'And to you, sir.'

'How are you managing?'

Hughie shrugged. 'We're getting by. Belle worries a lot. We have no money and not much food.'

'Did you cull the barren ewes?'

'Not yet. Belle isn't so sure.'

'You are the man around here now.' Ethan glanced at the house then took a deep breath. He stepped towards Hughie. 'Shall we go into the shed and talk business?'

★   ★   ★

'You did what?' Isabelle stared at Hughie as if he'd lost his mind. 'How could you go behind my back like that?'

Hughie squirmed in his chair. 'Mr Harrington said I was the man around here now and wanted to discuss things.'

'You are not in charge!' She stamped her foot in exasperation. 'He had no right to do that. He took advantage of you because he knew I wouldn't let him do as he pleased.'

Hughie straightened his shoulders. 'Why can't I be involved in what happens here? I work as hard as you.' His defiant look reminded her that he was no longer a boy but quickly becoming a young man.

'I'm not denying how hard you work, and I will always consult you on my decisions regarding the farm. I'm angry at Harrington.'

'He wanted to help. What's so wrong about that?'

Isabelle leant over the table towards him. 'I don't need his help. We can manage on our own until Farrell returns.'

Hughie snorted in disgust. 'He'll not come back and I hope he doesn't. I'd much rather have Mr Harrington helping us than Farrell, who was useless to us anyway.'

Water boiled over the pot and sizzled on the hotplate. Isabelle gave her attention to it, but seethed inside. How dare Ethan Harrington. How dare he!

'I don't see what you're so angry about, Belle. Mr Harrington's butcher is coming at no cost to us. I thought you would be pleased.'

She stirred the chicken stew, the aroma made her stomach growl. She hadn't eaten all day. Cutting back on food to make it last longer seemed sensible in theory, yet in reality she was always hungry, which in turn made her cranky and irritable.

'Belle?'

'I don't want to talk about it, Hughie.' She sighed and then faced him. 'We only have each other to rely on. We can't afford to look elsewhere for help.'

'Why?'

'Because we haven't anything to give back when they ask for help in return.'

'Mr Harrington won't ask for anything,

Belle. What could he possibly want from us?'

Isabella had the desire to laugh but hastily squashed it. Ethan Harrington would ask and expect something in return. She had no doubt about that.

8

Isabelle slashed at the mammoth climbing rose at the front of the house. Behind her a small fire smouldered after devouring her last toss of thorny vines. She stood back and surveyed her morning's work. She glanced at the pitifully few remaining geese, ducks and chickens that flittered about the front yard fighting over the insects and worms she had uncovered in her task of making the entrance to the house more presentable. She raked more clippings into a pile and the poultry ran for the pickings she revealed. 'Aren't you the lucky ones?' She smiled at them as they squawked and jabbed at each other. 'You survived the winter. So now you must behave and lay a dozen eggs a day and in return, I'll let you sit on some of them to hatch fine chicks.'

Weak sunshine crept from behind a cloud and brightened the house's brick walls, bare now from the thick covering of the climbing rose. Gardening gave her much satisfaction. She had always enjoyed helping her grandfather in his small garden between the vicarage and the church. Now, as she continued to rake the rose trimmings into the fire, she took pleasure in her achievement. After trampling down the long grass, narrow garden beds had emerged, lining the curved path from the drive to the front door. Daffodils and snowdrops materialized once she had removed the choking weeds from the beds. She pruned the old rose bushes into some semblance of order and dug manure into the soil between clumps of wild purple violets. The former mistress of Meadow Farm must have found some time to get pleasure from gardening. Isabelle knew that in the summer the roses would be a welcome delight after winter's bleakness.

'Here she is, Belle.' Hughie came around from the side of the house leading Mayflower. 'She'll benefit from cropping this down to a manageable lawn.' He let her loose on the grass amidst the poultry.

Isabelle patted the cow's large rump. 'If the other cows were as easy to lead as her, I'd like to have more in here to get it down sooner.'

'Mr Harrington said that the rest of the herd should go to market. They aren't milkers and are just eating grass that the lambs need.' He averted his gaze from Isabelle to Mayflower, the mention of their landlord was a sore point between them. 'Well, it does make sense. With the money we can buy more ewes or fix up the sheds, maybe buy . . . '

'Yes, I will think about it.' At the mention of Harrington, Isabelle raked furiously. She clenched her teeth, tired of hearing Hughie praise Ethan Harrington's every word. 'I feel uneasy about selling Farrell's animals without his consent.'

'It's not as if he cares.'

She shrugged. 'Even so.'

'Right, well, I'd better get back to chopping the wood.' After a last look at her from under his lashes, he left.

Isabelle nodded with a sigh. She was losing her sanity over Ethan. In the last two weeks he had arrived nearly every day on some pretext or another. The butcher slaughtered the four ewes at no cost to her and what meat she didn't want, the butcher bought from her, providing welcome funds. Ethan also arranged for the piglets to be sold at market, dropped off a cartload of vegetable seedlings, plus new hoes and spades. Whenever he arrived, he brought a hamper of food and small tokens of friendship like a wooden case filled with needles and thread, newspapers, books from his own library and clothes for Hughie which were once his own but no longer fitted.

At first, she had been mortified by his

149

charity. Her pride tempted her to refuse his gifts, but one look at Hughie's delighted face quickly dampened her self-righteousness. How could she deny her darling brother all the things she would have liked to buy for him? Things he had earned through hard work. She couldn't deny that Ethan's help eased their lot considerably. So, biting back her urge to tell Ethan she would rather swim in the midden than accept his gifts, she let Hughie bask in his attention.

It annoyed her that her body reacted to his presence. She craved his smile like a drowning man needing air. She knew with every look and word that he was simply waiting for her to surrender to their attraction. Every fibre of her being wanted to. She physically ached to touch him, but what would it achieve? Once she started down that road there would be no turning back.

'Ho there, missus. We're looking for Meadow Farm.'

Isabelle looked up at the stranger and the boy that walked through the gates. Each wore the haggard look of beggars. Their clothes hung loose, were torn and dirty. She frowned, glancing between the man and the boy. The man's lanky frame and the way he strutted towards her, as though he owned the place were vaguely familiar. He had an air of confidence, as though he led a charmed life, when in fact his appearance showed the opposite. Some instinct made her grip the rake and bring it against her chest in a gesture of protectiveness against the fragile organ that was her heart. He stopped a few yards away and studied her while slowly lowering his canvas bag to the ground.

'Looks like I found it then. I would know you anywhere, even though you are now a woman grown.'

Isabelle lifted her chin forcing herself not to show her trembling. A mixture of rage and longing warred within her, frightening in its intensity. Deep creases fanned from the corner of his eyes. His face was the colour of old leather, but his pale blue eyes were still as striking as she remembered. *Her* eyes.

'No welcome, my Belle?'

He had been the first to shorten her name. Tears sprang to her eyes and she blinked them away preferring the anger that quickly replaced her heart's first leap of joy. 'You deserve nothing from me. You relinquished that right eight years ago.'

He looked around the yard, his eyes searching. She noticed a tension had entered his body contradicting the lazy smile he wore.

'Looking for someone?' She sneered,

wanting to brandish the rake over her father's head.

He snapped his attention back to her and gave her the indolent smile that had made all the females in the household weak at the knees. 'I called in at the vicarage. Some woman told me that your grandfather had died.'

'What else did she tell you?'

'She didn't know what happened to you all, but she said that a girl by the name of Gibson had been married not so long ago to a Len Farrell of Meadow Farm. She had to copy the record in the register. It's a job she does every so often apparently.' He shrugged and again searched the yard. 'I was buying the boy something to eat and got talking to a fellow near the Piece Hall. He knew of Len Farrell and told me where the farm was.' He looked back at her. 'So here I am.'

'Here you are.' Isabelle echoed. Her anger disappeared, leaving her wrung out like a wet dishcloth.

'Where are they?'

Her face hardened, resentment mingled with pain. 'Who? Your family? The wife and children you abandoned?'

'Belle . . . '

She gave a derisive snort. He placed his hands out to her as in offering, but he had nothing to give her now. She wanted nothing from him. Not anymore. Once, a lifetime ago, she had been proud of Aaron Gibson, her tall, strong father. A man who was friends with everyone. A man who was loved by all for his easygoing charm and quick wit. Her knight. The one who dried her eyes when she fell from climbing a forbidden tree. The one whose arms held her tight when storms raged outside. Then he had gone. He walked away from her, from them all. She woke one day to hear her mother crying softly and Sally whispering that he would come back, he would come back.

She stared at her father and saw him properly for the first time for what he was. A weak man. Someone pathetic, past his prime and now looking for a family that didn't exist. For a second she felt sorry for him before coldness numbed her heart. He no longer had the power to hurt her. She simply didn't care.

Isabelle leant the rake against the house wall and, gathering up her skirts, stepped over the uneven grass and weed clumps. She walked around the side of the house and towards the sheds. After a moment's hesitation, he joined her with the boy silently walking behind. Concentrating on the boy for the first time, Isabelle noted he must only be about five years old. His legs and arms were as thin as sticks. As if sensing her appraisal the boy looked up. His pale blue eyes locked with hers. Her father's eyes. *Her* eyes. Shocked, she stumbled. 'Who is he?'

Her father ruffled the boy's black hair. 'Bertie. My son.'

Sudden anger rose in her chest. 'Your son?'

'Yes, and your half-brother.'

She closed her eyes momentarily and then walked on. *I can't cope with this.*

The sound of splitting wood came from the first shed. Her step faltered. She didn't want Hughie to be hurt, but she was powerless to stop him from meeting their father now. Besides, she knew that if she turned their father away without Hughie meeting him first, he would never forgive her. Hughie's soft heart still worshipped the man that left them for adventures unknown.

'Hughie.' Her voice croaked. She cleared her throat and tried again. 'Hughie, love.'

'Yes?' His voice carried out to her from within the shed.

'Can you come out here for a minute?'

He stepped out and glanced from her to the strangers. He dipped his head. 'Good day.'

Isabelle took Hughie's hand. She moved to stand beside him and together they looked at the man and small boy. 'Hughie, do you remember this man?'

He scratched his cheek. 'No, I don't think so.'

'This is the man you've often wondered about. Aaron Gibson.'

'Gibson?'

She squeezed his hand. 'Our father.'

Hughie jerked as if struck. His eyes grew wide.

Isabelle gripped his arm, pulling him closer. 'It's all right, dearest,' she said soothingly.

Their father stepped forward. 'You look well, son. All grown up.'

Hughie dragged his eyes away from him to stare at the boy.

Aaron thrust the boy in front of him. 'This is your brother, Bertie.'

'Shall we go inside?' Isabelle waved her hand in the direction of the house, hating the frozen look on Hughie's face. How could their father do this to them? Returning after eight years as if nothing had happened. He was meant to look after them, that was his role within a family. Yet, being the selfish man he was, he'd turned his back on them so easily. Walked away from a loving wife and adoring children. Simply walked away.

Aaron cleared his throat. For once his nonchalant expression slipped and his

Adam's apple bobbed. 'Where are your mother and Sally?'

Isabelle stared at him. Years of buried bitterness rose. Her lip curled back in hostility. 'Dead. Both dead.'

★ ★ ★

Ethan rode up the beech-lined drive, his mind on one issue only Isabelle. The last two weeks of visiting her, helping her, gave him enormous satisfaction. Additionally, it confirmed his stance on the feelings they both shared. Oh, he knew she tried to hide her emotions, but he wasn't fooled. She wanted him just as much as he desired her. His gut tightened at the thought of holding her, kissing her, loving her. As love her, he did. He made no apologies for it.

He rounded the corner and Bracken Hall loomed before him. In front of the sweep of steps leading to the double doors, a groom attended to a visitor's horse as the man dismounted. Only one man wore such an odd hat. His sister sent many sketches of that man and his hat. Ethan clicked his heels into Copper's sides to quicken his pace. The closer they got, the wider his smile became. 'Hamish MacGregor you old dog!'

The man in question spun around and

grinned. 'Ethan! You are a sight for sore eyes.'

Ethan dismounted in one fluid movement before throwing the reins to the groom and grabbing Hamish's upper arms. 'This is marvellous. Rachel's letter told us you had left Australia and returned to Scotland.'

'Indeed I did. Arrived back four months ago.'

'Four months ago?' He pretended to be shocked. 'And this is the first visit we've had? Mama will not forgive you for leaving it so long.'

Hamish laughed. 'Sorry, old friend, but business before pleasure and all that.'

Ethan leaned back to look at him better. 'You look well. Despite the hat!'

'I am. Very.' Hamish took off his battered, wide-brimmed hat and twirled it on one finger, leaving his red hair askew. 'Your sister, begged me to leave it behind when I left, but I simply could not. It's been on my head every day for the last six years.'

'Aye, it looks it, too.' Ethan chuckled. 'How is Rachel? Lord, I miss her, as does Mama.'

'She was in the best of health when I left.'

'John is looking after her for me then?'

Hamish laughed. 'My brother adores his wife. Never fear about her welfare in that regard.'

Ethan chuckled. 'I don't. Besides, my sister

can take care of herself. Perhaps I should concern myself over John?'

Hamish shook his head and grinned. 'I've seen John tackle a wild bull and kill a deadly snake in one clean shot, but Rachel . . . Well, let us just say that he's putty in her hands.'

Ethan turned for the house. 'Come in. Come in. We've much to talk about. I want to learn all about Australia and my sister's new home. How long are you staying?'

'Not long. I have to be on my way to Liverpool and then London. I've much to do in my time back home.'

They entered the drawing room and found it empty. Ethan went to the drinks cabinet and poured them both a brandy. 'When do you return to Australia?'

Hamish sat at one end of a cream and green striped sofa. 'Hopefully in twelve months. It could be more though. Depends, on Mother.'

'How is she?' Ethan handed him his drink.

'Not well. She has missed both John and me these last few years since father died. The estate has fallen into disrepair. It is too much for her. I am trying to persuade her to move to Carlisle and be with my sister Joan, but she refuses.'

Ethan swirled his drink in his glass. 'Difficult situation for you.'

'Enough of me.' Hamish sipped his drink. 'What about you? Where is your delightful mother?'

Ethan looked through the doorway. 'I believe she is out calling.'

'And your wife.'

'I neither know nor care.' He swallowed the rest of his drink and returned to the cabinet for more. 'I might as well tell you that soon my marriage will be no longer.'

Hamish spluttered and choked on his mouthful of brandy. 'No more?' he cried hoarsely.

'I am to divorce Clarice.'

'Good Lord. It's as bad as that?'

Ethan nodded and sighed. 'I have fallen in love with another, and I wish to be with her.' He rubbed his eyes, suddenly tired. 'It's all such a mess really. Totally unexpected.'

'Rachel has worried constantly ever since we left England. She knew you had made the wrong decision in marrying Clarice.'

'I should have listened to her, but Father's voice was stronger. My responsibility to the estate was more important than any of my needs at the time. After Father's death, I focused only on the estate. The rest of my life remained dormant. Then I met Isabelle.'

Hamish crossed his legs and tapped the side of his glass softly. 'Divorce is so untidy.

There's always gossip and court hearings; wrangling over money and property and the reasons why, etcetera.'

'I have no choice. I have spent the last seven years living a half-life. I could be an old man before Clarice dies. I want children. I want to be happy. Naturally, I'd make certain that Clarice had everything she wanted.'

'There is no hope for the two of you?'

'None at all.' Ethan shuddered. 'I don't love or desire her. I never did. She feels the same as I do. Father wanted our union and I wanted the estate to prosper with Clarice's dowry.' He flopped down on his mother's wing-backed chair. 'For seven years the estate has been my life, my love.'

'Is she worth it? This Isabelle?'

A tide of adoration enveloped Ethan like a soft, warm embrace. 'She is worth everything to me.'

Hamish raised his eyebrows. 'I've never seen that expression on your face before, dear friend. She must be a madonna?' He grinned.

'She is. She's beautiful and clever and warm.'

'Where does this wonderful woman reside?' Hamish laughed. 'She sounds so delightful I might marry her myself!'

Jumping to his feet, Ethan paced the room. The walls seemed to be closing in on him. He paused to stare unseeing out the window, and then turned. 'She is married to a tenant of mine.'

Hamish jolted in surprise and twisted on his seat to gape at him. 'Are you mad? A married woman? A working-class married woman?'

Ethan lifted his chin, defiant and ready to argue. 'Her status is of no importance to me.'

'Good God man!' Hamish leaped to his feet. 'You are willing to sacrifice your family's reputation and everything a divorce entails for such a woman?'

'You don't understand — '

'I understand you have lost your mind!'

Gritting his teeth, Ethan glared at his oldest friend. 'Hamish, you are a valued friend, but you have no right to speak — '

'Where is she?' Hamish strode to the door.

Startled, Ethan went after him. 'What are you doing?'

'I'm going to call on her. I must see for myself what spell she has put you under.'

Ethan grabbed his arm, stopping him in the entrance hall. 'You'll do no such thing.'

'I have to wonder at what hold she has over you. Won't she lift her skirts until you've married her, is that it?'

Anger licked at Ethan's insides. 'You are pushing the boundaries of our friendship.'

Hamish, his face pale, blue eyes pleading, looked at him. 'I can't let you make this mistake. Rachel will never forgive me. I cannot let you ruin your life.'

'Ethan?' Clarice stood at the top of the stairs dishevelled with her hair hanging in long childish braids. She leant her bulk against the banister and puffed as though she had run a mile when she'd only walked across the landing. One hand held a jar of boiled sweets. Ethan hung his head and swore.

Hamish stepped towards the bottom of the staircase. 'Good day, Clarice. You might not remember me. I'm Hamish MacGregor.'

'MacGregor?'

'My brother John married Ethan's sister and the three of us left for Australia six years ago.'

She wrinkled her nose, obviously trying to remember. 'Are you staying with us?'

'Yes. Just for one night. Ethan and I are going for a ride. Shall I see you at dinner?'

She stepped back and looked over her shoulder towards the bedrooms. 'No, I don't think so. I'm not feeling too well at the moment.' For one so large she turned swiftly and disappeared back along the landing.

Hamish looked at Ethan and his smile barely lifted the corners of his mouth. 'It is an impossible situation.'

Emotion clogged Ethan's throat. 'No, not impossible. Just difficult.'

★ ★ ★

Isabelle took the golden loaves out of the oven and dashed them out onto the table. Bertie's eyes followed her every move and she couldn't help but grin at him. 'They are too hot to cut.' She turned them upright in short movements. 'You aren't hungry again, are you?'

The boy shook his head but seemed hesitant to admit it.

She sighed and took the lid off the jar in the middle of the table. 'Here, have one barley sugar and then go and help Hughie and your father.'

Bertie took the sweet and ran out of the kitchen. Isabelle stared after him as he passed the window and ran across the yard. Six days. Her father and new brother had been at the farm for only six days, yet Hughie and Aaron Gibson had formed an immediate bond. This did not surprise her really, for Hughie had a soft heart. Aaron might be older and his good looks may have dimmed a little, but he could still charm the birds from the trees. She threw another log onto the fire and closed the oven door. Bread was all she was to bake today.

Four pies sat on the shelf in the larder, unsold from Saturday's market. Marge Wilmot's lies had begun again the moment she set up her stall table, but at least the woman herself didn't resort to physical violence this time. Isabelle ignored her threats and fist waving from the end of the market. Hughie and their father kept close by and so the day passed without further incident.

Isabelle sat at the table and rested her chin in her hand. Ethan came to mind and her heart swelled. He arrived again yesterday after an absence of a week. With him he'd brought his friend, Mr MacGregor, who was staying at Bracken Hall. MacGregor had studied her as though she was the first woman he'd ever seen. Instantly she knew that Ethan had spoken to him about her. She didn't know what to make of the tall Scotsman. She sensed his protectiveness towards Ethan and his disapproval of her. Thankfully, MacGregor's scrutiny of her was cut short when she introduced them both to her father and Bertie. Ethan kept his shock in check, but she didn't miss his meaningful glances. They stayed for an hour, talking with Hughie about the animals, checking the lambs and finally asked her opinion about the small herd. Plans were made for the spare cows to be taken to market next week.

She glanced at the small, tin carriage clock on the mantle above the fire. Ten minutes to noon. As Ethan mounted his horse on leaving yesterday, he had bent low to whisper in her ear. 'Meet me below Lee Bank at the edge of the wood tomorrow. Midday.' Her legs nearly buckled at his closeness. She didn't reply and watched him ride out of the yard with her skin alive with awareness.

Now, as she twisted the cloth in her hands, she watched the minutes tick by on the clock. Lee Bank. Ethan. Alone. The words sounded in rhythm to the clock's ticking. No. She couldn't go. He disturbed her senses, filled her mind and body with longing she couldn't control. She couldn't be his mistress. *One meeting couldn't be so harmful could it?*

Abruptly, she jumped up and ran into the scullery. She washed her hands and face, dried them and then tidied her hair. After taking off her apron, she slipped off her house shoes and put on her boots. Her blood singing in her veins, she grabbed her black shawl and tossed it around her shoulders. In the next moment, she was out the door and striding up the yard.

'Belle? Where are you going?' Hughie held a dead rabbit in one hand.

'Just for a walk. I'm tired of being in the kitchen.' She didn't pause, for if she hesitated just slightly she'd not have the courage to go.

Hughie smiled and held up the rabbit. 'Dinner.'

'Lovely. Skin it and put it in the pot. I'll see to it later.'

'Be careful.'

She waved and glided out through the gate. Ethan. He spurred her on. Invisibly calling her, beckoning. She lifted up her skirts and ran across the fields to the stile. Once on Draper's Lane she slowed, not wanting to be out of breath when she met him. At Lee Bank, she entered the wood. The dark coolness halted her for a moment before she once more lifted her skirts and tripped lightly down the slope, winding between thick, fungus-covered trunks. She skidded a few times on loose dirt as the ground sloped sharply closer to Hebden Water. She could hear it now, bubbling and churning, swollen from the melting snow high on the moors.

Out of breath, she stumbled into the sunshine again and walked to the bank. The sunlight reflected off the water like a thousand stars. She scanned the area, looking for him, but there was nothing save the birds wheeling from the woods on each side of the river. Insects chirped in the grass and a butterfly quivered near her skirts. Isabelle frowned and steadied her breathing. *Where was he?*

She followed the water and rounded a slight bend. Ethan stood throwing pebbles into the river, further away his horse cropped at the grass by the water's edge. He was unaware of her presence and she took the opportunity to study him. He wore dark brown cord trousers with a lighter shade jacket. A cream shirt showed every time the jacket gaped open when he raised his arm to throw. Warmth spread from the pit of her stomach throughout her whole body. As always, the urge to reach for him, to touch and caress him consumed her like a blaze. She shouldn't have come. This was madness. He bent to select another pebble and caught sight of her. Slowly, he straightened and smiled. Within the space of a heartbeat he was in front of her.

'You came.'

She nodded, not able to do anything else but gaze at him.

He took her hand and led her into the shadow of the trees where Gyp lay panting and wagging his tail. Her eyes widened at the picnic before her. Chicken, ham, cheese, crusty bread, pickled pears, macaroons and what looked like a jug of cider, all spread out on a thick woollen blanket, beneath which was a canvas sheet to protect them from the cold ground. Everything was as it should be and it took her breath away.

'Will you join me?' He swept his hand over the blanket clearing it from imaginary dust.

She answered his question with a tender smile and sat down, tucking her feet under her. Gyp sidled over to her and nudged her hand for a pat. 'How are you, boy?' She tickled under his chin. Content, Gyp flopped down beside her, resting his large head on his paws. Isabelle turned her attention to Ethan. 'It all looks wonderful.'

'I hope you are hungry?' He lay on his side opposite her, stretching his long legs out towards the river. 'I wanted it to be perfect, for you.'

'Why?'

He poured a glass of cider and passed it to her. 'I want to show you how much you mean to me.'

She swallowed nervously. 'This changes nothing.'

His gaze pierced her heart. 'I want you to be happy. I can make you happy. If you let me.'

'No, you cannot.' She lowered her lashes and peered at the drink in her hand. 'It was silly of me to come here.'

'But you did.'

'Something overcame me. I couldn't resist it.' She shrugged and gazed at the water. 'We are wrong to do this.'

'I see nothing wrong in loving someone.'

She whipped her head back and stared at him. 'You can't love me. You don't know me.'

An ironic smile lifted the corners of his mouth. 'I adore you, but,' he opened his arms to encompass the picnic, 'all this is so we can learn more about each other.' He picked up a plate and forked slices of chicken and ham on to it. 'We'll talk and eat. Nothing more. Agreed?'

Isabelle swallowed the lump of emotion blocking her throat. 'Just talk?'

He nodded, his eyes bright with subdued mischief. 'Absolutely.'

The look that passed between them was full of charged understanding. Isabelle raised her chin accepting the challenge, and a challenge it would be. To be so close to him and not give in to the temptation of touching would be torture, but she could do it if he could.

'I want to know all about you.' He passed her plate over. 'And I hope you want to learn about me?'

'I do, yes.' She nibbled a piece of ham and he sucked in a breath as he watched her. She lifted her glass towards him. 'To friendship.'

He grinned at her salute and lifted his own. 'To us.'

* * *

Isabelle threw her head back and laughed. She gripped Ethan's waist tighter as Copper surged on, eating up the ground, thundering over Wadsworth Moor. Sheep darted away bleating in fright. The wind teased her hair from her hat and her skirts billowed out like a flag behind them. She closed her eyes, enjoying the thrill of the ride, the closeness of Ethan.

They had met again two days after the picnic and walked through the wood, just talking, learning ever more about each other. Not once did Ethan touch her in any way that was unchivalrous. He helped her over tree roots or fallen branches, but other than that he remained a good three feet from her at all times. For over an hour they talked, before parting with a promise to meet today at noon.

It was Sunday. The surrounding mills were quiet and deserted. Isabelle's heart fluttered a little at the risk they took, but it was overshadowed by the prospect of spending time with Ethan. She met him on Horse Bridge that crossed Crimsworth Dean Beck. Thankfully at that time, no one was using the old Limer's Gate packhorse trail. On arriving, she found Ethan mounted on Copper and Gyp nowhere in sight. At first she thought he was to tell her that something kept him from their meeting and he would have to leave. Instead, he slipped his foot out of the stirrup. 'Put your foot in there and give me your arm.' His loving smile broadened as he reached down, grabbed her arm and hoisted her over the saddle behind him.

The shock of riding pillion, of even being on a horse, kept her silent for a few minutes. That, mixed with his nearness, sent shivers of excitement through her. Never had she experienced something so primal as hugging her arms around his waist. His corded muscles bunched under her touch and she heard his sudden intake of breath. Then, before she could gather her scattered thoughts, he was urging Copper out of Crimsworth Dean and up onto the surrounding moors. Copper's thundering hooves matched the thud of her heart. Every ounce of her being sang in glorious exhilaration. It was all new to her; the speed, the ride. She wanted to shout, to scream, to cry at such a simple joy.

Soon enough, Ethan gently reined Copper in until he walked and then wheeled him back southwards down across Shackleton's Moor and towards the valley they'd come from. They rounded a stone wall bordering a lane and Ethan halted Copper and slid off his back. Isabelle put her arms out for Ethan to help her down and grinned when he swung her about him.

'Put me down, what would people think?' She laughed.

'There is no one to see except the crows and sheep.' He winked and released her. 'I want to show you something.' Taking her hand, he led her over to a small monument on the left.

She peered at the two ancient pillars. 'What is it, a wayside marker?'

Ethan knelt to look closer. 'They call it Abel Cross.' He straightened and walked around it. 'See how on each pillar there is a simple Latin cross?'

'How fascinating.'

'I'm not certain of its age, but it is old.' He came to stand beside her. 'There is a legend about it.'

She grinned, relaxed in his company in a way she never thought possible. 'Of course.'

'They say each panel represents a man's grave. They fought over a lady, who, after they killed each other, threw herself into the waterfalls from Lumb's Bridge. Legend has it she still haunts the bridge on misty nights.'

Isabelle shivered. 'Poor woman. Indeed it would be difficult to be responsible for such deaths.'

Ethan took her hand and kissed it. His gaze sought and held hers. 'It is easy to imagine the despair of being torn asunder by love.'

She swallowed, feeling his passion and intensity like a physical force. 'Ethan . . . '

'Yes, my love?'

'Don't call me that.'

He took her other hand and held them both to his chest. 'Do you feel my heart, Isabelle?'

She nodded, unable to speak, unable to breathe.

'It beats for you. Only you.'

She tried to pull her hands away, not needing the evidence to know of his sentiments, but his grip tightened. His eyes told the story, his body played out the actions of his soul. He loved her. His every deed confirmed his words.

Tears pricked her eyes. 'What are we to do?' she whispered, afraid of acknowledging her heart.

'We trust each other. Do you trust me?'

Again she nodded.

Ethan smiled, a glorious smile that melted her bones. His eyes mirrored the happiness that possessed him. 'I promise you, here at

Abel Cross, under this blue sky, surrounded by sheep, birds, and heather that I will always be yours in my heart until I am free to make it legal by law and God.'

Her eyes widened at his sincerity. 'Oh, Ethan . . . ' She reached up on tiptoes and kissed him softly on the lips. 'I promise you, here at Abel Cross, under this blue sky, surrounded by sheep, birds and heather that I will always be yours in my heart until I am free to make it legal by law and God.'

'Weehoo!' He picked her up and swung her around and around.

She laughed, cupped his cheeks in her hands and kissed him. It felt so right, so pure.

9

Isabelle, humming tunelessly, swept the path from the scullery door to the water pump. Along the path, herbs released their fragrance as her skirts brushed against them. Pausing, she heard Hughie's laughter from inside one of the barns. He did a lot of that these days. Bertie idolized him and was a willing follower. Their father and Bertie's arrival had been a blessing to Hughie, if not to her. Her heart, although softened from Ethan's love, still remained cold and hard towards her father. Despite his attempts to fill the breach between them by helping around the farm and gestures of courtesy, she couldn't forgive him for the past. Her cool reserve towards him did not extend to Bertie, however, for the boy was loveable, with a shyness that reminded her of Sally. And he had grown in these two months on the farm. Bertie responded quickly to any chore she requested of him and on many occasions surprised her by doing a task before being asked. He was no hardship to love.

Isabelle believed her father knew why she took frequent long walks into the wood, and this only gave her more reason to be barely civil to him. She tried to make sure they were never alone together, never able to talk. Yet his eyes sometimes told her things that his mouth never uttered. It didn't concern her if he approved or not, but nevertheless, she felt uncomfortable every time she donned her shawl and slipped away to met Ethan. *Ethan.* An inner glow of bliss warmed her and she sighed. For short moments during the day while she did her monotonous chores, she allowed her mind to concentrate on only him; his laughter, his wit, the way he smiled at her, the way his eyes lingered on her face. His kisses sent her to heaven, and she knew with an inborn logic that it wouldn't be long before they took the next step and loved each other in the full sense of the word. Her skin tingled at the thought.

She turned and carried the broom back into the scullery and then ducked her head into the kitchen to check the time. Nearly noon. After quickly washing her hands, she tidied her hair and dusted off her skirts. She wrinkled her nose at the washed out colour of them. Ethan offered many times to buy her new clothes, but to do so would cause comments from Hughie. She recoiled at the thought of him finding out about her and Ethan; the shame would be too much.

'Going out again?' Aaron walked into the kitchen from the hallway.

A guilty flush crept up her cheeks. She paused on the kitchen step, her hand on the door handle. 'Just for a walk, while the weather is fine.'

'Be careful, lass.'

She stared at him. 'I'm only going for a short stroll.' Her words sounded false even to her own ears.

He lowered his gaze. 'Aye, if you say so.'

Isabelle raised her chin. 'You think otherwise?'

'What you do is none of my business.' He shifted his weight from foot to foot. 'All I'm saying is that if you play with fire be prepared to get burnt.'

She hated him for guessing her secret. Knowing that another knew about her and Ethan's friendship somehow defiled it. 'The time has long gone since you were allowed to have a say in what I do. I am answerable to my husband only and since he has abandoned me, then I am answerable to myself.'

He inclined his head in acknowledgment of her words. 'I just don't want you to be hurt.'

'You don't want me to be hurt?' She mocked him with a humourless laugh. 'You mean hurt like when you walked out on us? Hurt when Grandfather died? Hurt when we

177

were forced to enter a private workhouse? When mother stopped eating and died of a broken heart? Hurt when Sally no longer cared enough to fight a common cold and allowed it to weaken her lungs? Is that what you mean?'

'Belle — '

'Don't call me that!' She yelled. 'You have no right!' Pain and disappointment ate at her. She denied her tears an outlet and let them burn within her heart like a cancer.

As though he were an old man, Aaron stumbled to the table and sat down. 'If I could leave now, I would.'

She turned away from him in disgust. 'Leaving is what you're good at, isn't it?'

'I stayed with your mother for as long as I could, but I wasn't made to stay in one place all my life. Being a husband, a father, smothered me. It wasn't as though I didn't love you all; I did, but I couldn't breathe.' He shook his head, his eyes not seeing the kitchen, but locked somewhere in the past. 'The responsibility was too much. Your mother never understood my ways. She met me at a fair. I lived and worked within a travelling fair. I loved her at first sight. We both thought I could live in one place and be happy.'

'I don't want to hear your pathetic excuses.

What kind of man abandons his family?' Isabelle steeled her heart against him. She had loved him, adored him — once. And he had left without even a goodbye. She wouldn't give him the power to wound her that way again. 'If you want to leave, you can. I will take care of Bertie. He doesn't deserve to be dragged around the country, always hungry, always tired.'

'I can't go.'

She shrugged, desperately trying not to care.

'I am a coward.'

'Yes, you are.'

He cleared his throat. 'I came looking for my family because I didn't want to die in a roadside ditch somewhere.'

Isabelle turned to stare out of the window. 'The saying goes, 'Only the good die young.' I am sure it will be many years before you meet your Maker.'

'Not true. I am ill.' He scraped back his chair and stood.

She glanced at him over her shoulder as he pulled up his shirt and vest. A large lump in his side distended his stomach. Her eyes widened at the ugly misshapen bulge. She gasped, her hand flying to her mouth. The swelling only highlighted his thin lankiness more.

179

Aaron grimaced. 'Not something you wished to see, I'm sure.'

'What is it?'

'Some cankerous growth I'm told. A doctor in Scotland told me last year that I'd not have long, a year or two at most.'

Abruptly, white-hot fury overcame her. 'So you came home to die? You came home to burden *us* with your illness and then death? You would have saddled Mother with all this after walking out on her?' She gripped the table to stop herself from scratching his eyes out. 'Have I not enough to contend with? Wasn't it enough that you returned with an illegitimate child? But now this!'

He stepped back at her ferocity. 'I . . . I — '

'You're not just a coward, you're a selfish, unthinking swine! And I hate you!' Isabelle picked up her skirts and sped from the kitchen. She ran across the yard, scattering geese and chickens, through the back gate that opened into the house field and dashed towards the woods. A sob broke from her. *I hate him.* Blind with tears, she scrambled over the stile to fall to her knees on the other side. A youth walked on Draper's Lane, but she ignored his questioning look and, scrambling up, flung herself into the dense trees. New leaves coated the branches and made a canopy over the wood like an umbrella, blocking out the sun. In the dim light, she skittered down the incline. With the back of her hand, she dashed away her tears. A tree root tripped her. She fell hard, knocking the air out of her lungs. The dank smell of earth filled her nose. She lay outstretched, numb and not wanting to move for the fear of the pain that would certainly break her heart. *He came home to die.*

'Isabelle!'

Ethan's cry jolted her upright and in seconds she was in his arms. Kneeling on the dirt, he held her tight, searching her face and body for evidence of an accident.

'I've been waiting for you. What's happened?'

She clung to him, sobbing.

He kissed her head. 'I have you now, my love. You're safe with me.'

'I hate him!'

'Who?'

Wordlessly, she shook her head and cried into his shoulder while he held and soothed her. It felt right to be here in his arms. His solid strength made her feel protected, safe. Ethan was the one person she could trust, depend on. At last, she hiccupped into silence. Her eyes felt sore and puffy and her nose ran.

'Can you tell me what upsets you so,

sweetheart?' He pulled out his handkerchief and wiped her eyes, then passed it over for her to hold.

'My father.' She blew her nose. 'He came to find us because he is dying.'

'Oh, my sweet.' He kissed her softly and held her close.

Snuggled into his chest, Isabelle sighed and closed her eyes. Being held, comforted, allowing another to hear her worries and wipe away her tears was paradise. A haven she hadn't known existed.

Ethan kissed the top of her head. 'Is there anything I can do for you? I can pay the doctor's fee or — '

'No. Thank you.' She cupped his cheek in her hand. Loving him so much was a physical pain she couldn't heal. He lowered his head and she welcomed his kiss. After a moment they pulled apart and she rested her head on his chest. 'I don't know how long he has. It may be months, a year even.' She shuddered, remembering the sight of her father's stomach.

Ethan ran his fingertips down her cheek. 'I'm here to help you through this time, my darling. I'm always here for you.'

'I know.'

He tightened his hold on her as he twisted them around together, so that he leant against a nearby tree. 'Lie quiet. Rest.' He kissed her ear. 'You gave me such a fright. I can't tell you what I thought when I saw you running and crying like that.'

Nodding, she closed her eyes. 'I'm sorry. It became all too much. I don't want to watch him die. I detest him for doing this to me and Hughie.'

'I understand. It's not going to be easy.'

'No.'

He sighed and stroked her arm, as she lay curled up against him. 'Sleep for a while, sweetheart.'

Suddenly, tiredness cloaked her like a heavy blanket. She wouldn't sleep, not really, but it was nice to close her eyes and relax in his arms. Overhead the birds twittered, skipping from branch to branch. Further down, the soft trickle and hum of Hebden Water wafted on the light breeze.

Isabelle opened her eyes slowly, dis-orientated.

'Had a good nap?' Ethan grinned down at her.

'I fell asleep?'

'Indeed, my pet, for at least an hour.'

She jerked upright. 'Lord!' Warmth flooded her cheeks. 'I'm so sorry.'

'Nonsense.' He laughed and gathered her back into his arms. 'I enjoyed holding you, watching you sleep.' He took her hand and played with her fingers, kissing them, nibbling them.

'They'll be worrying about me.'

'I will walk you home.'

She shook her head, recalling the scene in the kitchen. 'I don't really want to go yet.'

'Then stay here with me.' He kissed her with such tenderness, she felt as if all her bones liquefied.

Isabelle swallowed, knowing with an inborn logic that the mood had changed between them. Heat replaced her grief and awoke her to his sensual caresses. His breath shortened, she felt his heart beating beneath her hand. It pleased and frightened her that he could want her so much. 'Ethan . . .'

He nibbled her neck. 'Hmm, my love?'

'Farrell and I have never shared a bed.'

Ethan raised his head to stare at her. 'Never?' His eyes widened.

'No, never. Our marriage hasn't been consummated. At first I did want it, only so he wouldn't look for an excuse to throw us out, but now I'm glad we didn't.'

He closed his eyes briefly before a slow grin escaped. 'That's the best news I could have hoped for.' He kissed her quick and hard and then laughed. Amazement glowed in his brandy eyes. 'This is magnificent news! Have you any idea how I've tortured myself thinking he has touched you?'

She shook her head, surprised by his response.

Suddenly, his expression grew serious, his eyes narrowed with longing. 'This means you are truly mine, Isabelle. Do you understand?' He kissed her lips, her eyes. His voice dropped, thickened. 'All mine, for ever.'

'Yes.'

'You mean everything to me.'

'I do?' She blinked in happy surprise. 'Truly?'

'Of course!' He pulled back to frown at her. 'You don't believe me?'

She glanced away with a shrug. 'It wouldn't be the first time a man in your position took a mistress.' Inwardly she cringed at that awful word.

He took her chin and turned her back to him. 'No, not you. Never a mistress. I promise you.'

'But that is what I am. Now. It's silly to deny it.'

'You will be my *wife*. You have my word, my bond, my heart.' He tucked a tendril of hair behind her ear. 'You do believe me, don't you?'

Isabelle squirmed closer. 'Yes, but it won't be easy. Nothing ever is. If I've learnt one thing over the last six months then it is that.'

'Agreed. However, I love you and I will never let you go.'

She threw her arms around his neck and pressed herself against him. Her body was on fire for his touch. An urgency, a wanting of completeness possessed her. She kissed him with a passion that surprised her. She needed him in a way she didn't entirely understand. Her body cried out to be fulfilled and her soul ached for warm refuge from the harshness of her life. Ethan offered the answers to her needs. Moreover, she knew she gave him the love he craved and could only find with her. The power was heady. She welcomed his kisses, soft at first, then becoming more demanding as his fervour grew like a consuming fire. She tore off his jacket, unbuttoned his waistcoat and helped him to shrug it off.

'Glory be, Isabelle, I must have you,' he whispered, hot against her mouth.

'We will have each other, yes?'

He chuckled. 'In every way, my darling, in every way.'

She tilted her head back as he kissed her neck, while his hands worked at the buttons of her blouse. His shirt soon followed the way of his jacket and waistcoat. Isabelle ran her hands over his chest. Delighting in his masculine shape, she clenched her fingers in the light sprinkle of chest hairs and bent to kiss him there. Ethan sucked in a breath. He quickly used his jacket as a blanket and laid her down. Reclining beside her, he assisted her in undressing. Soon her corset and chemise lay in a heap beside them. Ethan went to remove her skirt but she stopped him.

'No, darling. Leave it on.'

'But — '

'If someone should come, I can quickly cover myself.'

He nodded and then grinning, he slipped his hands up her thighs under her skirt to gently wriggle down her drawers. His voice became husky. 'Do you know how I've dreamt of this moment?'

Isabelle bit her lip as his fingers found her. Her breathing stopped as for the first time the most intimate part was touched by another.

'You're ready for me, my sweet.'

'I am?' She swallowed. His fingers, soft and gentle, worked to make shivers of delight spread throughout her body. Her hand hovered over his, wanting to pull him away, yet to also keep it there. 'Oh Ethan. I'm not sure . . . '

'I will stop.'

'No!'

He kissed her, flicking his tongue gently against hers. 'Touch me, Isabelle. Feel what you do to me.' He guided her hand to the bulge in his trousers. 'Free me, my love.'

Hesitantly, she unbuttoned his trousers and helped him pull them down to his knees. Her eyes widened at the sight of his arousal.

Ethan lifted her chin so that she looked into his eyes. 'Kiss me, Isabelle.' Taking a deep breath, she ran her fingers through his hair before raining light kisses over his face. He pulled her close, laying her head on his arm. 'I love you.'

'And I you.' Isabelle grinned, her skin tingling under his sensuous touch. 'I want this to last for ever. Just you and me in our wood.' She gazed up at the tree canopy. Dappled sunlight filtered through like hundreds of fingers. To be exposed in the open was such a wicked delight that she giggled.

Ethan raised his head from sucking on her nipple. 'What's so funny?'

'We are so immoral. I never thought I would say that about myself. Yet, I don't feel bad about it. I guess I am doubly damned.'

'Then we are both damned together. Perhaps this devil fellow isn't so bad after all?'

Isabelle spluttered. Her laughter rose and echoed through the wood. Ethan hugged her tight and rolled onto his back so that she lay on top of him. He released her hair from its pins and it cascaded down, covering their faces like a veil. Her laughter died as his eyes darkened with yearning.

'Let me love you, Isabelle, for the rest of my life.'

She kissed him gently, reverently. 'I will, my heart.'

He rolled back over, pinning her beneath him. His kisses deepened, urging her on to a new level of awareness. Arching up to him, she dug her nails into his back. 'Love me, Ethan.'

'Always,' he murmured. Using his knee, he gently opened her legs. Taking his weight on his hands, he paused a fraction before carefully entering her.

Isabelle bit her lip as he filled her and she moved slightly to adjust to him. Closing her eyes, she let out a pent-up breath. It felt like her heart had stopped beating. Every ounce of her was centred on this one moment. Ethan kissed her, whispered something she didn't hear. He withdrew a little and then slowly slid back into her, as he did so he lifted her hips up to meet him and she was shot with a sensation so startling her eyes flew open.

He smiled and kissed her again. 'Take the ride with me, sweetheart.'

10

Whistling, Ethan jogged down the staircase, fit to burst with happiness. The thick walls of the house kept out the hot August sunshine, but the day's brightness penetrated through the windows, beckoning him. As always Isabelle came to mind and his stomach knotted with anticipation. Soon, she would be in his arms, kissing him with a passion that empowered him. He had an insane urge to sing.

Elizabeth stepped out from the drawing room, glanced up and smiled. 'Why darling, I don't think I've ever seen you so happy.'

'It has been a brilliant summer, Mama.'

She laughed. 'Indeed it has, though I have hardly seen you these last few months.'

Ethan grinned and jumped from the third last tread. In one fluid movement, he swept his mother into his arms and waltzed her around the hall.

She squealed like a young girl. 'What are you doing, you silly boy!'

'I'm dancing with a beautiful woman,' Ethan declared, spinning her faster.

'Stop it at once.' Elizabeth giggled. 'What

has come over you?'

'Love!'

Elizabeth halted, her smile slipped a little. 'Love?' She stepped back and patted her hair into place. 'Have you bought a new horse?'

He laughed. 'No, not a horse, Mama. A woman.'

All colour left his mother's face. 'A woman? What can you possibly mean?'

He closed his eyes and shook his head, inwardly groaning. He straightened his jacket. 'It was stupid of me to mention it just yet.'

Elizabeth walked back into the drawing room, waited for him to join her and then closed the door. 'Explain yourself.'

Ethan pushed his hands into his trouser pockets and shrugged. 'It's rather simple really. I have fallen in love with a wonderful woman who loves me in return.'

'You are married.' Her tone turned to ice. 'Or had that escaped your mind?'

He snorted. 'It is forever on my mind, as it stops me from being with Isabelle.'

'Isabelle.' Elizabeth sat on the edge of the sofa, her back straight, her face impassive. 'Do I know her?'

'No.'

'I . . . I suppose it is natural for a man to have a . . . mistress when his own wife — '

'Isabelle will be my wife!'

Elizabeth blinked. 'Wife? What nonsense. How is that possible?'

'I am soon to leave for York where I shall be petitioning for a divorce and if I get no satisfaction there, I'll go on to London.'

His mother shot to her feet. 'Divorce?'

Ethan turned away and walked to the empty fireplace. A delicate and colourful Chinese screen stood upon the hearth. 'I cannot remain married to Clarice any longer. I wish her no harm but do not love her. I never did. I'm sorry.'

'But you married her!'

He spun to face her. 'Yes, for Father, for the estate, for the money, but never for me.' His heart pounded as memories of that time resurfaced. 'I never wanted her for me. It was a duty. My duty as a son and heir. Father was dying, he made me promise to marry her so that we could have her properties and strengthen our land holdings. You know we needed her wealth and she needed a home since her mother wanted rid of her so she could remarry and move away.'

'Clarice has done nothing to give you reason to divorce her.'

'I have grounds, or if not, I'll get her to divorce me. She has grounds now.' He ran his fingers through his hair. 'She is not a true wife to me, never really was. Clarice wanted a comfortable home and to be free from her mother's tyranny. She doesn't want to be a wife, a mother or mistress of this house. You know that as well as I do. We've both known it for years.'

'That doesn't make it right.' Elizabeth sat back down and Ethan noticed how her hands shook.

He didn't want this argument with her. Upsetting his mother was the last thing he sought. 'Try and understand, Mama. I'm tired of living my life without a woman beside me who I love. I've finally discovered what I've been missing.' He sat beside her and took her hands in his. 'I want children. I want to be loved and, sadly, Clarice cannot fill those needs.'

'But divorce? Do you wish to have scandal attached to our good name?'

'It's a sacrifice I am willing to suffer.'

'Will this Isabelle suffer it too?'

A wry smile escaped him. 'She has no choice either, since she must divorce her husband to be with me.'

Elizabeth launched to her feet once more, staring at him as though he had turned mad. 'She is married too?'

He nodded and ran his fingers through his hair. This wasn't going well. 'Mama — '

A knock interrupted them and the footman

stuck his head around the doorjamb.

'We do not wish to be disturbed!' Elizabeth snapped.

'I'm sorry, madam, but your seamstress has been waiting in the parlour for some time. Shall I send her away?'

'No.' Ethan took advantage of the escape. 'My mother will be with her shortly.' He turned and kissed his mother's soft cheek and left the room.

Elizabeth tapped her foot and nibbled her fingernail. She looked at the waiting footman. 'Tell Mrs Goodman that I shall be ten minutes more. Send in a tray of tea and cakes for her.' She swept from the drawing room and up the staircase. A slow anger simmered in her chest. She burst into Clarice's bedroom, startling the woman where she lay on her bed still in her nightwear. 'I must talk with you, Clarice.'

Her daughter-in-law blinked like a mindless ninny, a chocolate seashell half way to her mouth. Clarice had occupied the room from the very first day of marriage, surprising them all by asking to have a room to herself. Ethan had readily agreed. Elizabeth glanced around the bedroom. An assortment of sweets and chocolate boxes littered the bed. Clothes hung haphazardly, magazines stacked in piles by the bed, books lay where they had fallen.

Distaste curled in her stomach and fed her frustration.

'Do you allow the maids to clean in here?'

Clarice stared and popped the whole chocolate into her mouth.

'Good gracious me!' Elizabeth paced the room before stopping at the end of the bed. 'Now listen to me carefully, Clarice. Do you like your life here?'

Clarice paled. She clutched a sweet box to her ample chest. Her double chin wobbled as she nodded.

Elizabeth looked down at the girl-woman and suppressed a shudder. Clarice's dark hair shone in a greasy unwashed way. Over the summer she had kept nearly entirely to her room and Elizabeth felt guilty for enjoying the freedom of not having her in sight for days on end, but that absence only now increased her awareness of Clarice's size. She seemed to have doubled her enormous weight. 'Something has happened and together we must prevent it disrupting our lives further. Ethan wants to divorce you.'

Clarice's eyes widened but she remained mute.

'Now, he will have grounds to do this because you refuse to be a proper wife to him. Do you understand?'

'Yes.'

'Do you wish to be a wife in every sense to him?'

'No.'

Elizabeth sighed. 'Come, come, Clarice. Look around you, look at how well you live. You have every comfort. Do you want to lose that? If you simply cut down your weight and became more involved in Ethan's life, gave him a child or two, then you could continue to live here with your sweets.'

Clarice straightened slowly, spilling boiled sweets onto the bed. 'I . . . I cannot talk to Ethan.'

'You must! Do you want to be living somewhere else with no comforts? As a divorced woman your life will be over, you'll have nothing and no one.' Elizabeth took a deep breath to calm down. 'We must work together to see this doesn't happen. Yes?'

'Very well.'

'Good.' Elizabeth relaxed. 'All I want is his happiness and bringing divorce into this house will not grant him that.'

★ ★ ★

Isabelle squeezed the cloth over the bucket and shook the water from it before scrubbing the floor once more. Her sore knees reminded her that she had declined Ethan's offer to hire a maid to help with the chores. She smiled as his face swam into focus, her swirling movements dwindling until she knelt back on her heels, the cleaning forgotten. Her body responded to memories of his touch, his kisses, his loving that sent her reaching for the stars and beyond. What a summer it had been. Lazy days together, snatched after-noons, and secret meetings in the wood had occupied her every thought for months. The weather had remained fine for weeks, showering them with a golden haze of brilliance as they lay beneath tree canopies, loving one another. They wove a magical aura around each other. Ethan brought out such fire in her that at times she was frightened by its intensity. How had she lived without him in her life until now? In his presence, she laughed, talked, learnt and loved so much. Surrounded by his worship, she felt immor-tal. He was her first thought in the morning and the last one at night. She ached for his touch and listened for his voice. All was good in her world while ever he loved her.

'Belle, we're off now.'

Isabelle jumped at Hughie's voice. He stood in the doorway, knowing that to tread on her clean floor would earn him a clout around the ear. She rose from her position, throwing the cloth back into the bucket. 'Are

Father and Bertie going with you?'

'Yes. Will you be all right alone?'

'Of course.' She picked her way over the floor, trying to find the dry patches. From the table she took a list and a small pouch of money given to her from Ethan. 'Now remember, I need everything on this list. The clothes I ordered are from Mrs Bottomley in Bridge Gate. I've already paid her, so just collect the package.'

'What clothes are they?'

'Two new dresses for me and a flannel shirt each for you, Bertie and Father.' Isabelle double-checked the list. 'Your new boots need to be picked up from Mr Jackson in Market Street. You need to pay him the last instalment of two shillings.'

Hughie looked over her shoulder at the list. 'Did you write wool on your list? I need to knit some socks for winter.'

'Yes I have. And Father wants to knit a vest for Bertie.'

Hughie leant against the doorjamb. 'It's good to have a little bit of money, isn't it?'

Isabelle glared at him. 'Now listen, Mr Harrington is simply loaning it to me until — '

'I know, you told me.' He raised his hands to ward off her verbal attack. 'I didn't mean anything by it.'

'Then don't mention it.'

Hughie frowned. 'Why?'

'Because it's . . . unseemly.' She gave him the list and shooed him out the door. 'Don't forget to buy more twine for the jars. I want to start pickling and preserving this week.' She stood on the back doorstep and waved to Bertie, who sat up in the cart beside their father. 'Keep safe and return before dark.'

She watched as her father steered the old horse around the yard and they trundled down the side of the house and out of sight. Returning to the kitchen, she grimaced at the bucket and shrugged. 'Well, it's clean enough for one day.' She emptied the bucket out onto the herbs growing by the door. Looking up at the sky, she bit her lip. Grey clouds loomed and the cool breeze warned that summer had nearly run its course. From the scullery door, she grabbed her shawl and whipped it around her shoulders. She'd spent the morning inside cleaning and needed the fresh air. There was to be no meeting in the woods today, as Ethan informed her of his trip to Halifax for business.

Geese and chickens, scattered around the yard, took no notice of her as she walked towards the sheds. The breeze brought her the squeals of the new piglets delivered last week. Hughie was as proud of them as if he'd fathered them himself. Whereas, Bertie enjoyed Mayflower's presence better, which was surprising considering his smallness against her large size. When he milked her which he did with ease, he wore a dreamy expression and he always managed to get more from her than anyone else.

Isabelle lifted the gate latch and wandered through into the field. Two poddy calves, bought from the sale of the old heifers, joined Mayflower. Hopefully, the calves would be good milkers in the future.

The future.

She tried to shy away from the thought, as she did whenever her mind strayed beyond the present. What would the future bring her? Her husband? Ethan's divorce? Her divorce? How long would it be before they were both free? Throughout the last few months, she had ignored the possibilities of what was to happen and lived day-by-day. She could see no possible way as to how they would be together, but it didn't stop her from dreaming about it, hoping for it. Who knew when Farrell would re-appear? Even then, could she divorce him? She had no notion about ending a marriage.

Isabelle sighed deeply and found that she had walked to the edge of the field without realizing. She climbed over the stile. On the other side, the wood looked cold and unwelcoming today without the sun and Ethan to warm her. Depressing thoughts of living the rest of her life as she did now haunted her. She was an abandoned wife and a mistress. Never did she think her fate would be this. Despite that Ethan wouldn't be there to greet her, she slipped into the wood. It was so familiar to her now that it seemed an extension of her own land.

'What a lovely day for a walk.'

Isabelle nearly jumped out of her skin at the bodiless voice. She spun wildly, searching the dappled shade for whoever spoke. 'Who's there?'

'Your past.'

Twirling, seeking, Isabelle's heart thudded. Her hand touched a tree trunk, its rough surface a solid base to ground her. She took a steadying breath and leant back against the tree. Angry at being made to look a fool, she squashed her fear and found her courage. 'Aren't you brave enough to show your face then?'

From behind a large tree, some twenty feet away, Neville Peacock slid out.

She gasped. A shiver of dread ran down her spine.

'Isabelle Gibson.' A sly grin further distorted Neville's ugliness.

'Why are you here?'

He smirked and walked slowly in an arc through the trees, one second visible, the next hidden as though playing a game of hide-and-seek. 'Have you missed me?'

Her terror fed the fury blazing in her chest. 'Missed your games? Missed your vile advances?' She laughed, but quickly stopped when his face twisted in rage.

'You enjoy your squire's advances though, don't you? I hear your laughter. I watch you play with him. Even when you are both talking seriously, I still see what you feel for him.'

Isabelle closed her eyes for a moment and died a quiet death.

Neville leant against a tree and crossed his feet, portraying a man at ease. He plucked a leaf and carefully tore it into strips. 'What a life you lead, dear Belle. A wife to no one and a mistress to a man you can't have. You used to be so virginal, so pure. I remember how your lip used to curl in revulsion whenever you looked my way. It still does. Yet now, you are so free with your favours, you don't even hide the deed.'

Her breathing stopped. 'What do you want?'

'A little of what he has sampled.'

'Never!'

'You have no say in it.' The last shred of

leaf dropped to the forest floor. Neville crossed his arms and pierced her with his evil stare. 'So, your long lost father has returned then? Bringing with him a bastard?'

Her eyes widened. 'How do you know about them?'

'I know everything about you, Belle. I know how many pies you sold at your last market. They are good too, actually. I know you're hated by some of the stall women. I know you've been abandoned by your husband, stupid swine that he is. You would have been better off marrying me.' He paused, waiting for her response, but when none was forthcoming, he continued listing off his fingers what he knew. 'Your father and his bastard have returned. Your washing day is Monday. You beat the rugs on Tuesdays. On Wednesdays you work in the garden, and the changes you've made are very good by the way.' He grinned. 'You spend every Sunday after church, in the wood with Harrington and the odd times you can slip out and meet him.'

'Stop!' She covered her ears with her hands. Her stomach churned. He knew so much, too much. A fine sweat broke out on her forehead, despite the coolness of the wood. 'How long have you been watching me?'

He twitched one shoulder. 'Long enough.'

Isabelle shuddered, remembering the incident in the market when she thought she was being watched. 'What do you plan to do now?'

'I haven't decided just yet.' From his pocket he pulled out a small sharp knife and scored into the bark. 'It eats away inside of me, seeing you and him together. Watching his hands touch you, having him fill you. Do you carry his child yet?'

She whimpered deep in her throat. 'No. We . . . we try to be careful. I — ' *Lord, what am I saying?*

'I wouldn't be. I'd like to see you swell with my child.'

She took a step back, breathing fast.

He paused in his gouging. 'Look.' He indicated his artwork on the trunk.

She leant as far as she could to see without actually moving closer to him. Her eyes widened. IG + NP was crudely etched.

'See, Belle? While ever this tree stands, we are recorded as being here, alive, together.'

'It proves nothing.'

A flush crept up his neck. 'Go home.'

'P-pardon?'

He tucked his knife away into his trouser pocket and dusted his hands together. 'I said, go home.'

'You're allowing me to go?' A high note of hysteria came into her voice.

His smile was slow in coming, but full of wickedness. 'For now, yes. I have enjoyed our time together. I am in no hurry at the moment, to take our . . . friendship to the next stage.'

Isabelle's feet seemed rooted into the soil, unable to move.

'Unless you wish to invite me for some tea and a slice of your delicious pie?'

She backed away from him, watching him. Her foot caught on a tree root and she stumbled in her haste to put distance between them.

'Good bye, Belle, until we meet again.'

Stifling a cry, she turned and ran. Lifting her skirts high, she scrambled up the wooded slope. Her spine tingled, believing he pursued her, his hands outreaching, his face turning into the slobbering vicious face of a rabid wolf. Breaking out of the wood, she crossed the lane and nearly fell over the stile. Once on the open fields she increased her speed. Blood pounded in her ears making her deaf to his footsteps. Fear urged her on, but the instinct to look behind her was too strong. Tearfully, she glanced over her shoulder. Nothing. The wood receded. All that moved was the grass she disturbed with her racing.

Slowing, gasping for air, she staggered towards the gate leading into the house field. Her fingers were clumsy as she unlatched the gate and swung it open. When she turned to fasten it, she jumped. In the distance he stood atop of the stile, watching. Isabelle sucked much needed air into her lungs. Finding the strength and courage she didn't know she owned, she gradually turned away and made herself walk, not run, towards the yard and the farm buildings.

Humiliation, combined with terror, opened the door to her rage. White-hot fury fed on her fear. Again he had scared her witless. Memories of the weeks leading up to her wedding came back to her vividly. If he had left her alone, she wouldn't have seen the need to rush into marriage with Farrell. She could have taken her time to advertise and maybe selected from a few other men . . .

Once inside the yard, Isabelle checked that the others hadn't returned. The quietness told her she was still alone. She hurried into the house and locked the kitchen door before shooting the bolt home on the scullery door. Exhausted, she laid her head against the door's cool timber. In silence she allowed the tears to fall.

11

Isabelle stirred the bubbling blackberry jam. The delicious aroma of sweetened fruit filled the kitchen. In the oven, three pear and apple pies cooked, while on the sideboard, five more pies cooled. Already packed in the larder were four dozen jam tarts and two currant loaves. Tomorrow, for the first time in months, she was to sit at her stall again. Ethan's handouts had kept her from trading at the market, but he was in York now on business and her money was running short.

At the table, her father sat quietly, peeling and seeding lemons for her to use in the lemon butter she was making next. The situation with her father hadn't altered. The ice wall she had erected between them stood firm, and since he showed little of the illness that plagued him at the moment, she had no inclination to soften her stance towards him. He treated her with polite respect and she him with frosty tolerance. The boys accepted this as an unspoken truce between them.

Outside, the late September sunshine assisted in keeping Autumn at bay. The nights had grown a little cooler, but the days remained pleasant for the last of the harvesting. Looking through the window, Isabelle smiled. Hughie and Bertie carried a full sack each. Noisily, they tumbled into the kitchen, bringing with them the scent of grass and squashed fruit.

'That's the last of the plums, Belle.' Hughie panted, placing the sack against the table leg. 'Flossy and her piglets are enjoying the windfalls. Though the new nanny goat isn't too happy at sharing the orchard with them.'

'Did you restack the stones on the west field wall?' Isabelle took the jam off the heat and started ladling it into jars. 'I don't want the nanny getting out again. She'll be close to delivering her kid soon.'

Hughie poured out two glasses of watered-down cider and handed one to Bertie. 'We fixed it.'

'And did you water those two new apple trees I planted?'

'Yes, Bertie did that while I fixed the wall.'

Isabelle opened the first sack and took out a purple plum. She smelt its ripeness and grinned at Bertie. 'How many did you eat, little brother?'

He tucked his chin on his chest and held up two fingers.

'Only two?' Isabelle laughed.

Slowly, he unfolded two more fingers.

'Yes, I thought so. Well, if your stomach gripes you, don't come crying to me.' She winked and took out more plums. In a large bowl filled with water, she washed them.

Aaron reached over for them. 'Here give them to me, Belle. I'll get them ready for the pot.'

She nodded her thanks and became annoyed when a blush warmed her cheeks. Why did he always make her feel guilty about the cool way she dealt with him? She had nothing to be guilty about. It was he who should be burdened with his conscience.

Isabelle checked the jars of cooling jam and then grabbed her oven towel, took the pies from oven and set them on the table. 'I'll go out and collect the last of the elderberry, now these pies are done. We might be able to make a bottle or two of wine. I asked Mrs Jackson, the cobbler's wife, for the recipe. If I make it now, we'll have it to drink in February.' She picked up her basket and snips, but paused near the dresser to sniff at the vase of roses. Flowers from the front garden filled the house. In each room, she left a bouquet that stood in anything that held water — jugs, tins, jars, and chipped glasses. At the doorway, she turned back to Hughie. 'You and Bertie can go pick the peas for dinner. Also, I need some mint for the potatoes and sticks of rhubarb. I'll stew the rhubarb and some apples for afters.'

Leaving the kitchen, she walked down the passageway to the sitting-room. This room she had transformed over the summer. In here, she had polished the furniture with beeswax until it shone, the rugs had been beaten, the curtains washed, the floor scrubbed. Ethan's presents added to the comfort. A landscape to go on the wall. A tapestry frame and silks. The fireplace had a shiny new grate and a fancy worked screen in a mahogany stand. Again flowers decorated every surface. Books, given by Ethan, sat in rows on shelves fitted to the far wall. On the new green sofa lay her rust-coloured scarf, another present from Ethan. He'd given it to her on the day he returned from London.

She sighed now, thinking of that day. His divorce hearing had been given the date of 21 April of next year. Ethan's emotions swung between satisfaction at receiving a date and the frustration of having to wait. Her soothing comments mollified him some, and he left her with a promise to meet after church on Sunday. Thankfully, her monthly curse had prevented him from becoming too amorous in the wood and she, forever keeping an eye out for the presence of Neville Peacock, cut their meeting short. Briefly, she thought to tell Ethan about her surprise visit from Neville, but knew only trouble would result from sharing her secret. Ethan would hunt Neville down and there would be bloodshed.

Tossing her head and dismissing her disturbing thoughts, Isabelle left the sitting room and unbolted the front door. Once out in the sunshine, her spirits lifted. The garden greeted her like an old friend. The little white briar rose still flowered by the gate, as did the climbing rose along the house wall. Beds of chrysanthemums grew well, ready for their burst of show in November. A magnificent old magnolia grew in the far corner and Isabelle loved to bury her nose in its cream flowers. Now cleared of choking weeds, the fuchsias' beautiful bells hung delicately and always raised a smile in her. Michaelmas daisies, so large and abundant with glorious colour, spilled out of their beds and crowded the path. After the drabness of the work-house, she revelled in the colourful glory.

Turning away from the garden, Isabelle headed down the rarely-visited right side of the house. All that grew here were bushes of gooseberry and the large elderberry tree. She had noticed the fruit on it from the upstairs bedroom window. The tree's top branches reached below the sill. A month ago, she had leaned out and touched the flowers and then detected the darkening berries. Placing her basket on the ground in the shade cast by the house, she picked up her snips and pulled the first branch to her. She hummed a little as she worked.

Since the episode in the wood with Neville she had not ventured further than the orchard behind the sheds, except for Sundays when she went to church in Heptonstall and met Ethan in the wood later in the afternoon.

In the last three weeks since Neville's visit, she had kept a constant vigil on the wood whenever she was outside, wondering if he watched from within its darkness. She looked for signs of his presence nearer the farm, but nothing revealed his existence. As the days went by and she saw nothing of him, she began to relax. He lived in Halifax. It would be impossible for him to be watching the farm every moment of every day. It seemed ridiculous that he should continue to stalk her. Never would she wander alone in the woods again. Surely he would know this now? What hope did he have of finding her alone when she lived with three others?

Anger filled her at Neville's deviousness. Her plans for putting him in his place grew large and rewarding. Only, in the quiet moments as she worked or dozed, his long sallow face would leer at her and her heart would beat as fast as it did when she ran from him.

The sound of carriage wheels and hooves on the dusty road before the house, alerted her to the present. Sometimes, Ethan called in on his way home from Halifax and her stomach twisted in expectation of seeing him. As the trundling sound slowed, Isabelle dropped her snips and walked back to the corner of the house. It was him! The Harrington coat of arms displayed in gold stood out well against the black paint of the carriage. Gathering her skirts with one hand, she tidied her hair with the other and ran across the garden.

She smiled at the driver as he climbed down and opened the carriage door. He was a pleasant fellow whom she always gave a drink to whenever he brought Ethan to the farm. 'Good day, Brown. It is a beautiful day, is it not?'

Brown's eyes widened and he hurriedly ducked his head, touching his fingers to his hat's brim in acknowledgment. Isabelle faltered, her smile slipped at his refusal to greet her. Swiftly, her attention was diverted to the tall woman descending the carriage step. The magnificence of her pale copper dress, her strands of pearls and the serene oval face Isabelle glimpsed from beneath a short veil blurred her senses. Her heart fluttered wildly in her chest like a caged bird. The blood drained from her face.

Standing straight and dignified, holding on to the ivory handle of a cream parasol, the woman stared about before resting her gaze on Isabelle. 'I am Elizabeth Harrington.'

'How ... How do you do, Mrs Harrington?' Isabelle locked her knees to keep from crumbling to the ground. The enormity of the situation hit her like a lightning bolt. *Ethan's mother!*

'You know who I am?'

'Yes, I do.'

'I would wish to speak with you in private, if I may?'

Isabelle sucked in a quick breath and stepped back. 'Of course. Shall we go inside?'

Elizabeth Harrington's gaze darted to the house and she hesitated a fraction before nodding.

Leading the way along the path, Isabelle sent a silent prayer of thanks that the sitting room looked at its best. Inside, she glanced up the hallway. Aaron stood in the kitchen watching her. Sensing her distress, he gently closed the passage door. She sent up another prayer and showed Ethan's mother into the sitting room. 'Please be seated.'

Elizabeth took note of the room and a little

colour came into her cheeks. She perched herself on the edge of the sofa. 'A . . . pleasant room.'

'Thank you.' Isabelle bit her lip and closed the door. In horror she noticed the purple fruit stains on her fingers and abruptly stuffed her hands into the folds of her grey skirt. 'Would you care for some tea, Mrs Harrington?'

'That is kind of you, but no.' Elizabeth gripped the parasol handle more tightly. 'This is not a social call, Mrs Farrell.'

For some reason this saddened Isabelle. She bent her head and sighed. What possessed her to think it would be anything different? She and Ethan flouted every social rule. Of course his mother and every other decent citizen of the area would be uncharitable towards them once they knew. Silence stretched and Isabelle didn't know how to break it.

Elizabeth lifted her chin. 'I am aware of the relationship you share with my son, Mrs Farrell. My visit here today has been planned for some time. Yet, I had hoped my son would come to his senses and disregard you to save me from this embarrassment.'

Isabelle bowed her head and searched for something to say.

Elizabeth stood and walked to the window.

'My son is weak where you are concerned. I confess I have never seen him behave this way before, and therefore I concluded that I must speak with you instead.'

Raising her eyes, Isabelle stared at the older woman. Instinctively, she knew what she wanted and pain lanced her heart. 'You want me to give him up.'

'Naturally! You are both married!'

Isabelle welcomed the other woman's heated emotion as it stirred within her a dormant frustration that the man she loved she couldn't have. Irritation at this woman's high-handed manner made her tone sharp. 'You do not have to remind me, Mrs Harrington, that I am married. It is a fact I live with every moment of every day.'

'But you choose to ignore it!'

'I didn't wake up one morning and decide to fall in love with another man!' Isabelle stared at her, defiant. 'Do you think that I wanted to love your son? That it is easy living my life loving Ethan as I do and knowing there is no hope for us?'

Elizabeth stiffened at the mention of his name. 'You should have been stronger and denied your feelings.'

She shrugged, the anger leaving her at the truth of the statement. 'Perhaps.' She stared blindly at the empty fire grate. 'You may not believe me when I say I tried, but I did, truly.' Her voice dropped to a whisper. 'Only the force of him was too difficult to resist. I couldn't ignore the care he had for me. His gentleness, his concern awakened a need in me I didn't know existed. He wrapped his love around me like a warm blanket. Then I realized that this was all new to him too. Ethan needs my affection just as much as I need his.' She turned to stare at Elizabeth. 'I suppose I am weak too for I cannot defend myself against his love. It's too powerful.'

Elizabeth's throat worked. 'It is wrong. This concerns more than just you and my son. He wants to divorce his wife! Don't you see what is happening here? All that we know, all that makes us who we are is at stake. He threatens everything this family stands for. All because of you.' Furious tears glistened in her brown eyes. 'I cannot let him do this.'

★ ★ ★

The cries of the stallholders faded into nothing. Isabelle sat on her stool in a small world of her own. She served her customers in a daze, her mind constantly replaying the meeting with Ethan's mother. She knew Ethan's family would not be pleased with his decision to divorce Clarice, but she hadn't expected the guilt she would feel over her part in it.

Without warning something hit Isabelle on the side of her head. Stunned, she touched the spot as darts of pain made stars dazzle before her eyes. Looking up, she just managed to duck another object, but not before she made out Marge Wilmot, laughing in the crowd.

Marge's fist held another piece of fruit and she flung it with increased effort. 'We don't want the likes of you here, Mrs Farrell! Trollop. Wait til yer husband's home, then we'll see what happens to yer then. He'll not be happy knowing that his wife has strayed.'

'Whore!' another voice shouted.

'Harrington's floozy!'

The gathering crowd paused in their shopping to stare at the spectacle. Murmurs of disapproval grew. Women closed ranks to nod and sniff condemnation at her. Isabelle felt all the blood drain from her face. *They know!* Her thoughts scattered as an apple skimmed her shoulder. She stood in frozen shock. A split mouldy orange hit her skirts, spraying juice over the material.

From out of the crowd, a lanky man pushed his way clear. Neville Peacock. He grinned like the devil and slowly approached her stall. Isabelle's eyes widened in apprehension. Cold sweat trickled down her back. Her mouth went dry as he leisurely picked up one of her lemon curd tarts and casually dropped it on the ground at his feet. His eyes never left hers.

Neville turned to the gathering. 'We must not sully ourselves by sampling the food this harlot sells. She is not fit to be among decent people. She brings shame to the respectable women of this town by flaunting herself before you. Brazen!'

She croaked a strangled cry as his hand reached for a pie and within seconds it joined the tart on dirty cobbles. Marge Wilmot's laugh rang out clear and loud over the stunned stillness.

Murmurs grew again, but Isabelle was trapped in a world of silent agony. She couldn't drag her gaze from Neville's as with a small shrug, he swept his arm wide across the table and sent the entire stock to the ground. A rock was thrown from the crowd at either Neville or her, she didn't know, but it hit her on the cheek and she stumbled back, reeling in pain.

'Here now, that's enough!' The old man in the stall next to her threw his arms up to shoo them off. 'Lass, for yer own sake, get down!'

Hardly able to think for herself, Isabelle

crouched low, using the table as a barrier. As if from a distance, she heard the old man yell and Marge's insults were now aimed at him for spoiling her fun. A final overripe fruit splattered at her feet and at last the hubbub quietened. The pungent smell of decaying fruit made her gag.

'It's safe now, lass. They're gone.' The old man peered over the table. 'Are yer hurt?'

She shook her head. She felt nothing. Somewhere in the far recess of her mind, a throbbing ache assaulted her, but she ignored it. Nothing had the power to hurt her like the pulsating hatred she had just faced.

He came around behind the stall and gently helped her up. 'Yer'd best be getting home, lass. There's nowt yer can do here now.'

Nodding, she glanced at the dwindling crowd. Some looked on with pity, others with scorn and a few grinned, having enjoyed the show. Humiliation finally clawed its way through her shock. Smothering a whimper, she jerked into motion. After ripping the sheet from the trestle, she stuffed it and the smaller baskets into her largest basket. Her arms full, she turned to escape and then saw the sympathy in the old man's watery eyes. She swallowed, not wanting to appear ungrateful for his help but desperate to flee this scene of her shame. She inclined her head. 'Thank you.'

'Aye, lass.' He gave her a half-smile and she brushed past him and away to the stables. This morning she had refused Hughie and her father's offer to accompany her to the market, wanting to be alone with her thoughts. How foolish had she been to forget the old hag who took pleasure in tormenting her at every turn, and to forget Neville.

At the stables she stumbled to the cart and dumped the baskets in the back. Not giving the stable lad a chance to help her, she unhooked the nosebag from the horse, led it out into the lane and climbed up onto the seat. Each passerby that glanced her way suddenly drew her focus. Eyes stared, mouths laughed, fingers pointed, babies cried. Whispers grew into shouts. She slapped the reins onto the horse's rump, urging it to go faster, despite the impeding traffic. Her skin tingled, aware she was being talked about, discussed.

She sagged with relief as they climbed up Heptonstall road away from the hub of Hebden Bridge, away from the market, away from Marge Wilmot's leering crudeness and away from Neville Peacock. But then, she would never be free from him. He made it his business to stalk her like men stalked game. He hunted her as though she was a deer and he needed meat for his table.

At the top of the hill, a stiff, cold wind slapped her face. The threatening rain, which had held off until now, fell. It was too much. One too many burdens she had to bear. Tears ran hot down her chilled cheeks. She tugged her coat closer and her hand smeared the mess on her skirts. The sickening stench of old fruit filled her nose. She gagged. Abruptly, she slammed her foot on the brake and jerked on the reins, halting the horse. Without thought, she scrambled off the seat and into the ditch by the roadside. She fell to her knees, heaving and sobbing at the same time. Rain lashed, stinging her face, trampling on her dignity.

'Belle!'

In her misery she looked up, not caring if the devil himself stood by her side. In fact it was. Neville Peacock.

'Belle, are you hurt?'

She stared at him and had the insane urge to laugh. His expression was one of caring, his hands reached out in helpless offer.

'Here, let me help you.' He stepped closer and placed his hand at her elbow.

That she let him touch her, help her, came as no surprise. After today, nothing could harm her. She was dead to all feeling and sense of worth. Her filthy wet skirts hindered her walk, but her fingers were too cold to hitch them up. Beyond the cart, his horse stood, its head hung low in misery at being out in this awful weather.

'I'll tie my horse to the cart and drive you home.'

She paused and stared at him. 'Have you lost all reason? Do you honestly think I can abide you near me?'

He stepped back, but a flush crept up his pasty face. 'I didn't mean to do any of it. I don't know what came over me. I didn't start the fruit throwing. Please believe me.'

She didn't care whether he spoke the truth or not. 'You didn't throw the fruit, but you planted the seed, yes? And then you destroyed my stock, added to my humiliation, killed any respect I held.'

His Adam's apple bobbed as he swallowed. 'I got carried away. Marge and I were drinking, she made — '

'Don't, Neville! Don't make all this out to be her fault. You enjoyed every moment of it. Well, let there be an end to it, yes? No more following me, harassing me. It's over.'

He wiped away the rain running down his face. Anger blazed in his eyes and he grabbed her shoulders, squeezing them like a vice. 'It will never be over. Not until you are mine!'

Isabelle sighed, tired and dispirited and not

at all frightened. 'I'll never be yours, Neville. Even if you threw me down in the mud right here and now and had me, it still wouldn't make me yours.'

Astonished, his grip slackened and she hoisted herself up onto the cart's seat.

Neville grabbed her trailing skirts. 'You *will* be mine, Isabelle Gibson! I'll not let Farrell or Harrington stand in my way! Do you hear?'

Without looking at him, she slapped the reins and trundled away as the rain pounded her and his threats grew wilder.

★ ★ ★

Whispers and mutterings dragged at her senses. Try as she might she couldn't open her eyes, but then, she didn't really want to. She was so warm, so tired . . . A loud bang jerked her into awareness.

'Bertie, you little oaf!' Hughie's outraged whisper boomed in her head like a drum.

'I didn't mean to.' Bertie's unhappy mumble forced her to open her eyes.

'Belle?' Hughie's anxious face hovered over hers. A lock of his hair fell over his forehead. 'Can you hear me? Are you better?'

Isabelle frowned. Better? What had happened? What were they doing beside her bed?

She went to speak but her mouth was dry, her throat parched. She mumbled something unintelligible.

'Bertie, get Belle some water, quickly now.' Hughie sat on the edge of the bed and placed his arm under her shoulders. 'Here, sis, drink some water.'

She sipped and allowed the cool water to slide down her throat. Whereas before she felt warm now shivers of cold shook her. Hughie's touch chilled her. Her head seemed too heavy for her neck to support and every part of her body ached.

'There now, you rest.' Hughie stood and tucked the blankets around securely. He added another pillow for her head and the coldness of it made her shake anew. He smiled. 'Want to sleep some more?'

Too exhausted to agree or deny, she closed her eyes and gave in to the welcoming blackness.

★   ★   ★

Isabelle opened her eyes to see the sun stream into the bedroom. *Morning.* This room only got the morning sun. Lying still, she watched the dust motes floating in the rays. The walls were so bare, so drab in colour. Mould in one corner looked like fine lace. Yellow. That would brighten the room. She could paint the walls yellow and give the ceiling a fresh coat of whitewash. Ethan once told her . . . Ethan! She jerked upright only to jump when her father leant over and pushed her back down.

'There's nothing to worry about, Belle. Rest easy.'

She turned to look at him. He appeared as ill as she felt. Eyes sunken, skin grey, hair even greyer. He shifted under her unblinking stare.

'You have some colour back in your cheeks, lass. We were worried about you.' He reached over and poured water from an earthenware jug into a glass. 'The boys have been working their fingers to the bone.' He brought the glass to her lips and she sipped it. 'They've done all the jobs around the farm. Kept the house clean.'

'How long have I been ill? I don't remember . . . '

'You've been abed for two days — '

'Two days?' She scowled. The incident at the market flashed before her eyes and a wash of mortification flowed over her. She could never show her face there again. 'I . . . I'll be back on my feet today.'

'You gave us such a fright, arriving slumped on the seat in the pouring rain with blood trickling down your face. I don't know how you made it home, but then you always were a brave one.' He leant back in the chair. 'The ground near shook with thunder and lightening. The storm didn't abate until near midnight.'

'I don't remember a storm, only rain.'

'Well, no. You were numb with cold and wet through. Hughie and I carried you in and put you to bed.'

She glanced at her nightgown and blushed.

He raised his eyebrows at her. 'I couldn't leave you in your wet clothes now could I?'

'I guess not.'

'Still, you're on the road to recovery now, aren't you?' Not waiting for an answer, he slapped his thigh and then stood. 'I'll have Hughie bring you up a cup of tea. The boys will be glad to have you awake.'

Isabelle nodded. 'Thank you.' She turned her face away. Through the window, the pale blue sky showed promise of a fine day.

By the door, Aaron hesitated. 'He came on Sunday afternoon.'

Her heart started up a rapid tattoo against her chest. Ethan. She'd missed their meeting in the wood on Sunday. Oh, how she ached for him. Longed for him to hold her and tell her everything would be all right.

Aaron cleared his throat. 'No doubt he wondered where you'd got to. I told him you

227

were ill. He wanted to come up and see you, but I suggested that wouldn't be wise. Hughie would think it odd that our landlord visited your bedroom.'

She closed her eyes, trying desperately to block out her father's disapproving voice. He had no right to judge her like the people in the market, had no right to make her feel guilty. Yet, she cringed inside knowing that once, long ago, she had sought his good opinion, had been his favourite child.

12

Ethan checked Copper's girth strap. It was a ritual he performed every time before he mounted. His mind wasn't focused on the strap, but rather limited to worrying over Isabelle. He would see her today, no matter what her blasted father said. He'd not be put off a further time. Every day for a week he had called, only to be told each time she was still abed and mostly sleeping. What's more, Isabelle's brothers happened to be hovering near the house on each of his calls and so he'd behaved as was expected, when he wanted nothing more than to push the older man aside and storm upstairs to see her for himself. What did propriety matter to him when his beautiful girl lay ill? In anxious frustration, he mounted and turned to the groom loading the last basket onto the cart.

'Is every thing ready to go, Dyers?'

Dyers gave one last look at the cart. 'All set, sir.'

At that moment, the butler opened the front doors and his mother walked out onto the top step. 'Ethan?'

He swore softly under his breath. 'Yes, Mama?'

'What is all this?' Her hand wavered towards the full cart.

'Gifts for a sick tenant. Now, if you'll excuse me I must be on my way.'

Her eyes narrowed, but then she lifted her head to peer down the drive. 'Someone comes.'

Ethan swore again, louder, on hearing the crunching sound of carriage wheels on the drive. *Please be a friend of mother's!*

The carriage slowed and Dyers hurried to open the door. Hamish MacGregor descended the step and grinned. 'Good day!'

'Hamish!' Elizabeth came swiftly down the last two steps and hugged him as though she hadn't seen him for years instead of only a few months. 'This is a lovely surprise.'

Ethan sagged in the saddle, knowing his visit to Isabelle would have to wait a few more minutes. He forced a smile as Hamish and his mother drew closer. 'Good to see you, my friend.'

'And you.' Hamish shook Ethan's hand and then glanced at the cart. 'What's all this?'

'For a sick tenant.' Ethan straightened defensively.

'Really?' A wry smile lifted Hamish's lips.

Ethan gathered in the reins. 'I'll not be long

and when I get back you can tell me all about London.'

A gasp came from Elizabeth. 'Come now, Ethan. Hamish is far more important than a tenant. Send Dyers to deliver it and your good wishes.'

'I think not, Mama.' His fingers tightened on the reins.

Elizabeth flushed and she turned to Hamish. '*See*, I told you it was a bad business. He's going to *her!*'

'Mama!'

Hamish looked up at Ethan. 'So that nonsense is still taking place?'

Ethan tried to keep his anger in check but his head throbbed with tension. 'It has nothing whatsoever to do with either of you!'

Elizabeth stepped forward, grabbing his trousers. 'You've been made a fool of and it has to stop.' She twisted back to Hamish. 'Tell him, Hamish, tell him that this will all end in trouble!'

Copper pranced sideways at the raised voices. Ethan steadied him, without taking his eyes off his mother. 'Did you write to Hamish and ask him to come here? Did you ask him to talk sense into me?'

She stepped back, yet still defiant. 'What if I did? Somebody has to make you see logic. Lord knows I've tried.'

'You had no right!' Ethan glared at his mother as Copper trotted sideways, snorting displeasure.

Hamish quickly stepped in between them. 'Stop this, please.' He glanced back at the groom and the cart's driver before gripping Copper's bridle. 'Ethan, your mother has every right to be worried.'

'Be quiet, Hamish,' he spat. 'You know nothing of it!'

'But *I* do.' Elizabeth folded her arms across her chest. 'I won't have my good name dragged through the mud because you can't act like any decent man and hide your mistress.' Her eyes narrowed. 'I've heard about the incident in the market last Saturday. It would be no surprise if there wasn't a soul in all of Heptonstall and Hebden Bridge who hasn't!'

Ethan paled. 'What incident? What are you talking about?'

'Your mistress was pelted with rotten fruit and chased out of the market. They shouted, 'Harrington's whore'.' Suddenly Elizabeth's fury died and her chin wobbled. Tears glistened. 'I'm so ashamed of you.' She fled into the house.

Ethan sat motionless, feeling like he'd just been punched in the stomach. His darling Isabelle pelted? It couldn't be real. Her father

232

would have mentioned it, surely, unless perhaps he'd been deliberately hiding it from him.

Hamish sighed. 'Ethan. Go in and comfort your mother.'

'I . . . I cannot. I must see Isabelle.' He wiped his hand over his eyes. 'Christ, I cannot believe it.'

'Then let me go.'

'You?'

'Yes. I'll ride over, the cart can follow, and I'll tell her you'll see her tomorrow. It's for the best.'

'Is it?' Ethan scoffed. 'I'm not a boy to ask for Mama's permission.'

'No, you're not, but you are all she has here.' Hamish looked him straight in the eyes. 'She doesn't understand the feelings you have for this woman. She's frightened of losing you.'

He glowered at his friend, knowing he was losing the argument. 'She must have said much in her letter.'

'Yes, she did. You've become distant to her and she's afraid. You need to repair your relationship with her. For the moment that is most important.'

As though an old man, Ethan slowly slid from the saddle. He looked at the house and then at Hamish. 'Tell Isabelle I love her and will see her soon. Tomorrow.'

Hamish nodded and swiftly mounted Copper. He indicated to the driver of the cart and then spurred Copper into a trot.

★ ★ ★

Isabelle sat in a chair in the front garden and blew her nose. The tiredness had left, but not the cough or running nose. Hughie had tucked a rug around her knees and Bertie had brought her knitting, but it lay untouched on her lap. The boys, satisfied she'd come to no harm, had left to do their chores while their father cooked the midday meal.

She gazed at the garden, her garden, now slowing down in readiness for winter. The sun, still warm, allowed the roses to continue to bloom, albeit sparingly. One of her few pleasures was tending to the garden. It saddened her that shortly the frosts would come, followed by the winter snow and her garden would be no more until next spring. Sighing, she nestled more comfortably in the chair. With accustomed ease, her thoughts turned to Ethan. Would he visit her today? She understood he'd called every day, but her father refused to let the boys see their landlord visit her bedroom. Aaron's last stand at respectability annoyed her. Despite his dubious past, he was shocked by her behaviour. The hypocrite. Well, she'd show him. She was improving every hour. Hence her insistence that she sit outside in the fresh air. She tilted her face to the sun, enjoying its warmth on her skin. Soon, she would be completely recovered, and nothing would stop her, come Sunday, to walk to the woods and her father knew it. Sunday and Ethan. She smiled at the thought. Then she frowned. Sunday would be the first day of October. Isabelle sighed. She had married in October last year. 'A wife of one year,' she whispered. 'And what a year it's been.'

A sound on the lane diverted her attention. She saw a lone rider and behind it a cart. Her stomach flipped. Straining to see over the garden wall, she ached for Ethan to come. However, even at this distance she knew it wasn't him. He didn't sit in the saddle in that way. Yet, she was sure the horse was Copper. In amazement she watched them turn in through the gateway. Visitors? She immediately put her hand to her hair and adjusted the white lace collar of her navy wool dress.

The rider dismounted and she noticed his dark brown trousers hugged his thighs before tapering into long leather boots. He wore his dun-coloured jacket loosely over a cream shirt. His wide-brimmed hat looked odd, but vaguely familiar. He looked like no Yorkshire man. He muttered something to the cart driver and then walked along the path to her.

Isabelle racked her brains to think if she knew the tall man. Why did he ride Copper? Did grooms wear such outlandish hats? He walked with a comfortable stride, confident in who he was. He was no groom, she was certain. Then it came to her. Ethan's friend, MacGregor or something.

A few feet from her, he took off his hat and bowed, displaying a thick crop of dark red hair with gold highlights. 'Good day, Mrs Farrell.'

She blinked. His Scottish accent threw her into disarray. 'Good . . . Good day, Mr?'

'Hamish MacGregor. You may not remember me.' He didn't smile and his gaze swept over her, assessing her every feature.

Isabelle stiffened. 'Is there something I can help you with, Mr MacGregor?'

'My good friend, Ethan Harrington, cares to know if you are well?' He waved his arm back towards the cart. 'I come bearing his gifts . . . to ease your recovery.'

She stared at him as though he'd grown a tail. 'Ethan sent you?' A pain lanced her heart. Ethan wasn't coming.

'Indeed. He sends his apologies for not

calling in person but pressing business detains him.'

'Oh.' Dumbfounded, she didn't know what else to say. She felt cheated and somehow robbed of dignity. This man's condescending stare and upright stance conveyed exactly what he thought of her and it filled her with a burning anger, an anger that had built, albeit unknowingly, since the market confrontation.

'Shall I have the cart unloaded at the back of the house?' MacGregor's tone was akin to disdainful mocking.

Her face grew hot with embarrassment. He knew! *Was there not a soul who didn't by now?* His whole manner revealed his awareness of what she meant to Ethan and he hated her for it.

She jumped to her feet, letting the knitting and blanket fall to the grass. 'No, thank you. Please inform Mr Harrington that I appreciate his tokens of assistance, but I am not in need.'

MacGregor's piercing blue eyes widened. 'You are refusing it? All of it?'

'Does that surprise you, Mr MacGregor?' She sneered. 'You think I am without morals or standards?'

'I . . . I do not know you, Mrs Farrell, to make such judgement.'

'Oh, come now!' She laughed harshly. 'You

237

had decided on my character before you arrived.'

He had the grace to flush nearly as scarlet as his hair. 'That is true. I do know about your relationship with Ethan.'

'At least you are honest.' She coughed and slumped back into the chair, her strength gone. The intense beautiful love she and Ethan shared was now soiled by everyone's knowledge of it. How had it happened? How had the purity of their feelings been destroyed, sullied?

Unease shadowed his features. 'Mrs Farrell —'

'My name is Isabelle.' She looked away. 'I have no marriage, my title is a falsehood.'

Unbelievably, he squatted down on his haunches beside her knee. 'I mean you no disrespect coming here today.'

She stared into his sharp blue eyes; eyes that missed nothing. 'No?'

He shook his head. 'No. My one thought was for Ethan and his family. To protect them.'

'From me?' She snorted. 'How can I possibly harm them? I want naught from them, except Ethan's love.'

'You have that, but are you content to be just his mistress? To bear his illegitimate children? To be scorned in public?'

'Of course not!' She rose and walked a few feet away from him. Her hands shook for she had already sampled public scorn and knew that she could stomach no more of it. 'But ... but as soon as we both are granted divorces then we'll be free. Ethan says we can go to Australia to his sister.'

MacGregor slowly straightened. 'And what if one of you isn't given a divorce?'

'We'll fight it until we do.' Isabelle raised her chin. 'Rest assured, Mr MacGregor, I am not some alley slut that you can toss a bag of coins to and hope I'll disappear.'

'How many bags will it take?'

The urge to slap his face was barely contained. She raised her eyebrows. 'My, my, you are skilled at these types of arrangements aren't you? Do you buy all your women?'

The blue of his eyes honed to ice.

Isabelle sighed, drained by the thrust and jab argument. 'Just because I have very little doesn't mean I want — '

'Ah, but you do have something.' He folded his arms and looked down at his boots, before pinning her with a glare. 'You have Ethan's love and he's never given that to anyone before. Therefore, the power is all yours. He's yours to do with as you please.'

'And you believe I will misuse my so-called power.'

'Many women do.'

'I am not as other women.'

He nodded. 'I am learning to understand that.' He looked away into the distance. 'This is not easy on either side. I realize this.' His eyes softened. 'I wish you and Ethan had met years ago and saved everyone this misery.'

She studied him for a moment. He was a tall, powerfully built man. Creases spread from the corners of his eyes and she had the inkling that he smiled a lot. Searching her memory, she recalled Ethan speaking of this Scot, who'd sailed to Australia and fashioned a life in the frontier. Suddenly, she wished they were friends. It would be pleasant to just sit and talk with this man and learn about his and Ethan's friendship. Sadness filled her. 'I'm sorry that you and I didn't meet under better circumstances, Mr MacGregor.'

He stared at her for a long moment. 'So am I.' A self-deprecating chuckle escaped him. 'I thought Ethan was mad to love you.'

'And now?'

'And now . . . ' His face became unreadable, closed from expression and emotion. 'And now I think he is equally blessed and cursed.'

★　★　★

Hamish gave his hat to the butler, and ran his fingers through his hair, steeling himself to meet Ethan. What would he say? His dispute with Ethan over giving Isabelle up rang hollow in his head, tasted nasty on his tongue. Isabelle Farrell had managed, without even trying or being aware of it, to find an unguarded place in his heart. All it had taken was one look from those pale blue eyes of hers and he had struggled to breathe ever since. He remembered their first meeting months ago, and if he was honest he would agree that he'd felt a stirring of attraction then, and immediately squashed it. There were rules in friendship and one of them was to not ogle your best friend's woman.

Today he had expected to feel attraction, but he certainly hadn't been prepared for the hit in the gut that he'd experienced the moment he saw her sitting alone in the garden. No wonder Ethan lived and breathed the woman, she was something exceptional, unique. Hamish shook his head at his own stupidity. He'd handled the situation poorly and, no doubt, left with her hating him. Somehow, her dislike caused him more distress than the fact he lusted after his friend's woman. *Lord, what have I done?*

The drawing-room door was wrenched open and Ethan stood there, tension lining his face. 'Well? Did you see her? How was she? Why are you standing out here in the hall?'

Sucking in a deep breath and squaring his shoulders, Hamish strode past Ethan and into the room, heading straight for the drinks cabinet.

Ethan followed him. 'I've been watching out for you. I noticed the cart came back still full. Why didn't Isabelle accept them? Did her father not let you see her? The bastard! I'll — '

'I saw her.' Hamish threw back the whisky and put the glass down. This was a nightmare he wanted to shake off. What possessed him to get involved? The image of Isabelle's furious face flashed before him. He groaned and turned to Ethan, who looked at him expectantly. 'She is well.'

'Thank God. I was so worried.' Ethan sagged. 'But why . . . '

'I have changed my plans. I'll not be staying a few weeks here, but shall return to Edinburgh tonight.'

'Oh?' Ethan frowned. 'Hamish, if it is because of Mama's lapse in manners and her writing to you, I do apologize. The last thing I wanted was for you to be caught up in this business. She should never have written to you.'

'It is none of that.' He felt the heat rise in his cheeks. 'I have other matters to attend before my return to Australia.'

Striding to the drinks cabinet, Ethan slapped his arm in good humour. 'Of course you have, my friend, but I'd really like your presence here for a day or two until Mama and I can look at each other without either of us losing our tempers.'

'I'm not certain . . . ' Hamish faltered. Until meeting Isabelle, he'd been looking forward to spending a couple of weeks or more at Bracken Hall. To go shooting, play billiards in the evenings, go drinking in town. He and Ethan enjoyed each other's company, behaved like brothers and he wanted to take some more memories back to Australia.

'Say you'll stay, old friend.' Ethan smiled with that boyish charm he'd always had and Hamish knew he would give in. Besides, he'd not meet with Isabelle again. He would pretend she didn't exist. It was highly unlikely she'd be calling in for tea.

13

Isabelle tested the heat of the iron and wiped her hair from her eyes. Her back ached from standing for the last hour. Pressing the iron over her father's shirt, she winkled her nose in distaste as cold winds blew outside causing the kitchen fire to smoke. A cool draught from under the hallway door circled around her ankles. The miserable weather had wreacked havoc for the last three days. Gales shattered roof tiles, blew down trees and simply became a nuisance. Any attempt at outside work ended in frustration and abandonment.

She glanced at her father and the boys as they sat around the table playing cards. After days of being cooped up inside she had run out of jobs for them to do. Still, she couldn't complain. They had accomplished much. The bedrooms received a coat of whitewash, the loose banister on the stairs was fixed, all the needlework was attended to and new knitted garments begun.

Her father dropped his cards on the floor and Bertie, laughing, bent down and scooped them up for him. Isabelle frowned, noting the blueness of her father's tight lips. In the last week she had noticed his pallor gain a yellowy tinge. His appetite had fallen, too. A trickle of fear crept up her spine at the thought of him becoming really ill. Until now, he'd shown no signs of the sickness that plagued him on the inside, but then her own recent illness had kept her from watching over them.

Aaron slowly looked up at her, as though the movement had cost him a great deal, his eyes wary as always of her rebuff. 'Don't be overdoing it, lass. You've only been on your feet a few days.'

'Yes, I know and just look at this pile waiting for me.'

He glanced down at the table.

She sighed and silently berated herself for her artless snipe. When would she ever stop cementing the walls between them? Each time her father tried to knock a brick down she was quick to replace it.

'Me and the boys can wear wrinkled shirts about the farm,' he murmured. 'No one can see them underneath our vests and coats.'

'Come sit and have a game, Belle.' Hughie coaxed, grinning. 'Those clothes won't mind.'

'You mind your manners, my — ' Isabelle broke off as her father gradually tilted sideways and fell to the floor. 'Father!'

In a heartbeat all three were fussing over

him. Hughie lifted him up and cradled his head. 'Da! Da!'

'Help me get him into the sitting-room, Hughie.' Isabelle lifted his legs by the ankles while Hughie strained under the weight of Aaron's top half. Shuffling, they carried him in the front room and laid him on the sofa. Isabelle threw a shawl over her father's chest. 'Make up a fire, Bertie, quickly now!' As Bertie ran from the room, she turned to Hughie, who was chaffing Aaron's hands between his own. 'You must go fetch the doctor, Hughie.'

He straightened immediately. 'Yes, I'm on my way!' He collided in the doorway with Bertie, who carried an armload of kindling.

Isabelle placed the fire screen to one side. 'Here, Bertie, give those to me and fetch pillows and blankets.' She set about making the fire. Fumbling and cursing, she managed a small blaze and was about to rush out for more kindling when her father moaned from the sofa. Hurrying to his side, she picked up one of his hands and patted it. 'It's all right. You're all right.'

Aaron's eyes flickered open and focused on her. 'B-Belle?'

'Yes, I'm here. Right here.'

He closed his eyes and his tongue poked out to wet his lips. His grip on her hand was feeble at best. Bertie, hidden beneath a tumble of pillows and blankets, burst into the room.

'Lord, Bertie, did you strip every bed?' Isabelle snapped, taking them from him. 'Tis a wonder you didn't fall down the stairs!'

'Is Da awake?'

'Not completely.' She squeezed his shoulder as he stood staring at their father. 'Listen, do you think you could make up a tray of tea without burning yourself?'

He straightened up and raised his chin. 'Aye, course I can.'

'Good, do that for me then, will you?'

When he had once more left the room she turned back to add the last bit of kindling to the fire and then crouched down beside her father.

As if sensing her there, Aaron opened his eyes. 'Not . . . too . . . good.'

'No, you're not at the minute.' She placed a pillow gently under his head and then covered him with the thickest blanket they had. 'But you soon will be again.'

'You know the truth.'

Bustling about folding blankets, she nodded. 'Yes, I do.'

'Don't waste good money . . . on doctor . . .'

'I'll waste my money in any way I see fit.'

She gave the fire a serious poke with the fire iron.

'Belle.'

'Yes?'

'Can you help me . . . up to bed?'

'I don't think that is such a good idea.' She studied him and although his face was grey, there seemed more life in his eyes now than before. 'Let us wait until the doctor has been, yes?'

He nodded and closed his eyes, obviously too worn-out to argue further.

Sighing, Isabelle knelt on the hearth and stared into the blaze. If this was the start of her father's end then she'd better prepare herself to nurse him. And to see less of Ethan.

★ ★ ★

Ethan plumped up his pillows and settled back against them. He checked over the end of his bed to make certain that the fireguard was secure and took a sip of whisky from the small glass on his bedside table. Lastly, he reached for his book, W.M. Thackeray's *The Virginians*. He wasn't one for fiction all the time, and liked to inject his reading habits with works on husbandry and, since Rachel's departure, books on England's colonies. Most nights he did his reading in the study or drawing room, but since the incident with his mother and the coolness between them, he had taken to his room of an evening and found a hidden pleasure in reading in bed.

A discreet knock interrupted him. He looked towards the door. 'Come in.'

Clarice sidled into the room and closed the door with a soft click. She nervously glanced around the room, as a blush crept up her face. Ethan stared in amazement. His wife had never been in his room before. He swallowed and hoped to God she didn't want to share his bed.

'Is . . . is there something you wanted, Clarice?'

She nodded, clearly agitated that she had ventured into his domain. Her fingers twisted the material of her nightgown and she couldn't quite meet his eyes. 'I . . . I need to talk to you.'

'And it cannot wait until morning?'

She shook her head.

Frowning, Ethan sat a little straighter and wondered if he should escort her downstairs, but abruptly she rushed forward and gripped the timber foot rail of his bed.

'You want to divorce me?'

He groaned. 'Clarice, please don't.'

'Your mother tells me I must not allow it to happen.'

Under his breath, Ethan swore violently. 'I understand — '

'I know we aren't as . . . most couples are.' She paused to pull at her hair that hung loose about her rounded shoulders. 'Only, I never wanted a husband.'

'I know.'

Her chin trembled. 'If you divorce me, where will I live?'

Pity filled him for this childlike woman. 'Please do not worry yourself, Clarice. I will always provide for you.'

'You will?'

'Naturally.' He forced a smile. 'You will have a house of your own to do with as you please, plus servants and an income.'

'Could . . . could I have a house in London?'

'London?' His eyes widened. 'Why London?'

'Because there are many shops there that will deliver and . . . and wonderful libraries. I wouldn't want to go about town much at all and in London everything can come to me.'

He was completely astonished. She had obviously been thinking this through. He nodded. 'I see. Well, I shouldn't think that would be a problem, you having a house in London.'

She seemed to sag and gave him a tenuous smile. 'Thank you, Ethan. You are a good man.'

'No, I am not.'

'Yes, you are. I am not the wife worthy of Bracken Hall. I . . . I know this will upset your Mama, but . . . but I never really wanted to be here. I'd rather be divorced and in London than here and married.' She hurried from his room and closed the door.

Ethan slumped back against his pillows. It was the most he'd heard her speak in all the time they were married. Wiping a hand over his eyes, shame washed over him. She had called him a good man. It was laughable really. He was divorcing her and she called him a good man. He cringed at the situation he found himself in. Yet, despite his unfavourable position, he could no longer change it even if he wanted to. A life without Isabelle was no life at all. His groin tightened at the thought of her. He needed to hold her, kiss and caress her, to fill her body with his. Smothering a moan of want, he threw back the blankets and jumped out of bed. It had been so long since he'd been able to see her that his mind was alive with her image and his body was on fire with yearning.

On impulse, he dressed, and then, carrying his boots, he swiftly descended the staircase and headed along the corridor to the back entrance of the house.

* * *

A tinkering noise woke Isabelle from her fitful slumber. She lay quiet, listening for sounds from her father's bedroom. Her room was fully dark and she guessed the time to be around three o'clock. The cockerel always started crowing around four, before dawn had even broken.

The noise came again; a ping against the window. Frowning, she left the bed and moved the threadbare curtain aside. She leapt back as something hit the window right before her face. Heart thumping, she stepped closer and looked down. A dark shape, a figure, moved below, it straightened and raised its arm again. A rain of pebbles tapped against the windowpane. Sliding the window up, Isabelle leaned out, her stomach clenching with excitement.

'Ethan?'

'Let me in.'

Biting her lip to stop a grin from spreading, she closed the window and ran from the room. Downstairs, she hastily lit the candle on the kitchen table and then unbolted the back door. Before she could speak Ethan had her in his arms and was kissing her thoroughly.

She pulled back. 'What are you doing here at this hour?'

He gathered her back into his arms. 'I've missed you more than I can bear,' he whispered and nuzzled her neck.

She ran her fingers through his hair to cradle his head and bring his lips back to hers. 'Oh, my love.'

He raised his head. 'Are you well, my sweet? I've been so worried.'

'I am well now, yes.' She kissed him.

'Hamish said you — '

Isabelle stilled. 'Hamish? What did he say?'

He kissed her eyelids. 'He said you had recovered. I've been so worried. Your father wouldn't let me see you.'

'No.' She hung her head back and he seared a fire-hot trail of kisses down her throat.

'I love you so much, darling girl.'

She gently pulled at his bottom lip with her teeth and then traced its outline with her tongue. 'And I you, my love.'

'It's unbearable being without you, I cannot go on.'

'We must at least for a little while longer.'

Ethan groaned deep in his chest. 'I need you, Isabelle. You make me whole.'

'I know, my heart, I know.'

He backed her into the scullery and closed the door. Pressing her against the cold stone wall, his hot mouth sucked her nipple through her thin cotton nightdress. The feeling was so sensual, Isabelle moaned, writhing against him. Her hands fluttered around his crotch, trying to find his trouser fastenings, but his assault on her body sent her mind spinning away from any coherent action.

His hands cupped her breasts. Urgency came into his movements. Panting slightly, he bunched her nightgown up around her hips. She was naked underneath and his fingers slid over her belly and down, seeking her moist warmth. He explored her inner core with his fingers, softly, slowly, building within her a raging torrent of sensations.

'Ethan . . . ' She arched against him, desperate for completeness.

'Christ, I must have you, Isabelle.' His groan was guttural.

In an instant he had freed himself from his trousers and she opened her legs for him, wanting him more than air at that moment. The cold stone scratching into her back was forgotten as he thrust into her, filling her, expanding her. She grasped his hair, curving herself into him, accepting and yet wanting more of him inside her. His tongue caressed hers as he strained, pulling her onto him as though he couldn't get enough. Her body lifted, her mind separated from reality. Closer and closer she surged. Then, when she thought she couldn't stand it another moment, he thrust harder, deeper and her whole being exploded into a thousand lights. She became dimly aware that he had tensed and shuddered to fulfilment, too. He moved leisurely now, each stroke a small goodbye until next time.

Ethan kissed her eyes, still inside her, still caressing her breasts, her hips. 'My love?'

She wriggled against him and the lingering throb slowly subsided. 'Mmm?'

'I didn't hurt you?'

'No, my darling.' She kissed his nose. 'Never.'

'Forgive me, this is not how I would want to treat you — '

'Shhh . . . ' She put her fingers to his lips. 'We are together, that is all that matters.'

'I should go . . . ' He glanced out of the small scullery window. Grey light streaked the sky chasing away the dark.

Isabelle sighed. 'How soon can you come back?'

'I don't know, but before I go, I must tell you that Clarice is not against the divorce as long as I provide for her, which I would naturally.'

They pulled apart as reality crept back into their world, which had, for a short time, been filled with only the delights of sensual pleasure. Isabelle smoothed down her nightgown. 'Of course you must provide for her, but it's not up to her whether you are granted a divorce, is it?'

Ethan sighed, shaking his head as he adjusted his clothes. 'You are correct. An unknown judge holds our future in his hands and he might not yet even be aware of it.'

In the cold shadows of the scullery, Isabelle felt a chill enter her heart as she looked into his eyes. 'And he could refuse you.'

'He may, but it won't stop me.' Ethan clasped her arms and held her close, whispering into her hair, 'nothing will stop us from being together, darling. If the courts deny us, then we'll leave the country and go somewhere else, where no one knows us.'

She nodded against his chest, swallowing back the tears clogging her throat for she knew that such a move was beyond them. They had families, responsibilities. Running away sounded so simple, but was, in all honesty impossible.

★   ★   ★

Isabelle wearily pushed her hair away from her face and leant her hip against the end of her father's bed. Changing his sheets on her

256

own was an exhausting task, but the boys had gone to the market and wouldn't be back until later. She looked at the man, now clean and shaven again, wasting away before her. His sunken eyes were closed, his skin yellow. She had hardened her heart to him so long ago that it was proving difficult for her to show or even know her true feelings concerning him.

October had disappeared into a haze of long sleepless nights easing her father's hurting and grey days of nursing him through each hour. Some days he rallied, and could hold a conversation, chuckle at the boys and their tales, but generally he lay looking out the small window at the sky or dozing between bouts of pain. His gaze would follow her around the room as she tidied or attended the fire. She cared for him because it was her duty to do so, and she left it at that. There was no time in her days to sit and analyse their relationship. They rarely spoke to each other, but at odd times he would catch hold of her hand and squeeze it, letting her know her attentions did not go unnoticed by him. Yet, she still could not, deep in her heart, forgive him for walking out on them.

Isabelle bent and gathered the dirty washing. Piles of it waited for her in the scullery and a deep sigh broke from her before she could stop it.

'Belle?' Aaron opened his eyes.

'I'm here. Do you need something? The bedpan?'

'No.'

'Go to sleep. Unless you want a drink?'

'No.' His eyelashes fluttered. 'I . . . Hope my time comes soon, to spare you from all this.'

'Don't talk such rot.' She bustled about, holding the washing tighter, her gaze flicking around the room making sure nothing was out of place. 'Go to sleep now and let me get on with it.'

Aaron's hand twitched on the bedcover. 'You will let the boys help you more?'

'Yes. Keeping them busy gets them out from under my feet.'

'You are so like your mother . . . '

She sniffed defensively. 'I'm nothing like mother. Sally was mother's image not me.'

'Sally had your mother's softness, but you have her looks. Such a beautiful woman she was. Only you are stronger than she is, have more spirit.'

'Go to sleep now.' Isabelle headed for the door. She detested it when he spoke of her mother, the woman he said he loved, but abandoned, just as he abandoned his children. And here she was discarded all over again, this time by her no-good husband. It seemed she was a lot like her mother; neither of them could pick good husbands. At the door he called her name again and she turned. 'Yes?'

'Don't listen to Harrington. Don't let him take you from here. The boys need you, and you've made a home here for them both. Farrell will come back.'

At the mention of Farrell her heart gave a sluggish thud. 'I don't need your advice, thank you, and I don't need or want Farrell back.'

Aaron swallowed, his gaze not leaving her face. 'Harrington isn't your future.'

'I didn't know you'd become a fortune-teller, was it a trick you learnt on your travels?' With that she left the room, indignant that he should try to tell her how to run her life when he'd made so many mistakes with his own.

She dumped the washing in the scullery and grabbed her cloak, the need to be away from the house, if only for a moment, was strong. The icy November wind whipped her hair from its bun and slapped her cheeks until they stung. Ethan came to mind but his last message, delivered only yesterday, told of his plans to visit London with Hamish Mac-Gregor and meant she'd not be seeing him for a fortnight. A spark of irritation surfaced for a second but she squashed it. What use was it to begrudge him his freedom? Men led different lives to women. Even if he hadn't gone to London, she still wouldn't have seen him today or even tomorrow or the next day. She was confined to the house, to the sickroom and her father. The stolen hours of pleasure she and Ethan shared in the summer had dried up to mere snatches of conversation at the back door when he called or sent the odd letter.

With surprise, she realized she had walked to the edge of the fields. The woods stood on the other side of the road, the stile before her. She dithered on the spot. Walking in the woods without Ethan held no pleasure. Besides, she should be getting back. As if an unknown voice called to her, she headed back to the farm, hurrying a little more with each step. Something wasn't right. She could feel it. Breaking into a run, she lifted her skirts high, focusing on the farm buildings as they grew closer. At the field gate, she flung it open and didn't stop to close it again. Her boots clattered across the stone yard and so intent was she on getting into the house she didn't see the figure who loomed up beside her. She screamed when a hand grabbed her arm. Another hand clamped over her mouth, cutting off her next scream.

'Be quiet, Belle!' Neville Peacock whispered in her ear. 'I'll not harm you.'

Her eyes widened in fear as he dragged her across the yard and into the closest barn. The dimness inside added to the suffocating feeling overwhelming her as Neville's hand covered both her nose and mouth. She struggled against his hold, frantic to escape, to breathe.

Neville stumbled over the uneven floor and they crashed against the post at the end of the stalls. 'Hold still, for God's sake!'

Her hands clawed at his, her lungs fit to burst. In one violent movement he flung her down to the straw-littered floor inside the stall. She gasped, gulping air, panicking like a stranded fish. Air wasn't filling her lungs fast enough, she floundered, terrifying herself further until Neville grabbed her shoulders.

'It's all right, Belle. Stop! Calm down, will you?' He softened his hold and put his arm around her shoulders. 'Breathe. Steady now.'

Slowly, unsteadily she relaxed enough to allow her lungs to work properly. She breathed in deeply, pulling at her bodice and corset, wanting them off her body. Edging away from Neville, she huddled near the wall, glancing at him uncertainly. 'What do you want?'

Neville sat back, his arms resting on his bent knees. 'Just to see you, to talk to you.'

'I must go inside. My father is ill, he needs me.'

'I saw your brothers in Heptonstall. I thought that I could spend some time alone with you.'

'No, Neville.'

'You haven't been back to the market.'

Astonished, she stared at him. 'You think I would return there after last time?'

He frowned. 'But you have to. You need to earn the money.'

She shook her head and rose to her knees. 'I have other ways of earning it.'

'No! You'll not whore yourself for *him* any longer!' He lunged for her and they fell backwards, knocking the breath from her again. Neville lay on top of her and, grabbing her hands he held them above her head. His face was only inches from hers.

'I don't.'

He cut her off by enveloping her mouth with his. His wet kisses swarmed over her face, hair and neck. 'You're mine, not his.' He clenched her wrists in one hand and ran the other over her eyes down her neck and over her left breast. His breathing grew hot and rapid.

'Neville, let me go!' She squirmed, trying

to wiggle out from under her him, but he pressed down harder, trapping her. His knee forced her legs apart and his intentions became horribly clear to her frenzied mind. 'No, Neville. Let me go.'

'I've waited too long,' he gasped, licking her cheek, sucking the tender skin beneath her ear. 'I've tried to be patient, me darling girl, you know I have.'

His hand inched up her skirts and then she felt his fingers grabbing the waistband of her drawers, pulling them down. The cold air on her thighs stunned her. She bucked, doubling her efforts to free herself. She screamed again, high and clear, startling him out of his intensity of getting his way with her.

'Quiet!' His hand left her drawers and slammed onto her mouth. Her teeth bit her lips and the metallic taste of blood coated her tongue. 'Lay still, Belle. I'll not hurt you. In fact you'll enjoy it, I promise.'

Breathing in short spurts through her nose, she tensed as his hand ventured lower. He was fumbling with his trousers, cursing at his hurried, ineffectual attempts when suddenly she raised her knee and in the same movement thrust him off her. Within the blink of an eye she was on top of him. The force of her push had taken him by surprise. He lay flat on his back and his eyes were wide in bewilderment.

'You filthy bastard! How dare you touch me!' Incensed, she smashed her fist into his face. Her knuckles met his nose and a sharp pain bolted from her hand up her arm.

Neville howled with a mixture of pain and outrage. He slapped her cheek hard and threw her off. 'You bitch!'

Her head snapped back and she landed on her bottom. She had no time to think or react as Neville hit her again. His right fist caught her a glancing blow to the side of her head at the same time she sprang for the doorway. Stars exploded before her eyes. Reeling, she put her hands up to ward him off as he punched her again. She fell back, her head banging against a timber post. Dry sobbing, retching, she crawled on her hands and knees, desperate to get away from him. She looked up. He was on his feet now and her scream echoed around the barn as his boot came at great speed and landed with a teeth chattering thud in her side. The air whooshed out of her lungs and she cried out.

'What the bloody hell is going on!'

Dazed, Isabelle peered up at the doorway, clutching her side in agony. She couldn't make out who stood there as the light came from behind, casting the face into shadows.

'Get yerself away from me wife!'

Farrell.

The shock rendered her speechless, momentarily shutting out her pain. She heard Neville behind her and closed her eyes, waiting for the blow to come. Instead, Farrell lunged for Neville and the two men fell to the floor. Fists flayed, curses and grunts filled the dim barn. Isabelle scrambled to her feet, gasping at the pain in her side. Tears blurred her eyes and she felt more than saw her way to the door. The crunch of bone on bone jerked her senses back to the fighting men. Farrell knelt over Neville pummelling his face. A wild, desperate rage brightened Farrell's eyes and this made her rush to pull him off the other man.

'Stop it! Enough.' She tore Farrell away and together they stumbled back, panting. Neville lay unmoving and Isabelle stared at him, horrified that Farrell had killed him.

'He's not dead.' Her husband's indifferent voice rang in her ears. Farrell looked around and, spotting a bucket, he picked it up and went outside.

Shaking, Isabelle stepped closer to Neville to check he breathed, fearful that he would suddenly spring up and grab her leg. Farrell re-entered the barn and lifting the bucket, threw the icy contents of it over Neville's face. Spluttering, gasping, Neville rose on one elbow and wiped the moisture from his rapidly swelling eyes. Blood streamed from his nose and he abruptly spat out a broken tooth.

'Get out and don't come back.' Farrell advanced on him and gripped his arm, hauling him to his feet and propelling him to the door. 'I don't know who yer are an' I don't care, but if I see yer here again, I'll have yer. Understand?' With a thrust he sent Neville staggering out into the yard.

Neville regained his balance and spun back to glare at Isabelle. 'Don't think I'm finished with you! I'll be waiting.' He looked at Farrell. 'All I was doing was sampling a bit of what she gives Harrington for free!'

Rage filled Isabelle. 'Shut your mouth, Neville!' she screamed, and ran for him, ready to tear his eyes out, but Farrell grabbed hold of her waist.

'Get off me farm, yer scumbag!' Farrell yelled at Neville.

Puffing, trembling, Isabelle watched Neville skulk down the yard and out of the front gate. Farrell released her and she stepped away, fighting back tears as the pain surged to the fore. She bit her lip to stop a moan from escaping. Isabelle peeked at her husband and saw him truly for the first time. Raising her head, she stared at his transformation. He looked older, haggard. The excess flesh stripped from him revealed a leaner, stronger-looking man. He'd been physically working, hard work by the looks of it. His blue eyes seemed duller than before. Deep lines ran down from his nose to mouth. He had lost his hat in the brawl and grey liberally sprinkled his hair. The months away had wreaked havoc on them both in more ways than one.

'Are you staying?' she whispered.

'It's me home ain't it?' He walked past her and into the house. Isabelle closed her eyes and this time let the tears fall.

14

Elizabeth tapped her foot, impatient with waiting. Ethan and Hamish were due home today and she longed to see them both. Two weeks away wasn't very long, but with Ethan afflicted with that Farrell women, she was worried that he might leave Hamish in London and hurry back to her side. She'd received no word from him since he left, and only two short letters from Hamish informing her that he was doing everything in his power to keep Ethan amused and entertained. It wasn't enough though. Elizabeth knew her son, knew how strong-willed he could be, especially when he was passionate about something.

She remembered one summer, when he was about six, he begged to be taught to swim in the river. She disallowed it of course, fearful of him drowning, but despite her protests, he had gone ahead and done it without her knowing. Her husband had found out and secretly helped Ethan learn the skill even though he could barely swim a stroke himself. It wasn't the only time Ethan had done as he wished and damned the consequences.

Elizabeth had tried her best to keep him safe, to keep him by her side. Oh, he loved her, she had no doubt of that. They were close, closer than she and Rachel, but that was because he was her son, her first-born. Still, it hurt and vexed her that he refused to listen to her advice. Stubborn. He was stubborn and wilful. Too used to getting his own way. No one ever resisted him. His charm, his smile always got him what he wanted. Until now he had led a blessed life, if you ignored his marriage, and Elizabeth wanted it to stay that way. *Is it so wrong of me to keep things as they are?* Elizabeth paced the drawing room, tormented by her thoughts. That Farrell woman was no good for Ethan, no good for the family. She paused, momentarily at a loss for if Ethan and Isabelle had been unwed, she would have encouraged the match. To see Ethan so happy would have been a balm to the disappointment of Isabelle's low status. Naturally that would have been forgotten as children arrived . . .

'Oh, you stupid woman!' Elizabeth chastised herself for her wayward imaginings. Such thoughts wouldn't do her any good. 'Ethan is married to Clarice,' she whispered, knowing that just saying the words weren't enough. Her darling son was unhappy and it hurt her.

She turned to stare at the miniature portrait of her husband. He'd been a sensible man, she'd cared for him deeply, yet never had she experienced the passion that now gripped her son. Had she missed out? What would it have been like to be so desired that a man was willing to give up everything for you? Weary, Elizabeth crossed to the window. She admired Isabelle Farrell, she had courage, if not sense. The lower classes couldn't be blamed for making hasty, unworthy marriages. They knew no better. Elizabeth worried what the recent gossip concerning Isabelle Farrell would do to Ethan when he found out. At that same moment, the sound of a carriage coming along the drive made her heart race. He was home.

Straightening her shoulders, Elizabeth waited by the fireplace for her son and Hamish to enter the drawing room. There was a rush of footmen attending to the luggage and the low murmur of the butler's voice, then the door opened and Ethan strode into the room. Behind him came Hamish.

'You both look so well!' Elizabeth declared, hugging them in turn. 'Were the roads very bad? At least we didn't receive any early snow.'

'The roads were indeed very good.' Hamish smiled and settled himself onto the sofa. 'Are you in good health, madam?'

'Oh yes, perfect health.' Elizabeth's eyes strayed to Ethan. 'Are you hungry? Shall I have tea brought in?' She didn't wait for his answer before hurrying to tug the bell-pull. She noticed Ethan and Hamish frown at each other and she tried to calm down. Her son was very astute. Taking a deep breath, she forced a smile to her face. 'So, do tell me about your trip.'

Ethan stood behind the sofa and stared at her. 'Mama you're as nervous as a chicken in a hen house with a fox on the prowl. What is the matter?'

Elizabeth swallowed and turned thankfully towards the door as the maid brought in the tea tray. 'Why, nothing is the matter, dear. I'm pleased to see you home safe, nothing more.' Her hands fluttered over the teapot. 'I do so worry about you in London. It's such a large city and full of desperate — '

'Has something happened here?' Ethan's eyes narrowed.

She picked up a teacup and saucer. It wobbled in her hands. 'Why, of course not.'

Ethan took one step towards her. 'I don't believe you.'

Hamish reached out for the teapot. 'Come along good fellow, we've had a long journey and I'm — '

'There is something I should know, isn't there, Mama?' A muscle pulsed along his clenched jaw.

'Dearest . . . ' Elizabeth felt the warmth fade from her face.

'Tell me.' Ethan paled under his tan. 'Is it Isabelle?'

'Well . . . You see — '

Within two strides Ethan was standing inches from her. 'Tell me!'

'He's back.'

Ethan blinked. 'Who?'

'Her husband.' Before Elizabeth could say another word, he was running from the room. She heard him shout for his horse to be saddled and, deflated, she collapsed back against the sofa.

Hamish took her hand in his. 'Perhaps this will be a good thing. Ethan must accept Farrell has rights to her. She is his wife, not Ethan's.'

A dull pain seized Elizabeth's heart. 'Ethan will kill him. I know it.'

★ ★ ★

272

Isabelle wiped the hair from her eyes and stirred the stew simmering on the range. Her swollen eye made her vision lopsided. Her right eye, the good one, viewed the bubbling concoction without much enthusiasm. Boiled bacon scraps and a handful of vegetables would hardly satisfy the boys, especially when Farrell seemed determined to work them to death. She wondered briefly if her life could become any worse. Her father lay dying upstairs, her brothers were outside working in all weathers, thankful to be out of Farrell's way, and Ethan gone from her life as if he'd never existed. Lord, how she missed him. Needed him.

Behind her, sitting at the table, was her husband. Sullen and betrayed. On learning how Ethan had helped her with the farm, Farrell had gone mad and smashed his fists into doors, walls and anyone who came close. He'd kicked holes in the dresser, smashed plates and cups and dragged Isabelle around the room by her hair until Hughie stepped in between them to take the brunt of Farrell's anger. Her darling brother still wore the bruises and walked with a limp.

Farrell had done an excellent job of putting her back in her place — as his wife. Whereas before he'd been uninterested in her, shown no intention of touching her, or of being a real husband and wife team, since his return, he hadn't let an opportunity go by to remind her that she was no longer Ethan Harrington's whore. If she wanted a bed partner, then her husband was willing. Her heart fluttered now at the thought of Farrell's torture, his mental cruelty. She did her best to ignore his jibes, his insults. Each night, and sometimes during the day he would catch her by the hair or arm or skirt and drag her into whatever corner was at hand and fill her body with his revolting seed. At first, she had fought, but he hit harder and she couldn't tend to her family while ever nursing her injuries. With reluctance, without going totally mad, she accepted his rough handling and ignored his presence the best she could.

Four days. That's all it had been, four days, but it felt like he'd been back for years. Whatever he suffered while on the run had turned him into a hate-filled fiend. He scowled continually, shouted orders, was abusive and belligerent.

From the first day she met him at the workhouse, she realized he would never be someone she could share her heart's secrets with, but she had hoped for friendship. Although he rejected her friendship, he had been civil enough, and definitely not the outright evil monster he'd become now. One day she would be free of him. She had to believe it.

'Can yer shut him up!'

Isabelle jumped as Farrell's yell filled the kitchen. Shaking, she blinked, wondering what he was talking about. Then she heard it. Her father calling her from above. She left the room at a run and bounded upstairs.

'I'm here now.' She hurried to his bedside and peered at him. 'What is it?'

'Drink.'

After filling the glass with water from the jug on the bedside table, Isabelle lifted him up to help him sip from it. Aaron nodded and rested back against the pillows.

'Everything all right?'

'Yes. I'll bring you up something to eat soon.' She avoided his gaze and straightened the blankets. He had lost so much weight in the last few days, she could easily turn him by herself now, which was good since the boys were never inside if they could help it. 'Do you need the pan?'

'No.' The whites of his eyes held a yellow tinge, similar to his drawn skin. 'If I do . . . I'll call Hughie.'

'Right, well then . . . ' She lingered by the bed, not wanting to face Farrell in the kitchen again.

Her father lifted his hand and gently

touched hers. 'Get word to Harrington.'

'I cannot. He's away and Farrell watches my every move. He won't allow me beyond the yard.'

He coughed for a moment and she eased him up higher on his pillows. Pain showed in his eyes. He gripped her hand tighter, his eyes imploring. 'When I'm . . . gone, you and the boys must get away.'

She nodded and sighed at his change of heart. He no longer advised her to stay with her husband. 'I know.'

'Harrington will help.'

'Yes.'

'I . . . was wrong, Belle . . .'

Commotion downstairs had her stiffening. She strained to listen and heard raised voices. 'I must go.'

Lifting her skirts, she ran downstairs and into the kitchen, skidding to a halt on seeing Ethan standing in the doorway. 'Ethan!'

Farrell's chair lay tipped over, he stood with his hands clenching by his sides, his face purple with rage and hate. He spun around to face her. 'Get upstairs!'

Shocked, Ethan stared at her, his eyes wide at the sight of her battered face. 'My God!' He lunged for Farrell. 'You bastard! I'll kill you!'

Ethan's momentum knocked Farrell against

the wall. Isabelle gasped, flinching at the contact. The plates rattled on the dresser from the force. The crunching sound of skin on skin, bone on bone filled the room. Grunts and curses accompanied the tussling and thumping as each man tried to better the other.

Locked together for a moment, Farrell bit Ethan's arm. Swearing, Ethan flung him off and then quickly followed him to lay a right hook on to Farrell's jaw.

Farrell hit the kitchen door and bounced back to grab Ethan by the shoulders and drag him down to the floor. With a twist, Ethan dislodged Farrell's grip and stumbled to the table, using it to haul himself up. Farrell grabbed his leg but Ethan kicked him off before turning on him and laying a boot into the man's side. Ethan lifted his boot again, but Isabelle sprang towards him. 'No! Stop!' Isabelle flung herself on to his back, pulling him away. 'Enough.'

Puffing, Ethan used his sleeve to wipe the blood dripping from his mouth. 'Only death is good enough for him.'

'Get out of me house!' Farrell spat from where he lay sprawled on the floor. 'And get yerself away from me wife, yer whore's son!'

Ethan lunged, fury twisting his handsome features, hauled Farrell to his knees and punched him repeatedly in the face. Blood spurted and ran free from Farrell's nose. Again, Isabelle reached for Ethan. 'Stop. No more.'

With a look of contempt, Ethan threw Farrell away from him like a rag doll. Tentatively, Isabelle touched his torn sleeve. He turned and his troubled eyes softened to warm toffee, he was puffing and sweat glistened his brow. 'I'm sorry.'

She didn't know if he felt sorry for her or for what he'd done to Farrell, but she had no time to ask as the boys entered the scullery and stood in the doorway. Hughie took a step forward, staring at the unconscious Farrell. 'Belle?'

'It's all right.' She nodded, but winced at Hughie's innocent gaze. The enormity of the whole situation hit home. She staggered back and leant against the table. 'Go upstairs, both of you.'

Hesitant to leave her, Hughie grudgingly ushered Bertie before him and they disappeared along the hallway. Isabelle gazed at Ethan, tears filling her eyes.

'Oh, my love.' Ethan gathered her into his arms and crushed her into his chest. 'I'm so sorry. I didn't know he had returned. I've just arrived home today and mother told me. How long — '

'Just hold me.' She squeezed him tighter,

sighing into the soft material of his grey coat. 'I've missed you so.'

He leant back a little to see her better. 'You must collect your things. I'm not letting you stay here another moment.'

The joy blotted out everything for a moment before despair quickly filled its place. 'I cannot. Father is ill, dying. I cannot leave him.'

'He and the boys will come too.' Ethan cupped her face in his hands and kissed her lips. 'I will take care of you all.'

Farrell moaned and moved his leg. Isabelle shuddered.

'I want to kill him for touching you.' Harshness entered Ethan's tone and his eyes narrowed to hate-filled slits. 'I'll make sure he suffers for the rest of his days.'

Isabelle stepped back, aware that nothing would ever be the same again. Her heart pained, spreading a dull ache throughout her body as if it knew what was to come and preparing her for it. 'Father cannot be moved. The boys don't know about us . . . '

'They see what Farrell has done, they will understand what you tell them. As for your father, if he is to die anyway, do you think he would stop you from escaping this hellish life?'

She twisted her fingers together. 'You don't

understand. To move him an inch causes him so much agony. I cannot make him endure a carriage ride. Besides, going with you will only make matters worse.'

'How so?'

'Because *I'll* hunt yer both down and *kill* yer.' Farrell spoke from the floor.

Isabelle squealed and jumped back. Her eyes widened as Farrell, wheezing, wobbled upright, using the wall as support. She gripped Ethan's arm, preventing him from attacking and killing the other man.

Ethan's lip curled back in a snarl. 'You will soon find yourself rotting in a cell and be unable to do a thing about it.'

Farrell's eyes narrowed. 'Report me to the authorities and she'll be dead by dawn. The moment they arrive I'll put a knife through her gut.'

Isabelle bit back a whimper, knowing full well her husband meant every word. 'Go home, Ethan. Please,' she whispered.

He looked at her as if she were mad. 'I'm not leaving you here with him!'

Fighting panic, she forced herself to talk reasonably, to silently beg him with her eyes, to listen to her, believe in her. 'I'll be all right, but you mustn't go to the police. Farrell won't touch me again. He knows if he does you'll kill him.'

'No — '

'Yes.' She squeezed his hand. 'Trust me. Everything will be well.'

'Isabelle . . . '

She shook her head. 'I must take care of father and the boys.'

Ethan strode to Farrell and lifted him by his jacket lapels. 'Touch her or even look at her in the wrong way and I'll have you swinging from the nearest tree, understand?'

Victory glowed in Farrell's blue eyes. 'Get out of me house.'

'It's *my* house!' Ethan threw him away and wiped his hands on his trousers as though he had touched something repulsive. 'Remember, this is my house, my land. You are *my* tenant. For now you are safe from a prison cell, but it won't always be that way.' He turned away and took Isabelle's hand and led her outside. In the yard he pulled her against him and kissed her softly. 'Send word the minute he starts — '

She kissed him hard, stopping his words of tragedy and despair. 'I will. I promise. Only, don't come here anymore, my darling.'

'But — '

'No, you mustn't. I beg you not to. If I need you, I'll send Hughie, but otherwise stay away for all our sakes. I can handle Farrell.' She kissed the broken skin on his knuckles. 'I love you and we will be together, but not yet. Once father has . . . gone. We will come to you. I'll escape him somehow.'

He crushed her to him and kissed her hair. 'Promise me?'

'I promise.'

★ ★ ★

Isabelle opened her eyes and for the second time that week dashed to heave into the wash-basin on the little table under the window. After emptying her stomach, she peeped over her shoulder at her father who slept in the bed, grateful she hadn't woken him. She stumbled back to the small pallet by the wall and curled up into a ball, tugging the blankets up to her chin. The truth hit her with the force of a hammer.

With child. The words, the meaning went around in her head like a spinning top on marble. She hadn't had her curses for a while; long before Farrell returned three weeks ago. After some quick calculations, relief poured out of her as she realized the child wasn't her husband's. Inside her grew Ethan's baby. It was a comfort to her, knowing that their love grew in her womb, but it also brought its own problems. A child changed things. It was another responsibility she could do without.

How had they let it happen? They were usually so careful . . . The stolen moments in the scullery.

Isabelle swore under her breath a word she'd often heard Farrell say. The thought of her husband made her gag again, but she fought it. She mustn't let him suspect. She shied away from the notion of telling anyone, even Ethan. No one could know, not yet. For a little while longer the secret was hers alone as she dealt with this new change in her life.

'Belle.'

Her father's weak call filtered through her thoughts. 'I'm coming.' Within moments she had clipped on her front-fastening corset over her chemise and pulled on her petticoats and grey service dress. How she looked was of little importance now. Her hair she drew into a tight bun at the nape of her neck and she slipped her feet into worn, low-heeled shoes.

Gaps in the drawn curtains allowed weak morning sunshine to light the room. From outside came the sounds of the farm awakening to a new day. Another day of Isabelle trying her best to keep Farrell away from tormenting her brothers. Another day of wondering whether her father would live to see the sunset.

'Did you sleep well?' She propped her father up with more pillows and then helped him sip a spoonful of the foul-smelling medicine the doctor left yesterday.

'It no . . . longer . . . matters.' He coughed and moaned in pain from the action.

'Do you need the pot?'

He shook his head a fraction and closed his eyes. 'Sore . . . '

'Where?'

'Backside . . . '

'I know, Father, but it hurts you even more when I turn you onto your side.'

He sighed. 'So sore . . . '

Isabelle turned as the door opened and Bertie stuck his head into the room. 'Come in, Bertie and sit with Father while I go make breakfast.'

The small boy sidled into the room and sat in the chair by the bed. 'Is he better, Belle?'

'No, darling. Remember what I said?' She ruffled his hair, hating to see the sadness in his eyes.

He nodded and gazed at the man who hardly resembled the father they both knew.

'I'll call you when your breakfast is ready. Has Hughie gone out?'

Bertie nodded. 'He's milking.'

She patted his shoulder and left them. Downstairs there was no sign of Farrell and with a prayer of thanks sent heavenward, she began making their breakfast of porridge, fried ham and eggs and a large pot of tea.

Since the fight with Ethan, Farrell had taken to drinking heavily every night. Most times he went out to the public houses in Heptonstall and came back in the small hours of the night to stagger upstairs and into bed, or sometimes he would fall asleep at the kitchen table. Not once had he touched her, for which she was deeply thankful, but instead he'd started arguing with Hughie. He picked faults with everything Hughie said or did. So far she had managed to come between them and prevent Hughie from losing his temper and trying to lash out at Farrell. Isabelle shuddered to think what Farrell would do to him if he did. How long she could continue living like this she dreaded to think. Against all odds her father clung to life, delaying her and the boys flight to freedom.

The bubbling porridge drew her attention from where she stood at the table cutting slices of bread. Food was becoming short, as was her money. She lifted the pot from the range and sat it on the table. At the same time Hughie walked in from the scullery with a bucket of milk. He quickly looked around, she knew, for Farrell.

'He's still asleep.' She gave him a tight smile and ladled porridge into one bowl for him and another for her.

Nodding, Hughie placed the bucket on the floor and then pulled out a chair. 'One of the pullets died in the night, but the other eight are doing well. I think there's three cocks and the rest are hens in that last hatching.'

'Good.' She sat down and ate, surprised by how hungry she was. 'The cocks will do for the winter pot.' It occurred to her suddenly that they might not be here come next winter. Their father wouldn't last much longer and then she'd be with Ethan. She held onto that glimmer of hope.

Hughie ate in silence for a while before lifting his gaze to her. 'What's to happen, Belle?'

'I don't know, pet.'

Determination entered his eyes. 'I'll not stay here much longer if he doesn't stop bothering me.'

'But — '

'Nothing you say will sway me from leaving.'

Her stomach tightened at the idea of him leaving, roaming the streets looking for work, for shelter. 'Things will change once father . . . '

'You think so?' Hughie sniffed. 'I doubt it.' He lowered his spoon. 'Why hasn't Mr Harrington had him arrested for stealing?

286

Surely he hasn't forgotten last winter when he stole his wife's jewellery?'

Isabelle stiffened. The mere mention of Ethan filled her with a desperate longing. 'Mr ... Mr Harrington holds us in high regard ... I believe he wouldn't like to see us ... shamed by Farrell's actions.'

Hughie's eyes narrowed, and at that moment looked very much like their father. 'You and he ... I mean what Farrell accuses you of being ... with Harrington ... Is it true?'

She closed her eyes and sagged against the back of the chair. He asked the one thing she didn't want him to. Hatred for Farrell rose, blocking out all rational thought for a moment. His drunken, filthy shouts of her whoring herself was often a daily occurrence and most times she had tried to shield the boys from hearing him, but obviously she had failed.

'I want the truth, Belle. I'm not a child any more so don't treat me like one.'

She looked at him. It was true. He had grown into a young man and worked like a full-grown one. Still, no matter his age or maturity, she hated him thinking any less of her and being a mistress was nothing to be proud of. 'Very well, yes, I love Ethan Harrington and he loves me.'

Hughie nodded just once.

Isabelle ached inside for disappointing him. 'I'm sorry, Hughie.'

'So why hasn't Farrell been arrested then? Who cares about scandal as long as we're free from him?'

'Farrell has threatened to harm me if Ethan comes near. I . . . we can't take the risk of Farrell hurting one of us. While ever father lingers we are stuck here, but the minute the funeral has taken place, I'll plan for us to leave. I promise.'

'You better, because I'll not stay after the funeral.' He shifted uneasily in his chair, his expression haunted. 'With or without you, I'm leaving. I've had enough.'

'I know it's been difficult. Awful. I'm sorry.' She paused, hearing footsteps on the stairs.

Hughie sprang to his feet. 'I'm off to check the traps.' He was out the door before she could utter a word.

As silent as a shadow, Bertie sidled into the room and to her side. 'Da's asleep. Can I have something to eat now?'

Isabelle let out a long breath and relaxed her tensed shoulders. 'Of course, dearest. Sit down.'

'Belle?'

'Yes, pet?' She passed a full bowl of porridge over to him.

'Will Da die today?' His pale eyes seemed large in his small face.

'I don't know, sweetling.'

'Will you send me away if he does?'

She stopped wiping her hands on her apron and stared at him. 'No. Never. You are my brother and will live with me always or at least until you're grown and married.' She smiled at him, hoping to ease his worry. 'Don't ever think I don't want you.' She kissed the top of his head.

Bertie's chin wobbled. '*He* said that soon I'll be living in the boys' home.'

'He? Who said that?'

Bertie ducked his head to his chest as Farrell lumbered into the room, scratching his stomach and scowling. 'I want tea.'

Isabelle's stomach clenched. 'There's plenty in the pot.'

Farrell's hand lashed out and caught her a stinging blow to the side of her head. Isabelle stumbled, moaning in pain. Stars danced before her watering eyes. Calmly, as if nothing untoward had happened, Farrell pulled out a chair and slumped into it. Infuriated and totally astounded that he had dared hit her again, Isabelle picked up the carving knife and waved it in front of his face. 'Don't you ever touch me again! Do you hear?'

Farrell yawned and dismissed her with a flick of his fingers. 'Put that down and get me some tea.' He smirked at her outrage. 'Do you honestly think I would listen to Harrington?'

The knife wavered in her hand as she frowned. 'You aren't to touch me or Ethan will go to the authorities.'

Farrell scratched his crotch. 'Harrington will never know.'

Isabelle swayed. 'What do you mean?'

'As of this moment, you aren't to leave the house.' He glanced in Bertie's direction. 'Any of you.'

The colour drained from her face. 'Don't be ridiculous. It's not possible. The animals — '

'Once yer father has met his maker, and I've sold all the livestock, we'll be leaving here.' Farrell casually inspected his fingernails and then looked up at her. 'I hear America is called The Land of the Free.'

15

Hamish rubbed his finger around the rim of his glass, watching Ethan pace the drawing room floor. Fine lines etched the skin from Ethan's nose to mouth. A colourful bruise blackened one eye, but his split lip had healed. He'd lost weight, grey peppered his hair now, and he was edgy the whole time.

With a sigh of resignation, Hamish placed his whisky on the rosewood occasional table and stood. 'Right, my good fellow, time for a game of billiards. I have the need to thrash you once more.' He tried to joke, to bring Ethan out of his brooding mood, but he might as well have spoken to the potted orchids in the conservatory for all the response he got.

Ethan, frowning, his mind obviously elsewhere, kicked at a fallen log in the fire grate. 'I don't understand it, Hamish. No word from her in over a week.'

'I'm — '

'I know she told me to stay away but I assumed she would go to the wood whenever she could. She knew I'd be there waiting for her every day.' Ethan banged his fist on the mantelpiece. 'I should have told her to meet me there. What a fool I was to not arrange a time each day.'

'She — '

'What a fool I was to agree for her to stay there!' Ethan, his face ravaged by pain, flung his glass into the back of the fire and turned for the door as a footman rushed into the room at the sound of smashing glass. 'I cannot stand to wait a minute longer!'

Hamish swiftly strode to his side and grabbed his upper arm. 'Enough man! You must stop this obsession.'

Ethan stared at him as though he had two heads. 'Obsession? You call my love for Isabelle an obsession?'

'Yes I do and it is.' Hamish ran his fingers through his hair and, confident that Ethan would remain in the room, he dismissed the servant and went to the drinks tray. 'She has a husband. You have a wife. What do you plan to do? Run away together? What about your responsibilities here? What about your mother and Clarice?'

Ethan flopped down on a leather-backed wing chair that had been his father's favourite. 'I want her safe, Hamish. I can install her in one of my houses somewhere and know that she is away from him until we can sort out this mess.'

Hamish poured them both a brandy and walked over to hand Ethan his. 'I understand that, of course I do, but you charging over there, all hot-blooded will not help her. If he saw you, who knows what he'd do to her? You've said yourself, he's a madman.'

Ethan sipped the drink and a little colour washed his cheeks. 'I cannot bear the waiting. It tears at my guts like a knife.'

Sitting back on the sofa, Hamish gulped his drink and summoned his courage. 'What if . . . What if I was to pay a visit on her?'

★   ★   ★

Hughie smiled as Isabelle entered the bedroom. His gaze flickered to their father's face. 'Father's sleeping.'

'Good. I've put yours and Bertie's dinner on the tray and it's in your room. Go eat before it gets cold.'

'Where's Bertie?' Hughie stood and stretched his cramped muscles.

'Already eating.' Isabelle kissed Hughie's cheek. 'Go now.'

'Will you be all right?'

'Of course. Farrell is downstairs haggling with some fellow over the sheep price and after that he'll have his dinner. We shouldn't hear from him for at least an hour or two.'

Once Hughie had left the room, Isabelle checked on her father and then took the chair to the window. From her knitting basket she took out the small item she worked on whenever no one was with her. It gave her a secret thrill to work on the baby's first garment, although she was quick to hide it in the bottom of her basket should anyone disturb her. Aaron made a small noise, and she paused to peer across the room at him. Confident he didn't need her, she took up her needles again and let her mind drift.

For the last seven days, Farrell had been true to his word and kept them within the confines of the house. He had locked every door and pocketed the keys. He watched the boys do their chores, milking, fetching wood or water, collecting eggs, all the while carrying a horsewhip in his hand should they try to escape, and she could do nothing but observe and worry from the window of her locked prison.

Thankfully, he hadn't hit her again. She placed her hand over her stomach. She had to be careful and do nothing to antagonize Farrell into lashing out, not that he ever needed an excuse to cause her harm, but the child required her protection. Farrell refused to enter the sickroom and so it had become their sanctuary. At night, the boys quietly sat in the corner and played cards or dice. Sometimes, Hughie read from the husbandry book. Their father was barely conscious now and floated in and out of wakefulness.

Another noise came from the bed and her head lifted again. She replaced her knitting in the basket and went to soothe him.

'Belle?' His voice was only a whisper, his eyelids fluttered.

'Yes, Father, it's me. Rest now.' She sat on the edge of the bed and laid his hand on her lap and stroked it. His paper-thin skin had a sallow tinge.

'You . . . no longer . . . hate me?'

Her heart somersaulted and goosebumps rose on her skin. 'No, Father. I don't hate you any more.' Admitting it felt good, a release. She didn't know when she had stopped hating him. It had been a gradual thawing.

'Never meant . . . to hurt . . . you all.'

Tears pricked her eyes. 'It's all in the past now.'

'Love . . . you.'

A tear trickled down her cheek and dropped onto their joined hands. She bent over and kissed his forehead. 'And I love you.'

He looked at her for a moment, his pale eyes, the mirror of her own, glowed with a special message of love and then slowly his eyelids closed.

She went and fetched her chair and sat down beside the bed, holding his hand as he slept. Outside the window the shadows lengthened and twilight called the birds to roost. Isabelle snatched a few minutes of sleep between her father's twitching and the boys coming in to add wood to the fire and bring her cups of tea.

Close to midnight, she rose and lit the lamp. Her neck was stiff and, while rubbing it, she gazed down at her father. A chill covered her skin, for she knew the signs. She had witnessed both her mother's and sister's deaths. Each inhalation her father took had a long pause between. She began to count the seconds after each breath, holding her own breath until she was forced to gulp air. She couldn't keep the same rhythm he had.

The time stretched. Beyond the window the world was silent and black. Isabelle dithered, wondering if she should waken the boys, but their father was past conversation now, past saying goodbye. Blinking back tears, Isabelle sat on the edge of the chair and held his hand, watching his face closely.

After a few minutes, she realized he hadn't taken a breath. His chest didn't move. Slowly, she bent over and placed her ear over his heart. Nothing.

Isabelle rested back against the chair. It was finished. He had left her again.

★   ★   ★

Hamish lifted his hand and rapped three times on the front door of the farmhouse. After a moment he heard rustling, cursing, a key in the lock and the bolt sliding back. The door opened and the man he guessed to be Isabelle's husband peered at him with bleary eyes.

'Aye? What yer want?' Farrell barked. 'Yer the undertaker?'

Undertaker? Hamish stiffened at the insult. 'No. I'm here to speak with Isabelle Farrell.'

The other man's small eyes narrowed and his expression changed to one of wariness. 'Oh aye, what yer want with her?'

Hamish thought quickly, worried he wouldn't be able to get past this bull-headed husband. If they were expecting an undertaker then someone had died. 'It . . . It is about the funeral service. Does . . . does she wish for flowers? Lilies perhaps? And hymns?'

Farrell stepped back, blinking and shaking his head. 'Christ, how am I ter know? I don't care either. I ain't paying for it, I've told her. He can be buried in a pauper's grave

297

as far as I'm concerned! He's her father, let her deal with it.'

'I understand. Perhaps I could speak with Mrs Farrell?'

'Well, yer can't stay long as she's busy cooking me dinner.' Farrell opened the door wider and allowed him over the threshold. 'Wait 'ere.'

As Farrell disappeared down the far end and closed the door, Hamish glanced around the dim hallway. He smelt damp. His quick thinking had got him inside, but now the reality sank in. Isabelle's father had died and she'd be in mourning. Would she want to see him? She'd be expecting someone from the church.

The door opened from the kitchen and Isabelle stepped through. Her eyes widened when she saw him. Not wanting her to withdraw, Hamish smiled and hoped his eyes told her he came as her friend. 'Mrs Farrell. My sympathies to you and your family.'

She faltered, her pale eyes showing her uncertainty, and then she gathered herself and came towards him. 'Thank you, Mr MacGregor.'

Hamish let go of a pent-up breath and held out his hand, was pleased when she took it. 'Shall we discuss your needs outside? The day is not too cold and the wind has dropped.'

'Very well.' She nodded and took down a shawl hanging from a hook on the back of the door. It alarmed Hamish how thin she was and the much-worn black garments of mourning did nothing to give her colour. Indeed, they only added to her wan appearance. Dark shadows bruised under her eyes.

In silence, they walked to the front gate. The carriage stood in the drive and Brown inclined his head to Isabelle. Hamish stopped and looked out over the road and into the distance. Flat fields spread as far as he could see. He was very aware of her standing beside him. He realized he towered over her and fought the instinct to crouch so she wouldn't be intimidated. Suddenly, he recalled their last conversation and knew she would never feel that way with him. She had cut him down with words and a simple, unforgiving glare. An unfamiliar thud changed the rhythm of his heartbeat. He never wanted her to look at him that way again. Shame filled him at the thought. What did it matter how she looked at him? She would never be his.

'Ethan sent you, didn't he?' Her voice was soft, delicate, unlike the first time they met.

'I offered to call on you. To save Ethan from himself. His temper would rule him the moment he saw your husband.'

'You speak the truth and, to my shame, I cannot cope with more . . . upheaval at the moment even though my desire to see Ethan is very strong. My brothers need me, especially since Farrell . . . ' She gave a little shake of her head as if to clear her mind. 'I mustn't bore you with such things.'

'You don't bore me in the least.' He smiled. 'Ethan worries and, after his last confrontation with your husband, I felt it best that he remains at Bracken Hall. He does not know about your father, and I know he would want me to help you in any way I can.'

She blinked back tears and stared straight ahead. 'Farrell refuses to give me any money. I don't even know if he has money, though he did sell all the sheep yesterday, but they haven't been taken yet. I'm guessing he'd likely receive the money when they are collected.'

Hamish nodded and remained silent, instinctively knowing she needed to talk, to think things through aloud.

Isabelle sighed, a long sad sigh that pulled at Hamish's heart. 'I fear my father will lie in an unmarked pauper's grave. As bad as Mrs Peacock's establishment was, she allowed the dead a cross with their name on it. I would like for Father to lie next to Mother and Sally.'

He had no idea who Mrs Peacock was or anything about her establishment, but the depth of her unhappiness made him want to hold her to him and promise her the world, anything she desired just to take away the pain from her eyes. Instead, he lightly touched her hand where it rested on top of the gate. 'I will help you.'

She lifted her gaze to him and frowned. 'Farrell will never allow Ethan to — '

'No, you misunderstand me.' He stared into her eyes, captivated by the shadow of her soul he saw there. 'I, me, alone will help you bury your father.'

'*You?*'

He nodded, eager to please her, to have her need and depend on him like she needed and depended on Ethan.

'But you don't approve of me.'

'Let me help you, I beg you.' Hamish searched his coat pockets and brought out a small leather pouch. He gave it to her. 'I believe there are three or four guineas in there. Perhaps more. Use them.'

Isabelle gasped, her eyes widened. 'But I cannot repay you.'

'I do not need repaying.' He took her hand, kissed it and was rewarded by the relief in her eyes, the tender smile of thanks on her lips. 'I will call again. Soon.'

Isabelle folded her arms on the table and laid her head on them. The boys were upstairs changing out of their wet clothes. She knew she should do the same, but didn't have the energy to mount the stairs. Tiredness weighed down her limbs. Her stomach growled, forcing her to think of the child she carried and, with the pace of a snail she rose and set about making a pot of tea and slicing the bread. Outside the rain continued to batter against the windows and she shuddered to think what foul mood Farrell would be in when he came inside from putting the horse away.

At least they had buried her father without turmoil. Farrell's constant vigil over them failed to affect her today. Whether he guarded them like a gaoler or not wasn't the issue as she watched the coffin being lowered into the ground. In church, she prayed for her departed family but also prayed harder for her freedom. Mr MacGregor's money had bought a decent funeral and, due to her prudence, a few shillings left over now jingled in her skirt pocket. After several quarrels, Farrell allowed and believed the funeral bill to be sent to Ethan. It had given her some comfort to see Mr MacGregor standing outside the church today. Farrell hadn't thought anything by it, still presuming he was a church warden, but to her, it had been a sign that she wasn't alone in the world.

The door banged open and she closed her eyes. Farrell never did anything quietly. 'I hope yer've done enough for an extra guest?' Farrell laughed.

Her eyes snapped open, as did her mouth. Farrell grinned at her and next to him, looking pleased with himself, stood Neville Peacock. 'W-What is *he* doing here?'

Farrell pulled out a chair and flopped down onto it, indicating to Neville to do the same. 'He's staying a while.'

A wave of dizziness washed over her and she groped for a chair. 'You aren't serious.'

'Indeed I am, Wife.'

'I don't understand.' She stared from one to the other. 'You and he . . . '

'Are now friends.' Farrell took a piece of bread and applied a liberal spread of pickled onions to it. 'He's keepin' an eye on yer while I'm away.'

'Away?' She blinked rapidly. Her heart pounded. 'Away where?'

'We need a bit more capital for America.' He bit into the bread and chewed. 'The sale of the animals won't bring in enough funds. So, I need to try me hand at a few things.'

'You're going to steal?'

He gulped down the last of his bread and stood. 'Steal, poach, which ever takes me fancy.' Farrell shrugged, not caring. 'Peacock here will keep an eye on yer while I'm gone.' He went into the scullery and the larder.

The boys entered the kitchen and Hughie checked his step as he realized who sat at the table. 'Belle? What's *he* doing here?' Hughie came straight to her side and Bertie followed close behind.

Isabelle felt sick, her stomach churned. 'He's suddenly become Farrell's friend,' she sneered. 'He's here to watch us while Farrell goes away.'

Farrell strode in, stuffing a small sack with the last of her ham and a small tart. 'I'll be gone about three days.' He paused and glared at the boys. 'Peacock knows what's what. He'll not put up with yer nonsense. I've told him to crack yer skulls if yer try any funny business and if he lets you escape then I'll crack *his* skull!'

Bertie huddled by Isabelle's chair and his frightened face sent her into a fury. She jerked up from her chair and flew around the table to slap Farrell's surprised face before she realized she'd done it.

'Bitch!' He went to hit her but she stepped back quickly, bumping into Neville, who'd stood and now staggered, but kept both himself and her upright.

As Farrell advanced, Neville raised his hand. 'No. Don't mark her any more. If Harrington comes he'll think I've done it and I ain't' takin' your beating.'

Farrell stopped a foot from them. His breath came in short puffs. 'She needs puttin' in her place!'

'Aye, well, you can leave that to me. I'll enjoy it.' Neville grinned and pushed Isabelle back towards the range on the other side of the table.

Grabbing his coat off the hook on the back door, Farrell glared at her and then lunged for Bertie. The boy squealed.

'Get your hands off him!' Hughie ran for Farrell, but the older man raised his fist.

'Take one more step and I'll squash his nose over his face.'

Isabelle felt that her heart would surely stop. 'Let him go, Farrell, please. I'm begging you.'

Farrell grinned. 'I don't think so. He's my insurance, yer see. I know yer'll not be tempted to run if yer know I have him.'

'I promise I won't run. I *promise*.' She clasped her hands together, fighting to stay calm. 'He's only a little boy. You don't need him.'

'Take me instead,' Hughie demanded, glaring at him. 'I can live rough better than he can.'

Farrell laughed and plucked Bertie's coat from a hook. 'Yer think I'm stupid? I know yer'd open yer mouth the first chance yer got. No, this little chap suits me fine.' He gave him his coat as though they were going on a Sunday afternoon picnic.

'*Please*, don't take him,' Isabelle cried, gripping the chair, wanting to throw it at her husband's head. 'Let him go! Take me if you must.'

Bertie struggled against Farrell's grip and received a clout around the ear for his troubles. Hughie reached out to snatch Bertie back and in a split second, Farrell kicked him in the groin. Gasping, Hughie buckled to the floor. Isabelle ran to his side as he lay groaning.

Farrell glared at them in triumph. 'Yer think yer've got it hard here, just yer wait until we get ter America. Yer life won't be worth livin'.' With that he pushed a sobbing Bertie out of the kitchen and slammed the door.

Neville, hesitant and wary, inched forward and helped Hughie up and onto a chair.

Isabelle crumpled onto a footstool by the door. 'I'll make tea,' Neville offered and went to the range and placed the black kettle on the hob plate.

For a short time, the only sound in the room was of Hughie sucking in gulps of air and the muted noise of the fire shifting. Stunned beyond belief, Isabelle sat as still as a statue and let her mind swarm with the knowledge that Farrell had disappeared to God knows where with her little brother. She rocked herself in agony.

'Why did you marry him, Belle?'

Neville's question brought her head up to stare at him. Hatred and despair filled her. 'To get away from you!'

'And you think I would have treated you worse than he does?'

'I didn't know that at the time, did I?' She wrapped her arms tightly around her middle to stop herself from scratching his eyes out. 'I was the biggest fool. I trusted your she-devil of a mother, but I should have known better that she wouldn't do anything in kindness regarding me.'

He looked away. 'She was jealous.'

'Of me?' Isabelle laughed without humour. 'What could she be jealous of?'

'How I felt about you.' A flush crept up his neck. He scored into the table surface with his fingernail. 'Everything would have been so different if only you hadn't rejected me.'

Isabelle closed her eyes and a single tear ran down her cheek. No words could alter the situation or undo the hurt. After a moment, she sniffed and straightened. Wallowing wouldn't do her any good either. 'I'm going out, Hughie. I won't be long.'

'No, Belle.' Neville barred her way. 'I can't let you go.'

Her lip curled back in a snarl. He easily caught her hands as they came up to rip his face. They struggled for a moment, but she soon gave up, knowing she couldn't risk hurting the baby. Hughie had tried to rise, but lost all remaining colour with the movement and with a grunt collapsed back down on the chair. Isabelle flung off Neville's restraint and stalked back to the table. She covered Hughie's bent head with her hand. 'It's all right. Rest.'

Neville, watching her out the corner of his eye, poured cups of tea, adding plenty of sugar to each. He pushed two over to their side of the table.

Isabelle peered at him over the rim of her cup. 'How did all this come about between you and Farrell?'

'I saw you today, outside the church. Farrell saw me and when you were talking to the vicar, he called me over. We spoke and he asked me to come to the farm and watch over you all.'

'A chance too good for you to pass up?' she scoffed.

He shrugged one shoulder. 'He said that if I could gather the money I could go with you to America.'

She locked her gaze with his. 'I am not going to America. Do you understand? I am leaving here with Ethan Harrington and neither you nor Farrell will stop me.'

'He told me he hates Harrington more than any person alive.' Neville leant over the table. 'He'll *kill* you if go to that man.'

Isabelle's gaze didn't waver. 'And I will kill *him* if he tries to stop me.'

16

Ethan reined in Copper at the edge of the Meadow Farm's orchard. A couple of goats stared at him before returning to cropping the weeds by the wall. A sow rooted in the undergrowth by the back of the sheds, but other than that all was still.

He frowned. It was early, not long after dawn, and this was one of the busiest hours on a farm. Obviously, someone was up and about to have let the goats and sow out, but why was it so quiet? A tingle of fear held him still in the saddle. Copper snorted in the chill air, uneasy with Ethan's tense body.

With a soft click of his tongue, Ethan guided Copper around the orchard and to the back of the yard. Apprehension pushed Ethan on and into the yard itself, despite Isabelle's request to not return. But something made him ride here this morning. Instinct told him to. He stood in the stirrups and gazed over the fields. Empty. No sheep or cattle had been brought in close for the coming winter. Christmas was only a week away.

Scanning the yard, he noticed the general state of neglect. The quiet unnerved him. He contemplated what to do. Barging into the house could set Farrell off. He jumped as two chickens unexpectedly flapped their feathers as they emerged from one of the sheds. Peering at the kitchen window, he tried to make out movement within, but the room was too dark.

Slowly, he dismounted and, with Copper trailing behind him, he checked inside each shed door. Surely, someone should be milking by now? Dark, silent emptiness was all he could ascertain.

Ethan glanced at the house. A flash of movement at the window was so brief he doubted he actually saw it. Then, the back door opened and his heart soared as Isabelle ran across the yard and hurled herself into his arms.

'Hold me!' Her sobs shook her body and she clung to him, grabbing fistfuls of his jacket. She buried her head into his chest.

'Hush, my love. I'm here.' He smoothed her hair and noticed it was lank and tangled. He tried to pull back to see her properly. 'Isabelle . . .'

'It's been awful.' She was crying so hard he could barely understand her.

'My love.' Forcing her from him, he gasped as he searched her gaunt face. She was terribly thin and fragile-looking. Anger so

311

swift and furious ignited, blinding him to all sense and reason. 'That bastard, I'll kill him.'

'No!' She hung onto his arm as he marched towards the house. 'He's not here.'

Ethan savagely pulled free of her hold. 'Don't lie to me! Don't protect the coward. He'll not live to see another day.'

'He's gone.' Isabelle sank to her knees on the ground. What little colour she had, drained from her face leaving her ghost-like. 'He took Bertie.'

'Bertie?'

'My youngest brother, remember?'

Ethan's emotions swung from rage to tenderness. She looked like a broken flower flattened by a wild storm. Her black skirts billowed around her, the fading bruise on her cheek ugly against the paleness of her face. The light had vanished from her pale blue eyes taking with it her strength, her spirit, her soul. Her eyes had always told him her feelings and as he stared at her he knew she couldn't cope with much more.

In one stride Ethan was beside her, kneeling before her on the dirt and stones. He folded her into his arms and kissed the top of her head. 'Oh, my darling. Let me take you away from here. We'll go anywhere you want.'

'I can go nowhere until Bertie comes back.'

'Tell me everything.' He listened as she

spoke of Farrell's cruelty, the hardship of watching her father die, the house imprisonment, the selling of the animals to finance Farrell's plans to sail to America, the lack of food and finally of his departure two days ago with Bertie as his hostage. With every sentence, Ethan became more alarmed. He cursed himself for ever leaving her. Farrell was a madman and needed locking up. How she had suffered! 'I'm so sorry you have endured this.'

'I had no choice but to.' She kissed him and he held her tight. 'I would bear anything for you.'

He stood and drew her up and against him. He kissed her with a deep longing that he could no longer control. Her lips parted eagerly, wanting him, accepting him. She was so soft, so passionate. His tongue explored her mouth, familiarizing his mind to her delights once more.

Raising his head, he smiled down at her. 'I love you and we will never be apart again.' She nestled into his shoulder and sighed. Ethan rubbed her back. Her body fit into his naturally, as though they were made from the same mould. When he thought of Farrell touching her, bile rose in his throat. He imagined knocking the man's teeth down his throat and grunted with satisfaction at the idea.

'But that is not all I have to tell you.' Her voice brought him back from his tortured thoughts.

'There's more?'

She nodded and traced her finger across his bottom lip, a faint smile played on her mouth. 'I am with child. Your child.'

The news stunned him. It was the last thing he expected her to say. Ethan rocked back on his heels, staring at her in disbelief.

Her eyes narrowed and her chin rose. 'You are not pleased.'

'No. Yes.' He blinked to clear his befuddled mind. 'I didn't anticipate such an announcement.'

Her expression hardened. 'You are angry.' She stepped back out of the circle of his arms.

'Isabelle.' He took her hands in his and kissed each one in turn. 'I am happy.' The stiffness of her stance told him she didn't believe a word. He brought her back close to him and kissed her eyes, her nose and her mouth. 'I'm shocked, and the timing isn't ideal . . . ' A wry grin lifted one corner of his mouth. 'But I'm delighted you carry my child.'

'Really?'

'Absolutely.' His grin widened and sucked in a deep breath. 'This changes everything.'

'Ethan — '

'No, you must listen.' His hands gripped her shoulders tight. 'I'll not be discouraged in this. You are to gather your things and leave here today.'

'I cannot!' She shook her head and a desperate look came into her eyes. 'Farrell has Bertie. If he returns and sees I'm not here . . . Well, I dread to think what he'd do to my brother.'

Frustration fired Ethan's anger. 'You believe I will let you stay here and await that madman's return?'

'We've no choice.'

'Farrell won't harm Bertie. He'll use him as a tool.'

'You have no notion of what Farrell is like. *You* haven't lived with him!' She flung herself away from him, her voice rising. 'I won't forsake Bertie. He's a little boy, who is terrified and alone with Farrell. I cannot bear to think how he's been treated these last two days. It's my fault he's out there!'

Abruptly, Neville Peacock strode from the house. 'What the hell is going on? How did you get out, Belle?'

She shrugged. 'I stole the keys while you were sleeping.'

Ethan frowned. 'Who the hell is this?'

'He's Neville Peacock, Farrell's new

315

helper.' Isabelle stepped in front of Ethan and faced Neville. 'Go back inside. Mr Harrington is just leaving.'

'I am not!' Ethan pulled Isabelle out of the way with one hand and with the other he punched Neville on the jaw, knocking the man to the ground.

'No, Ethan!' Isabelle ran in front of Ethan again. 'No more fighting. I've suffered enough of it!'

He grabbed her wrist and headed for the house. 'You're leaving here. Now.'

'Ethan, no. I cannot.'

He swung her around to face him. 'I won't let you stay another moment.'

'And I won't go!' Her face crumpled. 'I need your help not your caveman antics.'

'You expect me to leave you here?' he shouted, aggravated at the helplessness he felt. 'Do you want me to ride away?'

'Please understand I can't be with you until Bertie is safe.'

'Then we'll go to the authorities immediately. They can search for him.'

Her posture sagged. 'We have no idea where they've gone. Farrell could be anywhere.'

'The waiting is . . . '

She put her fingers to his mouth, silencing him. 'I know, my love, I know. But there is nothing for it. I must wait until Bertie has returned and then somehow I'll send word or we'll escape and come to you.'

'It's dangerous. You're carrying my child.'

'She's what?' Neville had scrambled to his feet and now stared at her. 'It's not true?'

'It is.'

A look of disgust flashed across his face. 'Farrell doesn't know, does he?'

She shook her head.

'Farrell's wife is having a Harrington brat.' Neville laughed. The sound echoed around the still yard, mocking them.

★ ★ ★

Isabelle glanced at Hughie and Neville as she ate the tasty stew, thick with meat and vegetables. She was so hungry she had to control the urge to stuff herself in the shortest time possible. The food hamper from Bracken Hall arrived an hour ago and despite the delicacies that filled the basket, she had demanded that they would eat the stew first and leave the lighter, fancier food for later. She also insisted that both Neville and Hughie bathe before dinner and while they did so, she unloaded the appetizing goods and found, beneath a tray of apricot tarts, a small black velvet bag. Gold coins jingled inside.

'Can I have more bread, Belle?' Hughie asked.

Isabelle passed him the wooden cutting board on which sat the half loaf of bread and a knife. Against her thigh she felt the weight of the little bag every time she moved. She looked at Neville. 'So, you are keen to go to America with Farrell?'

He lifted his head, his spoon poised mid air. 'Aye.'

'And what does your mother think of this? I can hardly see her agreeing to her only child going abroad.'

'It's nowt to do with her.' Neville placed his spoon back in his bowl. 'Any road, I might not yet go.'

Isabelle raised her eyebrows. 'Oh?'

'Well, if you ain't going, there's not much point, is there?'

'You were only going because of me?'

'Aye.' He lowered his head and ate some more.

'Why?' She stared at him, trying to understand his thinking. 'If, for some reason, I did go I'd still be married to Farrell. He wouldn't let you touch me.'

'I could look out for you and make sure he didn't beat you all the time.'

Stunned, she leant back in her chair. 'Neville, *you* attacked me, hit me. There is no difference between you and Farrell.'

A red flush stained his cheeks. 'He doesn't care for you, but I do. I didn't mean to do what I did in the shed. Only, you pushed me beyond madness and I lost control.'

'You don't care for me! You want to own me.'

Neville glared at her. 'That's a lie. In America I will work hard to give you a decent life, better than the one you have here, better than the one Farrell can give you.'

'And what of Farrell?' She spoke low, menacing, for behind Neville, Farrell had just opened the scullery door and was quietly listening with interest. 'Where does he fit into your plans?'

'I'll make sure he has an accident. Then you'd be free of him. You'd like that wouldn't you?' Neville grinned.

With a roar of anger, Farrell whipped a rope around Neville's throat and pulled tight, making his eyes bulge as he flayed at the restraint. Isabelle jumped back from the table and Hughie ran around to her. She grabbed his hand and looked beyond the two struggling men for a sign of Bertie, but the scullery was empty.

Neville was choking, turning purple, and

fell backwards off his chair as Farrell kept the noose taut and dragged him across the kitchen floor. Farrell turned his back, straining to keep his wiggling eel from kicking out at him. In a flash, Isabelle lunged for the door with Hughie right behind her. In the darkness of the yard she bolted, not heeding that she wore only house slippers and no shawl. 'Bertie! Bertie!'

Hughie searched the shadows. 'Bertie!'

They heard a faint whimper from the first shed and then a crashing sound. Isabelle, closest to the building, ran inside and fell over something, landing on her knees. Bertie's whimpering had her scrambling back to him. Hughie lifted him up. The boy was tied and gagged. 'It's all right now. I've got you.'

'Untie him, hurry.' Isabelle yanked at the knotted handkerchief about his mouth and when freed, Bertie cried and talked at the same time.

'His feet are free, but I can't untie his hands.' Hughie puffed and swore at the tangled rope cutting into Bertie's slim wrists.

'Leave it, he can still run.' Isabelle rushed to the door. The light from the kitchen gave them a good view of the scene through the window. Neville and Farrell fought and crashed against the kitchen table.

'I'll carry Bertie on my back, Belle. We'll be

faster.' Hughie panted beside her.

'Quickly, we must make it into the woods before they stop fighting.'

They slipped out the door and along the wall, around the corner and into the orchard. The shadows of the night hid them periodically as they ran between the trees. A full moon slid out from a lone cloud and lit the countryside up like its own personal lamp.

On reaching the orchard's far boundary wall, Isabelle paused for breath. Before them stretched the flat, open fields. They'd have to cross them and take the chance of being seen before they could arrive at the wood and safety.

'Will we go to Bracken Hall, Belle?' Hughie gasped, placing Bertie on his feet for a moment.

'Farrell will think we've gone there. He may be stupid enough to go there and create havoc.' She sucked in a breath. 'We'll hide in the woods, circle around Bracken Hall and make for Hebden Bridge. We can hide in town for the rest of the night and then go on to Halifax.'

'Belle, look!' Bertie cried, pointing back to the farm.

She stared at the cluster of buildings. Above the sheds an orange glow haloed the house's roof. 'What is it?'

The sound of a muffled explosion filled the air and then another, louder this time. Bertie huddled against Isabelle and she wrapped her arms around him. The orange glow grew brighter. More noise came - crackling and splintering.

'It's a fire, Belle.' Hughie whispered. 'The house is on fire.'

Goosebumps rose on her skin. She was torn whether to return to the house or flee.

'We can't go back. You know we can't.' Hughie touched her arm. 'Please, Belle, we must go. Don't think about them.'

She hesitated. 'They . . . they might be trapped inside.'

'Good. They both deserve whatever is coming to them.' He gently pushed her on. 'Knowing Farrell, he's likely to have escaped.' Hughie snorted. 'He's got the devil's own luck.'

They helped each other over the wall and, after catching their breath, they made a run for it across the fallow fields. Behind them, the crack and whoosh of a hungry fire sent golden red sparks up to the silver moon.

★   ★   ★

Hamish kicked at a smouldering piece of wood and frowned back at where Ethan stood talking to the police from Hebden Bridge. His friend looked as old as a man of ninety. The stoop of his shoulders, the haggard expression on his face, the look of death in his eyes showed his suffering. For two hours they had searched the farm for Isabelle while futile buckets of water were thrown on the parts of the house that still burned. The thought of Isabelle, beautiful and spirited, burnt beyond recognition turned his stomach and left a foul taste in his mouth. He hated listening to Ethan's distraught moans and the policeman's drone of possible causes of the fire.

A piece of wall from the upper floor crashed into the ruins of the house, sending a billowing plume of ash and smoke into the early dawn sky. Hamish sighed and suddenly thought of Australia. He missed the harsh sounds of the native birds waking him in the morning, the heat, the tropical storms in the evenings, the strange wildlife and the idea that each day he got up and achieved something on the station he and his brother now called home. He wondered if the farming equipment John wanted him to buy in London and send back to Australia had actually arrived yet. He knew Rachel would adore the trunk he'd filled with bolts of muslin and cotton, the books, fans, gloves, the grey kidskin boots and stationery. Right now he wished more than anything to be there with them . . .

'Hamish!' Ethan's call jolted him back to the ugly present.

'What is it?'

Ethan pointed to two other policemen emerging from the blackened remains of what was once the kitchen. They carried a stretcher on which lay a body covered with a blanket.

Hamish's gut churned but he had the presence of mind to halt Ethan's headlong rush to see the body. 'Steady, my friend.' He gripped Ethan's shoulders so hard he could feel his bones. 'Let me.' Ethan turned away and retched into the bushes beside the drive. Clearing his throat, Hamish stepped up to the stretcher and nodded to the policeman in charge. Steeling himself, Hamish held his breath as the policeman gently folded back the blanket. The smell of charred flesh seared his nostrils. The victim's face was only burnt on one side, leaving the left side unmarked. A man. A man with dark hair. Not Isabelle. Not Isabelle.

Hamish staggered back, his hand over his mouth. Ethan was beside him in seconds, his eyes begging to be told the truth but not wanting to hear it. Shaking his head, Hamish gulped. 'It's not her . . . A man.'

Ethan coughed and spluttered, bending over to draw air into his lungs. 'I cannot bear it . . .'

'She might not even be in there.' He drew Ethan over to the carriage. 'Let us return to Bracken Hall. The constable can speak with you when they have confirmed she isn't in there.'

'If she isn't, then where is she?'

'We'll find her. Don't worry.'

Ethan's eyes were dark pools of wretchedness. 'She is carrying my child, Hamish, and I don't know where she is or if she's safe.'

The news hit him like a sledgehammer, Hamish swallowed the immediate denial that sprang to his lips and for the first time felt a spark of hatred towards his oldest friend. He wanted to smash his fist into Ethan's fine straight nose for making Isabelle with child. He turned away, sickened and terribly lonely.

17

Isabelle opened her eyes and fought the wave of nausea. Every muscle ached from the previous midnight flight. She carefully turned her head hoping not to disturb her upset stomach and, in the filtered dawn light, gazed at the sleeping forms of her brothers.

Against the odds they had made it into Hebden Bridge and found a landlord, who graciously let them in and gave them a room. Before sleep claimed them Bertie had spoken a little about his days with Farrell. He told her and Hughie that Farrell insisted they walk everywhere. They slept rough in barns and ditches and had little to eat. Bertie would hide in the gardens of big houses as Farrell sneaked in and robbed them. Then, when Farrell had enough booty, they took the train to Manchester where he sold it all. Bertie's information had been sparse, for Farrell wouldn't have told him any secrets, but it was enough for her to imagine their days. Soon after, Bertie fell asleep and didn't stir for the rest of the night while she tossed and turned.

Isabelle slowly sat up and breathed in deeply. The fire loomed large on her thoughts and she wondered what had happened to Farrell and Neville. If they had survived, they'd be looking for her and, when Ethan knew about the fire, he'd be worried too. Sitting on the edge of the bed, she pushed her feet into her torn slippers. Hughie shifted in the bed, then opened his eyes. 'Belle?' he whispered, rubbing a hand over his face.

'It's morning, but go back to sleep if you want.'

He shook his head and sat up, careful not to disturb Bertie who slept between them. 'Shall I go buy us some breakfast?'

'Yes.' From her skirt pocket she took out the little bag of coins. 'Take this and buy enough to last all day. I'm not sure what is to happen.'

'We're not going back to the farm are we?'

'No. Our time there has finished.' She sighed, feeling numb at the admission.

Hughie pulled on his boots. 'We are to go to Bracken Hall?'

'There is no other choice. We have nothing but the clothes we stand in.'

'Mr Harrington will help us, Belle, you know he will.'

She nodded and moved to the small window. In the lane below, people hurried to work, well wrapped up against the chill of the morning. 'It was never meant to be this way . . . ' she whispered.

Hughie joined her and placed his arm around her shoulders. He'd grown so much in the last year that he stood a few inches taller than her now. 'Mr Harrington will take care of us. He cares for you and you're having his child, I think. Our lives will be much better off so don't worry.'

'You don't understand. Until I can divorce Farrell I will be his wife whether we live with him or not. He has rights . . . He could take me away and Ethan could do nothing about it.'

'Mr Harrington won't let him anywhere near you.'

'Ethan cannot watch over us all the time.'

'Perhaps Farrell will run off now, to America, without us?'

'I'd like to think so.' She straightened and forced a smile to banish the gloom.

Hughie paused by the door. 'I think the worst is behind us, Belle. We'll go see Mr Harrington and let him deal with Farrell now. You've done enough.'

Isabelle stared after him as he quietly left the room. Hughie had become so sensible and mature beyond his years. She had done that to him. He shared the burdens of her unwise decisions. They were worse off than when they left the workhouse for now they

328

had Bertie to feed and take care of, plus the baby when it came.

She leant against the window and blindly gazed out at the awakening town. A cart rumbled by, a woman swept her doorstep, a dog peed against the lamp-post and slowly the sun rose above the rooftops. She shivered. The room was cold, but not nearly as cold as her heart. Ethan loved her, she had no doubt of that, but they were both trapped in loveless marriages. He couldn't run away with her and leave behind his responsibilities, which meant she had to stay close by, maybe live in a house he provided. She would spend her days waiting for him to call. Years would be eaten up with snatched visits and receiving letters as to why he couldn't make it on a certain day for whatever reason. Hughie and Bertie would be ridiculed and she'd be called a mistress or worse, a whore. Her child would grow up as 'Harrington's bastard'.

She stuffed her knuckles into her mouth to stifle a moan of anguish. Her mother and Sally came to mind and her pain grew. They would be devastated by her conduct. Blinking back tears, Isabelle hugged herself, knowing that she had another choice, a choice of leaving here and starting anew somewhere far away. With her brothers she could start again, pretend to be widowed or abandoned. No one would know their past and the child would be simply Farrell's . . .

The idea grew, took on a life of its own. They could go to one of the cities: York, Liverpool or Manchester. She could work for months yet and Hughie, being a strong young lad, would soon find a job. The prospect of beginning anew seemed wonderful and filled her with optimism. Since she couldn't be with Ethan, and it was very likely she wouldn't be for years, then she would have to make her own way.

The door opened and Hughie entered carrying paper-wrapped parcels. 'I bought bread, cheese and ham. I got them to slice the ham for us.'

Her mouth watered as the smell of fresh, warm bread filled the room. 'Hughie, I was thinking . . . '

'Oh aye?' He wasn't really listening and instead concentrated on unwrapping the food.

'I've been considering our situation. We should leave here and go to one of the cities. We can get rooms and work aplenty I'm sure.'

He looked at her as though she spoke a foreign tongue. 'Go to the city? Why? Mr Harrington will — '

'Mr Harrington is married, as am I. Nothing can change that. He believes that we both can achieve divorces, but I don't, at least not for years and after spending a lot of money.'

'Well, if you have to wait, then wait. It'll be worth it, won't it? I don't see how going to a city to live will help.'

Isabelle ate a piece of ham. 'We'll be free of Farrell. We'll have a life of our own without the disgrace of everyone around here pointing their fingers at us or calling us names. I don't want my child to be called a bastard, to be shunned.'

'Like me.'

Shocked, Isabelle and Hughie spun around to face Bertie, who rubbed sleep from his eyes and climbed from the bed. He looked at them so innocently it broke her heart.

'I've been called a bastard lots of times. In my mother's village I was called The Little Bastard.' He shrugged and eyed the bread.

Hughie automatically tore some off and gave it to him. 'No one will be calling you that while I'm around.'

Isabelle turned away. Her heart felt like someone was squeezing it with a vice. She loved Ethan, *adored* him, but the thought of spending years being spurned by the locals, her child being rejected by society, ripped at her soul. She'd already experienced a taste of it in the market with Marge Wilmot and she knew she couldn't put up with it indefinitely.

'Belle?' Hughie's voice was soft with sympathy. 'What are we to do then?'

Breathing in deeply, she raised her chin. 'We're to leave here and go to Manchester.'

'What about Mr Harrington?'

'I'll go and see him now. You stay here. I'll be back as soon as I can.' The thought of arriving at Bracken Hall, dirty and destitute, filled her with shame. What would Ethan's family think of her turning up like that? His mother would never accept her and wouldn't forgive Ethan for bringing such humiliation to the family name. A jug of water and a porcelain basin stood on a small table by the window and she quickly washed her face and tied her hair. She had no brush or even a hat to hide her hair under. Her black skirts and bodice were crumpled but there was nothing she could do about that.

At the door, Hughie and Bertie came to kiss her cheek and she left them to descend the inn's narrow staircase. Outside in the lane, the sun disappeared behind a sheet of grey clouds. She faltered then at the prospect of being with Ethan, of telling him she was to go away. He would argue, demand she stay, and, for a moment, she wondered if she was strong enough to resist him.

★ ★ ★

The cab bounded around the curve of the tree-lined drive and Bracken Hall loomed into view. The sun crept out from behind a cloud and shone its glory upon the grey stone building, lightening it, softening it. Isabelle soaked in the beauty of the house. Ethan's home. His birthright, his inheritance. The extensive gardens, mainly dormant in readiness for winter's snow, flowed around the house and out of sight like a woman's patterned skirt. *If things had been different, one day my child would have owned all this* . . . She pushed the thought away. It did no good to dream of the unattainable. The baby she carried would never be a legal Harrington, but for ever a Farrell, at least in name.

As the cab slowed, a groom came running to open the door for her. His face showed no expression and he assisted her down the step as though she was a queen. Isabelle fought the urge to ask him whether Ethan was about and instead walked up the wide shallow steps to the front door. She pulled the brass ring and heard the bell clank inside. After what seemed minutes but was really only seconds the door opened and the butler inquired after her business with a disapproving sniff.

'I wish to see Mr Harrington.'

'Mr Harrington?' He clearly didn't believe someone dressed as she was would be of any interest to his master. 'I do believe Mr Harrington is out. I suggest you return another day or leave a note?'

'No, thank you. I will wait.'

'I do not think that is necessary. Mr Harrington — '

Isabelle lifted her chin and stared at the man. 'I *said* I will wait.'

His gaze raked over her in the most insulting way. 'And your name?'

'Isabelle Farrell.'

The butler's eyes widened and he straightened his already stiff back. 'Farrell of Meadow Farm?'

She nodded.

The door was instantly pulled wider and the butler almost fell over his own feet ushering her into the hall. 'Please come this way, Mrs Farrell. Mr Harrington will be so delighted to see you. I'll see if Mr Harrington has returned home.'

She followed him at a swift pace into the drawing room where he indicated that she sit on the chair closest to the fire before departing on close to a run. His behaviour astonished her. She looked around the room. High ornate ceilings, large paintings in gold-leaf frames on the walls, thick damask curtains, several sofas and delicate chairs, a wide patterned rug on top of polished floorboards, occasional tables, ornaments, a roaring fire. She'd never seen such a room before, yet she wasn't in awe. It was a fine room, a beautiful room, but she felt no yearning for it and wondered why. This was Ethan's home.

It hit her then, and she knew why the room or indeed the whole house left her unmoved. It was Elizabeth Harrington's home. Clarice Harrington's home. She would never live here. How she knew this with such intense certainty she didn't know, but it was clear in her mind. The truth was in her heart, her soul. Too much had happened. Too many people would be hurt by her and Ethan's relationship for them to ever be comfortable here, to be at peace. Somehow this made her visit and the words she must say easier to bear.

She sighed deeply, accepting the dull pain that accompanied her reasoning. Her future wasn't here at Bracken Hall and it begged the question whether her future was with Ethan. She shied away from further reflection; it was too painful. Instead, she let herself hope that perhaps . . . perhaps something could be saved from this mess. If Ethan could survive with not living at Bracken Hall, then they could conquer anything in their path, but again doubts reared their ugly head. Could Ethan shun his home, leave his mother?

Running echoed in the hall. Like a whirlwind, Ethan flung himself across the room and, with a shout of joy, dragged her up from the sofa and crushed her into his arms. 'Oh, my darling. My darling. I thought I had lost you!' He rained kisses over her face.

She sagged in his arms, only now did she realize how much she needed his embrace, his love to envelope her. Reasoning went out the window when she was in his arms. Their devotion rendered everything else redundant.

Ethan pulled back and cupped her face in his hands. 'Are you hurt? The child? Where were you?'

'We ran from Farrell.' Looking at him properly, she noticed the strain he wore like a cloak. Dark shadows were smudged under his eyes, his shoulders were tight and knotted beneath her fingers. He had aged somewhat since their first meeting. Grey now sprinkled his hair at the temples. *I have done this to him.*

'When they brought out the body, I nearly had a heart seizure.'

She frowned. 'Body?'

'From the fire.'

Isabelle gasped, reeling at the enormity of his words. 'I had no idea . . . '

'Sit down, my love.' Ethan gently lowered her onto the sofa and sat beside her, holding her hands.

'I thought they would get out . . . or douse the fire . . . ' Her heartbeat raced. She swallowed. 'The body . . . was it Farrell?'

He shook his head, the light dying in his eyes. 'No. It was that other fellow, who was watching over you, Peacock.'

Isabelle closed her eyes. Neville dead? It made no impact on her. She was numb to all thought and feeling.

'When they couldn't find any other bodies I felt relief.' Ethan kissed her hands. 'Then I wondered whether you had come here, to me, and so we hurried back. I didn't know Farrell and Bertie had returned. When there was no word from you, Hamish and I split up and started searching. I had only just returned to the stables when I was told you waited in the drawing room.' He smiled a soft, haunting smile. 'I couldn't bear not knowing what had happened to you.'

She licked her dry lips and he leaned forward to kiss where her tongue touched. Reaching up, she ran her fingers through his dark hair. 'Farrell is still out there. He'll be looking for me.'

'You don't have to run anymore, sweet-heart. You're safe now.'

'Am I?' She took his hand and placed it against her cheek. 'He's my husband and has rights. I will always be looking over my shoulder, Ethan, always.'

'We'll go away.'

She stared at him, silly, stupid hope building despite her earlier planning. 'We will?'

'Of course.'

He said it so easily but she wasn't fooled. 'Are you able to leave here for good?'

'For good?' He frowned. 'It won't have to be for good.'

'It might be. I cannot stay in this area. Farrell would never give me a minute's peace. He could snatch me at any time and before either of us know it, I'd be on a ship to America.'

Ethan shuddered. 'Don't even think it.'

'It's a possibility we cannot ignore. The boys and I have to leave here and not come back.' She gazed into his eyes. 'Can you do the same?'

'Once we're divorced — '

'You say that as if it is as easy as purchasing a newspaper.' She glanced away to the fire. 'Farrell will never divorce me and who's to say you can obtain a divorce so easily?'

'I'll fight the courts until I am free.'

She watched the embers glow and spark. 'And that could take our entire lives.'

'Nonsense.'

'You don't know for sure, Ethan, and until we are free we must live apart. I'd be your mistress, your child will be a bastard, not your heir. I don't know if I can tolerate it.'

He jerked to his feet and stood before the fire. 'What alternative is there? This isn't how I want it, Isabelle, believe me.'

She rose and went to him, slipping her hand through his arm. 'I know, my love. I'm not blaming you.'

Ethan swore softly and looked away.

Tears filled her eyes, blurring his image. 'You can't leave here, can you?'

He wrapped his arms around her and held her tight. 'For you I will do anything,' he whispered. 'I mean that.'

'Are you certain you can leave Bracken Hall?'

'Yes.'

Relief flooded her and she realized that saying goodbye to him would have been the hardest task she'd do in her life. 'How soon can we go?'

The sound of someone clearing their throat pulled them apart and they turned towards the door. Hamish gave them a tight smile, his face showed no expression. 'You are safe then?'

'Yes, thank God.' Ethan smiled down at her and hugged her to his side. 'She and the boys fled.'

'Boys?' Hamish frowned at her in misunderstanding. Again, he had mastered the art of making her feel unimportant, unworthy. Why the reversal of opinion again now?

Isabelle straightened under his scrutiny. He was a strange man, one she didn't feel at ease with. It was as though he demanded something of her and she had no idea what. 'Farrell had returned. We escaped him and stayed the night at an inn in Hebden Bridge. We didn't know how bad the fire was or that it had claimed a life.'

Ethan's eyes widened. 'Hebden Bridge? You walked all that way in the dark?'

'We had no choice. I wanted to put some distance between us and Farrell.'

'Why didn't you come here?'

'Because I was frightened he would predict such a move and come here and cause havoc.'

Ethan raised his eyebrows at her in admonishment. 'At least I would have known where you were!'

Hamish slapped his broad-brimmed hat against his thigh, distracting them from each other. 'Any word on Farrell?'

Isabelle shrugged helplessly. 'He could be anywhere. That's what worries me.'

'He won't come here,' Ethan fumed. 'He wouldn't dare.'

Isabelle said nothing, but she didn't feel as confident. Farrell was capable of doing anything to stop her and Ethan being together.

'Well.' Hamish's gaze lingered on her and instinct told her that what he saw was of little significance to him. He turned for the door. 'Now the emergency is over, I'll go and pack.'

'Pack?' Ethan stared at him. 'Whatever for?'

'I am leaving for Edinburgh today. I've much to do before I return to Australia in a few weeks.'

'A few weeks? You aren't serious?' Ethan shook his head. 'When did you decide this?'

Isabelle watched the two men argue over Hamish's decision and suddenly her mind came alive with a plan. 'Mr MacGregor.'

Both men stopped their heated discussion and looked at her. 'Yes?' Hamish's eyes widened with interest before narrowing so quickly she thought she had imagined it. She faltered. He looked at her as though he might not even like her.

She lifted her chin and braced herself for the hurt she would bestow on Ethan. 'Mr MacGregor I was wondering, if maybe, and, it may not even be possible . . . ' Her voice died out as his gaze never wavered.

'Wondering if what is possible, Mrs Farrell?'

Isabelle took a deep breath. 'I was wondering if my brothers and I could travel to Australia with you?'

Stunned silence was her answer. She didn't look at Ethan who had gone rigid, only Hamish had her attention for his shock was in his blue eyes.

She hurried on. 'I wouldn't be a burden, Mr MacGregor. Once there my brothers and I will — '

'You'll do no such thing!' Ethan exploded. Outrage etched his features. 'You're going nowhere without me.'

'Ethan, it will take you months to settle your affairs. I thought that I can go out there first and you can join us later.' She watched him fight for control. He looked as if he wanted to throw himself about the room like a child having a tantrum.

Hamish stepped forward. 'What about your husband, Mrs Farrell?'

Isabelle frowned. He'd done it again, made her feel undeserving. Hamish MacGregor had a shrewd way of subtle needling. His poison darts pierced her skin. *Why is it he always makes me feel in the wrong?* 'My husband, if

342

I can call him that, is of no concern to me.' She glanced at Ethan's tormented face and back to Hamish and her hope faded. 'Obviously, I've spoken out of turn. I shouldn't have placed you in such a position, Mr MacGregor. Forgive me.'

'Isabelle.' Ethan took her hand in his and at that moment they heard carriage wheels on the drive. He swore softly. 'Mama has returned.'

Cringing inside at the thought of meeting Elizabeth Harrington in her present state of disarray, Isabelle looked around for another door to slip out through. As if reading her mind, Ethan's grip tightened. 'No more hiding.'

Elizabeth glided into the room, but her step checked for a second on seeing Isabelle. She wore a dress of deep green brocaded silk and a small black hat with one pheasant feather sweeping along the side. Her smile wavered and her eyes silently sought Ethan for information before remembering her manners. 'Good morning, Mrs Farrell.'

Isabelle felt as uncomfortable as the older woman appeared. 'Good morning, Mrs Harrington.'

'Did you enjoy your call on Mrs Freidman, Mama?' Ethan assisted her to a chair by the fire.

'Indeed, it was very pleasant. Thank you.' She arranged her skirts and then gazed up expectantly at Isabelle. 'How did Meadow Farm fare in the fire, Mrs Farrell? I see you are safe.'

'There was one death, Mama,' Ethan answered. 'One of Farrell's friends apparently.'

'Oh dear, dreadful news.'

An awkward silence descended and before anyone could break it Isabelle took a step towards Elizabeth. 'If you'll excuse me, Mrs Harrington. I must return to my brothers.'

'Why, of course.' Elizabeth held out her hand and as Isabelle shook it she added, 'Family is very important. One must protect it at all costs.'

Ethan stared at his mother and took Isabelle's elbow. 'I shall escort you back to your lodgings.'

'There is no need.' Isabelle smiled at him and wished she could kiss away his sadness.

Hamish fiddled with his hat. 'Perhaps I should escort Mrs Farrell, Ethan?'

'No thank you, Hamish.' Only, Ethan faltered when his mother agreed.

Elizabeth rose. 'Ethan do let Hamish go in your place. I must discuss — '

'No!' Frustration covered Ethan's face. 'For once can you both keep quiet and leave

344

me alone! I love Isabelle. I want to spend time with her. We have much to discuss. I'm tired of being told what to do and what to think as though I am a child!'

'You are causing a scene,' Elizabeth hushed.

'It's my house and I will cause a scene if I bloody well wish to.' Ethan's voice had dropped to a menacing growl. 'For God's sake, Mama, let me live my life.'

Elizabeth lost all colour. 'Is it my fault that I love you and want what is best for you?'

'Isabelle is the best for me.' Ethan sighed, dispirited. 'Why can you not see it?'

'You are married to Clarice!'

'And Isabelle is having my child!' he yelled.

Isabelle lowered her head, shutting out his mother's amazed expression. Tears slipped over her lashes and she hurriedly dashed them away.

Slowly Elizabeth returned to her seat. 'You foolish, foolish — '

'Don't, Mama!'

The pain on both the mother and son's faces made Isabelle want to cry out in denial, to tell them she hadn't meant for this to happen. 'Ethan . . . '

He spun round to look at her and the look of love in his eyes rendered her speechless. Tenderly he touched her cheek with the back of his hand. 'We'll be together, I promise. Do you believe in me?'

'I believe in you.' She nodded, knowing it to be the truth and hating herself for being weak.

18

'Well, madam, do you like it?' The seamstress stepped back and admired her work. 'I do think the blue and white stripe is most becoming on you. Though, if I may say so, you've gained a small amount of weight since your last fitting.'

Isabelle grinned. Indeed the dress was a tight fit now, but Mrs Harris didn't know a child was the reason not overeating. Though under Ethan's care, she had done plenty of that, too. She smoothed the linen material of the skirt. Four inches of white lace at her cuffs whispered with each movement. 'I'm sure I'll lose the pounds again, Mrs Harris.'

The older woman tutted and helped her down from the low-standing stool. 'Do you wish to change now?'

'Yes, of course. If you would be so kind to assist.' It was a little depressing to replace the beautiful blue and white dress for her mourning clothes again, but at least she now owned new black clothes instead of the old worn dress that had seen her through three funerals.

Once suitable to leave the room, Isabelle

collected her umbrella and gloves. 'You will have my clothes ready by next week, Mrs Harris?'

'Absolutely, Mrs Farrell.'

'Thank you. You have been very good. I am pleased with my purchases.'

'And everything you ordered today is to be billed to Bracken Hall as before?' Mrs Harris's bushy eyebrows shot up in question.

Isabelle sighed. Despite being in Halifax — a large town with enough gossip of its own — scandal, big or small, still made its way into the fashionable shops as fodder for bored wives. 'Yes, thank you, just like my previous bill.' She refused to elaborate further to satisfy Mrs Harris and her clients' curiosity.

The older woman made a great show of tidying bolts of material on a wide table. 'Are you spending the New Year at the Hall, Mrs Farrell?'

Isabelle faltered in donning her black fur-lined woollen coat, wondering if she should lie or not. It would give them all something to speculate about if they knew some half-truths. 'I'm not sure. I shall be sailing to Australia with my brothers soon. Hence my need for dresses made in lighter material. I'm told it is summer over there now.' She wanted to giggle at Mrs Harris's surprised expression.

'You are certainly full of surprises, Mrs Farrell! Is your husband accompanying you?'

Her laughter faded abruptly. 'Not this time.' She headed for the door. 'Good day, Mrs Harris.'

Leaving the back room of the dressmaker's shop, Isabelle adjusted the short lace veil on her black hat and headed straight for the carriage Ethan had left at her disposal, complete with his own driver, Brown. A man he trusted implicitly to care for her in Ethan's place.

'To the house please, Brown.'

She settled back against the leather seat and shivered, though not because of the coldness of the day. Any mention of Farrell sent her nerves jangling. In the two weeks since the fire, her husband hadn't been seen or heard of. Ethan had people on the lookout for him, but so far had drawn a blank.

Thinking of Ethan put a tiny smile back on her face. Her life had changed again. The day after the fire, on leaving his mother and Hamish wordless at their reckless behaviour, Ethan had taken her in his carriage to a house he owned on the outskirts of Halifax. Later the boys joined her and it was to be their home until they sailed for Australia with Hamish. After a discussion with Hamish, before he left for Edinburgh, it had been decided that she and the boys would travel with him to Australia and Ethan would join them as soon as possible once his business and estate concerns were in order.

Knowing their time together was limited they spent hours alone everyday, either going for drives in the countryside if the day was pleasant enough or they stayed at the house. Sometimes, Hughie and Bertie joined them to discuss the future, but most often than not, Ethan would give them money to spend in town with Brown as their protector.

Brown slowed the horses and they turned into a short drive. At the side of the red-bricked house, Isabelle alighted and Brown continued on to the small yard and stable block at the back. Recent rain had littered the drive with wide puddles. Isabelle hitched up her skirts to navigate them and heard Ethan's laughter.

'Don't you slip, my lovely. You look too delightful to be spoiled.' He winked and helped her over the last remaining puddles.

She grinned at him. 'I wasn't expecting you until later.'

'Inspecting mills compares poorly to spending time with you, my love.' He kissed her soundly and led her inside the front door. 'Did you enjoy your shopping?'

'Yes. I've parcels arriving this afternoon for

350

the boys. Things that they will need for the journey.' She unpinned her hat and then peeled off her gloves. Placing them on the hall table she paused and glanced up the staircase. 'I wonder where they've got to?'

Doris, the maid that Ethan had insisted she have, hurried along the hall from the back of the house, ready to assist her. 'So sorry, Mrs Farrell, I didn't hear you come in.'

'It's all right.' Isabelle handed Doris her coat. The young, plump woman was a great find. Ethan had done well finding such a pleasant woman, whose sunny nature put everyone in a good mood.

'You'll be wanting a nice cup of tea, Mrs Farrell?'

'Absolutely, Doris, I'm fair parched.'

Ethan stepped forward to whisper, 'We'll have some of your delicious macaroons too, if you have any.'

'Certainly, sir.' She grinned like a conspirator and bobbed her head before disappearing the way she came.

Ethan took Isabelle's arm and they entered the small parlour. 'Hamish took the boys off for the afternoon.'

'Hamish? He's back from Scotland already? I thought he was to arrive on the Monday before we sail?'

'He returned earlier than expected, yes.

Instead of meeting us in Liverpool, we'll be all travelling together. Hamish mentioned it might be easier for us to say goodbye here rather than Liverpool, but I disagreed. I couldn't miss the chance of spending a few more days with you before you embark.' He stoked the fire into a more cheerful blaze and added more coal. 'The man mustn't have slept the entire time he was away so quickly did he attend to his concerns and return here. I believe he is very eager to return to Australia. It is more his home now than Scotland is.'

Excitement fluttered in Isabelle's chest. 'I am keen to see the country myself.'

Ethan took her in his arms. 'Not too keen to leave me though?'

'No, I'd never be that, my dearest one.' She kissed him, but pulled away when Doris walked in with the tea tray.

Sitting down on the green sofa placed at right angles to the fire, Isabelle nodded her thanks to Doris and after the maid departed, poured out the tea. 'How is your mother?'

Ethan sighed. 'Barely talking to me, and when she does speak to me she soon dissolves into tears.'

'I'm sorry to hear that.' She added a lump of sugar to his tea, a drop of milk and then passed it to him. 'She will miss you very much.'

'I know, and I will miss her, but there is no alternative.'

'No.' Despite the warmth of the fire, she shivered. So much pain, so much upheaval and she was responsible. 'And Clarice?'

'She will have a house in London, as promised. I'm sending out inquiries this week.'

'I am surprised that she won't stay with your mother.'

Ethan shrugged. 'Clarice prefers her own company and to not have to listen to Mama's criticism, which once I leave will be directed at Clarice for failing to be a proper wife.'

'Failure as a proper wife.' Isabelle mused. 'That is something that could be labelled on me.'

'My love, your situation is far different.'

'Is it though?' She stirred her tea deep in thought. 'Perhaps if I had . . . '

Ethan set down his teacup and saucer and enfolded her in his arms. 'I won't have you blaming yourself for his actions.' He rubbed his nose against hers. 'Farrell should never have married you.'

'I shouldn't have been so eager for a husband.' She gave him a wry smile. 'Well, it is done with now and soon the boys and I will start a new life in a new country that will be complete once you have joined us.'

He gazed deep into her eyes. 'Amen.' A faraway look came into Ethan's brown eyes and he stroked her stomach, which hinted at the life she carried. 'My wish is to be by your side when our child is born.'

She cupped his cheek in her hand. 'Then I suggest you hurry and complete your preparations.'

Taking her hand, he kissed each finger in turn. 'If all goes to plan I should sail a month after you.'

Isabelle leant her head against his shoulder. 'I hope so for I hate to be without you.'

★ ★ ★

'Do make haste, Bertie dear.' Isabelle coaxed from the doorway. 'The carriage will be here any moment.'

He looked up at her from where he knelt on the floor beside his small trunk, his big, pale eyes imploring. 'I can't fasten my trunk properly.'

She grinned and went to kneel beside him. 'Could it be you have put too much in there?'

The slightest of smiles lifted his mouth. 'Perhaps, but I didn't want to leave anything behind.'

'We won't leave anything behind, don't worry.' Isabelle lifted the lid and raised her eyebrows at the assortment of treasures on top of his folded clothes. Ethan had bought most of them for him. Picture books, drawings, a spinning top, a case of chalk, a ball, the kite Bertie and Hughie made last week, string and a small bag of marbles.

He gently touched his belongings. 'I've never had so many things before.'

Remembering the day he arrived at the farm with her father, she realized that he'd only ever had the clothes on his back. She ruffled his hair and then smoothed it back down. His endearing shyness reminded her so much of Sally it hurt her heart and she loved him for it. Though he looked nothing like Sally, for Sally was the image of her mother, they did share the same nature, which was even more surprising since she would never have believed it came from their father. The family had always assumed Sally's quiet, studious nature had been a gift from their mother.

'What are you thinking about?' Bertie's whisper penetrated her musings.

'My family. The family I'll be leaving behind in a graveyard in Halifax.'

'And it makes you sad?' He slipped his hand into hers.

She gazed down at their joined hands. His was so small, so fragile. He was such a thin boy. No matter how much she fed him, he remained as slender as a reed. Protectiveness overwhelmed her. She was all he had in the world and it frightened her. If anything happened to her, Hughie and Bertie would be alone. She would have to speak to Ethan and beg him to promise her that he would take care of them should she die.

'Belle?' Bertie whispered. 'I'll look after you. I'll never leave you. I promise.'

She gathered him to her and held him tight. 'We'll promise to look after each other. Yes?'

He nodded and she felt his body relax. This brother of hers was so sensitive and no wonder, having lost both mother and father so early in his life.

Hughie burst into the room, so full of energy he couldn't contain it. 'The carriage is here!'

'Oh, good.'

'Brown's kept it out on the road as it's so large it won't fit in through the gate.'

'Come, help Bertie with his trunk while I speak with Brown about the luggage.' Isabelle got to her feet and left the room, smiling as Hughie whined about Bertie overfilling his trunk. Outside, she greeted Brown, who waited for her on the footpath, and marvelled at the size of the carriage, pulled by four glossy black horses. A groom sat up in the driver's seat holding the reins. 'We'll have no trouble fitting our baggage on this, Brown.'

'No, indeed, Mrs Farrell.'

She peeked inside the carriage window. 'Did Mr Harrington not come?'

'No, madam, he told me to tell you that there was a problem at one of his mills, a fire, I think. He said he'll be at Bracken Hall by the time you arrive.'

She nodded. 'Very well.'

'Shall Willie and I start loading up?'

'Yes, yes do.' She smiled and turned back to the house. The early morning sun climbed over the bare trees behind the house and although it held no warmth, it made her feel lighter in spirit.

Inside, Doris descended the stairs with a carpet-bag in each hand. 'I'll put these in the carriage, Mrs Farrell, and then bring down the rest from your room.'

'Thank you, Doris.' As the woman neared, Isabelle couldn't help but ask. 'Are you sure you want to go to Australia? I won't be angry if you wish to change your mind.'

Doris shook her head. 'No need to worry about me, Mrs Farrell. I've no family left now. There's nowt to keep me here and I know a good job is worth holding on to.'

Isabelle smiled and patted Doris's shoulder

as she went outside. She looked around the sparse hall, the small rooms leading off it, the narrow staircase. It was a nice house, nothing grand, but comfortable enough for her and the boys. It had shielded them from harm in the last few weeks and she'd been grateful for it, but now it was time to go. Time to start a new life.

★ ★ ★

When they arrived at Bracken Hall, Brown took Doris around the back to the kitchens for a cup of tea as Isabelle and the boys hesitated on the front steps. She'd been expecting Ethan or even Hamish to welcome them, but only the butler stood in the entrance.

'Is Mr Harrington not yet home?' She asked him, hovering on the threshold.

'No, Mrs Farrell.'

'Is Mr MacGregor about?'

'As far as I'm aware, he has gone with Mr Harrington.' He indicated for them to go into the drawing-room.

Isabelle heard Hughie gasp as he gazed around the ornate room and Bertie stood so close to her, she could feel him tremble through her skirts. She held his hand and smiled in reassurance.

'Mrs Farrell.'

Isabelle twirled around as Elizabeth entered the room. Making small talk with Ethan's mother was the last thing she felt capable of. 'Good morning, Mrs Harrington.'

'Please, won't you and your brothers sit down and I'll ring for tea?' Elizabeth tugged the bell-pull near the fireplace and then sat down on a chair.

Isabelle sat on the sofa between Hughie and Bertie and prayed that Ethan would return soon. She smoothed down the black silk of her skirts.

'You are all ready to travel?' Elizabeth asked.

'Yes.'

A maid knocked and stood just inside the doorway. Elizabeth gave her instructions for tea and cakes to be brought in and asked for the fire to be tended. She turned her attention back to Isabelle. 'Your brothers might like to go down to the stables? You have a long journey ahead, they might prefer to stretch their legs while they have the chance? I'm told a foal was born during the night.'

'Oh, er, yes.' Isabelle forced a smile to her face and looked at Hughie. 'Would you want to visit the stables?'

He nodded, perching on the edge of the

sofa, clearly uncomfortable in this splendid drawing-room.

Elizabeth rose with a smile. 'Come, I'll have a footman show you the way.'

The boys left and Isabelle's heart contracted at the sight of Bertie sticking so close to Hughie. The poor boy was frightened out of his skin amongst strangers and the enormity of the Hall. She understood how he felt, for being alone with Elizabeth was something she hadn't anticipated. *Where is Ethan?* When Elizabeth returned, two maids followed her carrying the tea service and a tall stand filled with sandwiches, cakes and tarts.

'I thought you might be hungry, Mrs Farrell. I'm sure you've been busy this morning with your packing.'

She nodded and smiled but the thought of eating made her want to gag. Waiting while Elizabeth poured the tea, Isabelle tried to summon some form of conversation to her brain.

'You know, I never thought you'd win,' Elizabeth murmured, offering her the teacup and saucer.

'Pardon?'

'I thought Ethan would tire of you.' Elizabeth bowed her head for a moment and then raised her tear-filled eyes. 'I never expected to be left here, alone.'

360

Isabelle anticipated the woman's anger, but not the quiet acceptance, which was tinged with sadness and regret. 'I'm sorry, Mrs Harrington. It wasn't my intention to hurt you.'

Elizabeth stared at her for some seconds before nodding. 'I believe you. If circumstances had been different I would have welcomed you into this house as my daughter-in-law.'

The words humbled Isabelle and, bravely, she reached over to take the other woman's hand. 'Thank you.'

'None of it matters now, does it? I mean, soon you'll be on the other side of the world.'

'Ethan says he will return often. He has to. He won't let Bracken Hall be without its owner for long.'

Elizabeth nodded and dabbed her eyes with a white handkerchief.

This new insight to Ethan's mother made Isabelle want to close the gap between them. 'It would gladden Ethan's heart if you were to join us. It worries him very much knowing you will be here on your own.' She smiled, hoping to win her over. 'If you came with us, you would see your grandchild when it's born.'

'But it won't be my grandchild will it?'

Elizabeth withdrew her hand and glanced at the fire. 'The child will be a Farrell.'

'Only in name. It's a Harrington by blood.' She stifled her spark of irritation. 'The child is Ethan's. He will be a father. Do you not want to share that with him?'

'You don't understand.'

'What is there to understand? Your son, your daughter and your grandchild will be in Australia while you'll be wandering around this great house by yourself.'

'I've been the mistress of this house for thirty-four years!' Elizabeth rose and paced the floor. 'This house is my home, my children's home. It was meant to be my grandchildren's home.' She stopped and stared at Isabelle. 'Is it wrong for me to think this way? Is it wrong for me to want the same things any other mother wants?'

Isabelle shook her head, saddened by the other woman's pain. 'You are not wrong to want that. Yet, I don't see your dilemma.' She stood and stepped towards Elizabeth. 'You can have your family around you in Australia. However, you prefer to place this house above them.'

A blush swept up Elizabeth's cheeks. 'That's a lie!'

'Is it?'

'You know nothing.'

'I know I wouldn't put a house before my family.'

'No, you put everything else before your family! Your reputation, your vows to your husband.'

'My marriage was a sham from the very beginning!' Isabelle blazed. 'Farrell didn't want a wife. He wanted a slave!'

'Then you shouldn't have married him.'

'Have you ever been hungry, Mrs Harrington, really hungry? Have you ever been homeless, friendless and so frightened that you'd do anything to make your life better?'

Elizabeth's eyes softened and she sagged. 'No.'

'No. You haven't. I wanted what was best for my brother and me. I made a mistake. But that mistake gave me Ethan and I would do it all again to have him.'

Sitting back on the sofa, Elizabeth picked up her teacup and saucer but didn't drink. 'I will not deny you have made Ethan happy. He was never happy with Clarice. But are you prepared to live the rest of your life in sin?'

Sighing, Isabelle walked to the fireplace and stared at the shifting logs. 'It's not the most ideal situation I agree. Actually, I seriously thought of giving Ethan up and going away. But I'm not strong enough. It was madness to even contemplate it.'

'It would kill him if you left him for good.'

'It won't happen. I'm too selfish. I want him with me.'

'Being a mistress will not be easy for you.'

'True, I know. Ethan will keep returning to England to gain his divorce, as will I. But with or without it, we will be living on a station miles away from the nearest town. We will be happy on our own.'

'And what about your children?'

Isabelle rubbed the slight swelling of her stomach. 'We will try our best to make sure this child I carry is the first and last until we are both free.'

Elizabeth's gaze was drawn to her action. 'That might never be.'

She shrugged. 'Then we'll treasure this one all the more.'

They both turned at the sound of horses on the drive.

'They've returned.' A look of panic flittered across Elizabeth's face. 'Saying goodbye to you will crucify Ethan.'

Isabelle smiled softly and looked through the doorway as Ethan entered, with Hamish following. 'It won't be for long and he has you to comfort him until he can join me.'

After half an hour, in which time Hamish changed his clothes and they all drank tea and ate cakes, it was time for the travelling party to leave. Hamish gave instructions for his trunks to be stowed on the carriage, while Ethan spoke with Brown about the journey to the Halifax train station.

Nervous, Isabelle hovered behind with Hughie and Bertie. Elizabeth touched her arm. 'Will you write to me?'

The request struck Isabelle dumb. 'Write to you?'

'Yes. I would like to know about my grandchild. I know Ethan will write once he's over there but a man can never say the same things, the important things, like a woman can.'

Isabelle leant over and kissed Elizabeth's soft cheek. 'I will write.'

Relief shone in Elizabeth's eyes. 'Good. Take care.'

'Remember, you will always be welcome in my home.'

Nodding, Elizabeth stepped back as Ethan came to Isabelle's side. 'Ready, my love?'

She nodded. 'I guess so.'

'Well isn't this a merry sight!'

They all turned as one and stared.

Farrell stood on the lawn beside the drive. He grinned as though it was a huge joke and sauntered towards them. Isabelle expected her heart to stop beating any second. She couldn't believe she was looking at him just when she was to be gone from here in mere minutes.

'So, Wife.' Farrell smirked and licked his lips. 'Yer've done well for yerself I see.'

Ethan stepped in front of her. 'Take another step, Farrell, and it'll be your last.'

Holding his hands up as if in surrender, Farrell stayed where he was. 'No need to be all protective, Harrington. I'm not here to cause trouble.'

'Then why are you here?'

Farrell shrugged. 'Simple really. I want me wife.'

Isabelle moaned and clutched at Ethan's sleeve. She'd been a fool to think it was all at an end. It would never end. Farrell would never let it.

Hamish strolled over to Farrell. 'I suggest, my man, that you leave. Your presence isn't wanted. There is nothing here for you.'

'Really?' Farrell's eyes narrowed and he stabbed his finger into Hamish's chest. 'And I'm not yer man.'

Leaning closer, Hamish's voice dropped. 'There are twenty men all within calling distance. Still willing to try your luck?'

Farrell chuckled. 'Bring on all yer men, if that'll make yer happy, but there's no court in the land that will disagree with me when I take my wife home.'

'Home?' Ethan scoffed, his eyes had nearly darkened to black. 'You don't have a home. It's burnt to the ground. Meadow Farm is no longer yours. I'm taking it back *and* I have the law on my side!'

'Have the stinking farm. It ain't no use to me in America now is it?' He grinned, showing missing teeth. 'I just want what's mine.' His gaze centred on Isabelle.

She lifted her chin, confident he could do her no harm with Ethan and Hamish around her. 'I will never willingly go with you.'

Farrell's eyes narrowed to slits. 'If that's how you want to play it.' He strode up to her, but before he had the chance to grab her, Ethan and Hamish reacted. They both lunged for him, yet Farrell, anticipating them, sidestepped and ducked. His years of running from the law gave him an advantage of knowing how to dodge and weave. He made it look so easy that Isabelle felt a distinct urge to laugh. Only, it wasn't funny when his large hand grabbed her wrist and flung her away from the group. She stumbled on her long skirts and fell to her knees.

'Leave her alone!' Hughie yelled, hitting Farrell on the back.

Elizabeth screamed. Men rushed from around the side of the house.

'Isabelle!' Ethan rushed to her side, but

with a roar of madness Farrell shook off Hughie and Hamish and charged for Ethan, knocking him to the ground. They rolled together on the grass. Ethan aimed a few good punches while astride Farrell's chest before they rolled again and Farrell was on top.

'Stand up, Belle,' Hughie said, assisting her to her feet as they both watched the two men try to get the better of the other.

Dazed, she let him hold her around the waist. The strength had left her. The scene played out in front of her was like something from a stage comedy. This couldn't be happening. It was all a joke; a nightmare and she'd wake up in a minute. *Stop it! Stop it!* She'd had enough. No more. 'Stop!' she screamed. 'Stop it, I say!'

Startled at her outburst, Ethan paused and glanced up at her. In an instant, Farrell seized his moment and with one fluid movement he reached down to his boots and pulled out a knife. He plunged it into Ethan's chest and jerked it up under his ribs as clean as a butcher boning a carcass. An anguished cry escaped Ethan as his eyes widened in surprise, he frowned and then a look of utter pain creased his face. Then he was falling, toppling backwards, away from Farrell and his bloodied hand.

Isabelle's world spun, whirled off its axis. Horror of a magnitude she had never imagined had her swaying, gasping. She broke free from Hughie. Stumbling, her heart thumped as though it would burst from her body. She crumpled to her knees beside Ethan, who lay holding his stomach and frowning as if in puzzlement as to what had happened to him. He groaned and she lifted his head and placed it gently on her lap. Behind them she was aware of running, shouting, the sound of a gun going off and screaming, but it drifted into a muffle as she concentrated on Ethan's toffee eyes. 'I'm here, my love.' She kissed him softly on the lips. 'You'll be fine, I promise.' She kissed his forehead and brushed his hair back. 'We'll get help.'

His gaze wandered beyond her to the sky. 'My . . . Isabelle . . . '

'Yes, my love.' She kissed him again. 'Lie still, darling.'

'I cannot . . . see you . . . ' Panic heightened his voice.

Isabelle bit her lip to stop herself from crying. 'I'm holding you sweetheart. You're in my arms.'

'Good.' His eyelids fluttered and closed.

'Ethan!' She shook him. 'Look at me.'

He groaned and a trickle of blood seeped

from the corner of his mouth.

She clutched him to her. 'Stay with me.' Her tears dropped onto his hair. 'Don't leave me,' she whispered.

'Belle?' Hughie's voice came from a long way away.

She stared up, trying to focus. So many people circled her and Ethan. Faces blurred and she dismissed them all. Bent over Ethan she cupped his cheek in her hand and silently begged for him not to leave her.

His eyes opened and he looked right at her. 'You and me. We stole . . . a piece . . . of . . . heaven . . . didn't we?'

Isabelle nodded, her throat tight with emotion. 'Yes, sweetheart, we did.'

Pain made him grimace and she held him closer. Kissing his forehead while stroking his hair with one hand, she whispered her words of love to him until he could no longer hear them. 'Yes, we stole a piece of heaven . . . '

Epilogue

Spring blossom, all delicate and soft, floated on the tender breeze to land reverently in fragile clouds on the lush grass. Nature's own perfume saturated the air and was made more intense by the warmth of the May day. Bees buzzed from flower to flower and apart from birdsong it was one of the few sounds.

The baby, trying her best to stand from where she sat on the white woollen blanket, gurgled in contentment. From somewhere beyond the small wood, a cow bellowed once, then twice.

'Isabelle!' Elizabeth called from the top of the slight rise leading up from the back of the house.

Sighing at the loss of her peace, Isabelle straightened on the bench and awaited Elizabeth's arrival. The soft swish of skirts brushing the long grass indicated when she was near and Isabelle turned, summoning a welcoming smile.

'I've come to spend a few minutes with you before Mrs Kirkland calls.' Elizabeth smiled and glanced at her before quickly swooping down to gather up the baby. 'Here's my darling angel.' She kissed the baby's plump cheeks and tickled her tummy.

Watching, Isabelle couldn't help offering up a silent prayer of thanks that Elizabeth loved her granddaughter. In the aftermath of that terrible January day last year, Elizabeth could have easily shunned her, but she hadn't. In fact she had gone to extreme limits to make sure she was a part of her and the baby's life. She'd taken Isabelle and the boys into her home and begged them to live there with her. She'd supported Isabelle throughout the pregnancy and birth.

Settling down on the seat beside Isabelle, Elizabeth nestled the drowsy baby against her shoulder. 'Isn't it a beautiful day?'

'Yes.'

'I never thought I would say that again.' Elizabeth rubbed her cheek along the top of the baby's head. 'I thought I would never experience a good day again.'

Isabelle plucked at her black skirts. Whenever conversation alluded to Ethan or his death she felt as though a weight pressed against her chest. She glanced up when Elizabeth took her hand and held it. They sat for some time in silence. Alone with their thoughts, their memories, their grief.

After a while, Isabelle could breath easier,

the pain of losing Ethan sometimes threatened to choke the life from her, but some days were better than others. The trial was over and the newspapers had stopped hounding them for information. The first anniversary of Ethan's death had been endured, and now summer was nearly here and she could rest. She could forget. Not Ethan of course, she could never forget him, for she saw him every day in their daughter's toffee eyes, but the horror of that tragic day was no longer as sharp as it was. The constant nightmares, the uncontrollable grief had lessened once Bethan was born.

Turning, Isabelle lightly touched her daughter, Bethan Elizabeth. Her arrival had softened the anguish, the hurt, the ache of Ethan's death. She brought smiles to the house and love back into her grandmother's heart. Isabelle adored her so much it frightened her. If anything happened to her baby, her and Ethan's baby, she knew she would leave this world also.

Elizabeth shifted on the seat, adjusting Bethan's sleeping form. 'Hamish will be here soon.'

'Yes.'

'I shall miss him. He has always been like a son to me.'

'Yes.' Isabelle glanced away to the left over

the lake and to the deer park on the other side.

Hamish. Poor Hamish. How he had suffered. He witnessed his best friend's murder, then shot the murderer. His trial had run only days after the inquest into Ethan's death and though he'd been found not guilty of murdering Farrell, the strain had taken its effect. The verdict of self-defence freed him, but his mind still held him prisoner. And today, he was finally leaving them to sail to Australia. Isabelle knew he ached to return to that strange country on the other side of the world and leave behind the disastrous events that altered his life. He'd stayed too long in England and wanted to go home. Isabelle envied him. For though she lived at the Hall, it was no home to her. Hamish knew of a contentment that eluded her.

She'd seen him often in the seventeen months since the accident, and, despite his initial aloofness, they soon created a tentative friendship. His quiet presence whenever he called soothed her agony. He'd become close to the boys, helping them through another difficult period and she was so very grateful for that.

'I'm jealous of him seeing Rachel again.' Elizabeth sighed. 'I miss her so much. We all should have listened to her when Ethan and his father first mooted the idea of Clarice becoming a part of this family. Rachel was against it. She said Clarice wasn't enough for Ethan, but we wouldn't listen. All we cared about was the money she brought with her. Money that refurbished the house and restocked the fields with crops and animals.'

'We can have no regrets, Elizabeth.' Isabelle spoke without hesitation. She regretted nothing, except that Farrell managed to steal Ethan from her. 'Fate deals with us how it wishes, we cannot fight it.'

'I guess you are right.' Elizabeth patted Bethan's back. 'I have to be grateful for Bethan. Oh, I know I shouldn't be. I should have nothing to do with my son's illegitimate child, but . . . ' Tears formed in her eyes. 'I love her so. If I cannot have Ethan then his daughter is a wonderful gift that I will treasure even if it does offend some of my friends.'

Isabelle raised her chin, hating the gossip about her and Bethan, hating people who judged her tiny daughter. 'Bethan is indeed a gift. If others want to reject us, then let them. I care not.'

Elizabeth nodded and smiled through her tears. 'We have each other, we need no one else.'

'Yes . . . '

'But, of course, we cannot forget the boys,' she chuckled. 'The house hasn't been so full in years.'

'They adore being here. Hughie shadows the estate manager's every move, the poor man.' Isabelle smiled. 'Saying thank you feels so inadequate for all that you've done for my family.'

'Well, I couldn't turn my back on the woman Ethan loved more than anything else in the world. He loved you even more than this estate, which I never thought possible. I couldn't ignore that. In my heart I knew I had to do what was right by him.' Elizabeth gazed at her. 'Besides, I have gained much more than I ever expected.'

'This is a lovely picture.' Hamish called out to them as he walked closer. 'A beautiful grandmother, a delightful mother and the sweetest baby.'

They both turned and smiled in greeting. Elizabeth held out her free hand and Hamish lavishly swept off his wide-brimmed hat, bent over and kissed it.

Isabelle sat straighter. 'Welcome back, Hamish.'

The smile he gave her was a little awkward and he returned his attentions to Elizabeth. 'Sweetest Elizabeth, as I arrived another carriage was coming down the drive. I

376

assisted a most charming lady out of it.' He flashed a rakish grin.

Isabelle frowned. She knew he was play-acting, but still it surprised her that he found another woman charming. Giving herself a mental shake she glanced away to watch a butterfly hover near the blanket. Why wouldn't Hamish be attracted to someone? He was a single man in the prime of his life. It's only natural he'd want a wife, a family . . .

Elizabeth sat forward. 'Lord, it'll be Mrs Kirkland. Are you coming in, Isabelle?'

'No. Not yet. You know I'm not . . . easy in company.'

'All right, my dear.' Elizabeth carefully handed Bethan to Isabelle and then squeezed her shoulder. 'I'll not encourage her to stay long and then we'll have some afternoon tea on the terrace.'

Nodding, Isabelle smiled her thanks and Elizabeth left them.

Hamish raised his eyebrows. 'May I sit with you?'

'Of course.' She tucked Bethan more securely in her arms and gazed down at her.

'She's beautiful.' He touched Bethan's hand where it curled against Isabelle's breast.

'Yes . . . ' Isabelle stared at Hamish's large,

tanned hand so near to her.

As if sensing her discomfort, he straightened and crossing his legs at the ankle he stared over into the wood. 'I settled Clarice in a good house. She's near shops, the library and everything she needs.'

Isabelle swallowed, remembering her first sight of Clarice, obese and gasping for breath as she lumbered down the staircase. Ethan's wife had greeted her with warmth and shyness that morning, the morning of his funeral. 'Will she be happy there?'

Hamish nodded. 'She seemed content the moment she walked into the house and met the cook and housemaid. Everything was as she wanted.'

'Good. Ethan would approve.'

'Yes. It was what he planned for her when she originally requested to leave. She is now free to do as she pleases.'

'Just as I am . . . ' Isabelle sighed. Yes, she was free from Farrell but her future was very dim indeed. She had no money and three dependants. She lived by Elizabeth's goodwill.

'Will you stay with Elizabeth?'

She shrugged one shoulder. 'I'm not sure. I feel like I'm taking advantage of her. We all live here at her expense. The boys — '

'Ethan would want it this way.' His blue

eyes became tender.

'What of you, Hamish? Are you to return to Australia and never come back to England?'

He sighed and it sounded sad. 'Want I want is impossible to have.'

'Oh?'

He bent down and snapped off a blade of long grass. He inspected it for a long time and she wondered if he was going to answer her. Finally he threw the stalk away and stood to stare out over the fields. 'Peace of mind. I would like that back.'

His softly spoken words crushed her. He had killed a man. Because of her, he had shot Farrell and endured a trial that sullied his good name.

'I am so sorry, Hamish,' she whispered, tears gathering on her lashes. 'I am so ashamed I caused you such hardship, such embarrassment and such loss.'

For a moment he said nothing, didn't even turn around, then carefully, as though weighing up each action, he resumed his seat and faced her. 'You have nothing to blame yourself for. I didn't have to involve myself, but I did, mainly because I loved Ethan as a brother and wanted to help him, but also because of you . . . ' he swallowed, 'and my feelings for you.'

Her eyes widened and her heart somersaulted in surprise.

Hamish chuckled softly. 'I have nothing to lose telling you this, as we'll never meet again.' He took her hand closest to him and kissed it. 'I fell in love with you the moment I saw you in the garden at Meadow Farm. I've fought those feelings since then. I've tried to ignore them or at best hide them from everyone else. You were Ethan's. He loved you and you loved him.'

'Yes . . . ' She couldn't think straight. His honesty stunned her into numbness. 'I thought you hated me. You used to look at me with coolness . . . '

'No, I never hated you. I hated *myself* for wanting you though. I felt I wasn't being a true friend to Ethan. If I appeared rude at times, it was because I was trying desperately not to show I cared for you. Unfortunately, I wasn't very good at it.'

She blinked in wonder. Hamish wanting her? It was unbelievable. How could it be? Yet, somewhere in the distant part of her being, something stirred.

'I was so excited when you asked to travel to Australia with me. I was going to try so hard to make us firm friends. I knew Ethan would join us and that you would never be mine, but having you in my life as a friend was better than nothing. At least in Australia I knew you'd be safe, I'd be able to watch out for you.'

'Oh, Hamish.' She bit her lip and a tear trickled down her cheek. 'I don't know what to say.'

His gaze was full of loving, revealing the inner emotions he'd hidden for so long. 'You don't have to say anything at all. I do hope you'll write to me though?'

She nodded. Bethan stirred and lifted her head to smile sleepily at her. She was such a happy baby that an overwhelming surge of love for her filled Isabelle.

'Can I hold her one last time?'

Isabelle frowned as she passed Bethan to him. 'Won't you ever return?'

'No. Australia is my home now, my future.' He stood and jigged Bethan up and down to her delight. 'Who's a precious girl? Yes, you are.'

Isabelle watched them both. He was so tall, Bethan looked like a doll in his arms. Her heart constricted as he blew bubbles against Bethan's neck and she squealed in pleasure. *He has feelings for me.* She shook her head, amazed by his confession. She stared at him, really looked at him and analysed what she knew of him. He was kind, generous, loyal and caring.

'Isabelle?'

Startled out of her thoughts, she blinked. 'Yes?'

'I must go.' Hamish smiled. 'The train leaves in an hour and this little girl is wet.'

He was going. The gentle man who been such a strength to her since Ethan's death was leaving her. She was so tired of being left. Dazed, she rose and gathered the blanket. Together they walked back to the house, but with every step, Isabelle felt the urge to slow down. She wanted to think, to halt his plans until she was ready to accept what he'd told her. He had hit her with such a powerful revelation and was now going away. It was all too fast. Too confusing. Too emotional. She wasn't ready to think or feel yet. The numbness that encased her after Farrell killed Ethan had been comforting, reliable. It stopped her from feeling pain. But now she felt it slipping from her like a cloak, revealing her to the world again. She couldn't breathe . . .

'Isabelle? You're panting.' Hamish stopped and took her elbow, ignoring Bethan's attempts to pull his hair. 'What is it? You're pale. Do you feel unwell?'

She backed away a step, searching his face for answers. 'Why? Why did you tell me?'

He knew what she meant and as he

shrugged, she braced herself. 'As I said I had nothing to lose. We'll never see each other again and I've been carrying this heartache for a while now.' He grinned to lighten the situation and took a step.

'What . . . what if . . . if we were to meet again?'

He paused at the edge of the terrace and looked at her.

Isabelle took a hesitant step forward. 'What if we were to travel to Australia one day?'

'Is that likely?'

'Perhaps.'

Hamish stood very still.

She took another small step, her blood pounding in her ears. 'In time . . . when I feel able to . . . to move on . . . I might like to see where you live.'

His smile was slow in coming but it reached his blue eyes, turning them to azure. He kissed Bethan's cheek and then gazed at Isabelle. 'Then you'd be very welcome.'

We do hope that you have enjoyed reading this large print book.

Did you know that all of our titles are available for purchase?

We publish a wide range of high quality large print books including:
Romances, Mysteries, Classics
General Fiction
Non Fiction and Westerns

Special interest titles available in large print are:
The Little Oxford Dictionary
Music Book
Song Book
Hymn Book
Service Book

Also available from us courtesy of Oxford University Press:
Young Readers' Dictionary
(large print edition)
Young Readers' Thesaurus
(large print edition)

For further information or a free brochure, please contact us at:
Ulverscroft Large Print Books Ltd.,
The Green, Bradgate Road, Anstey,
Leicester, LE7 7FU, England.
Tel: (00 44) **0116 236 4325**
Fax: (00 44) **0116 234 0205**